THE ALCHEMICAL WEDDING

Other books by Dennis Klocek

Colors of the Soul
Physiological and Spiritual Qualities of Light and Dark (2016)

Esoteric Physiology
Consciousness and Disease (2016)

Sacred Agriculture
The Alchemy of Biodynamics (2013)

Climate
Soul of the Earth (2011)

The Seer's Handbook
A Guide to Higher Perception (2004)

Knowledge, Teaching, and the Death of the Mysterious
(2000)

Seeking Spirit Vision
Essays on Developing Imagination (1998)

Drawing from the Book of Nature
(1990)

THE ALCHEMICAL WEDDING

Christian Rosenkreutz, the Initiate of Misunderstanding

DENNIS KLOCEK

Lindisfarne Books | 2021

2021

Lindisfarne Books
An imprint of Anthroposophic Press/SteinerBooks
PO Box 58, Hudson, NY 12534
www.steinerbooks.org

Cover images by Dennis Klocek
Interior images by Dennis Klocek and
traditional alchemical images in public domain
Design by William Jens Jensen

Published with generous support from the

Coros Institute

www.coros.org

Library of Congress Control Number: 2021936590

ISBN: 978-1-58420-921-8 (paperback)

Printed in the United States of America

Contents

To my friend and publisher

Gene Gollogly

A rare, bright, and passionate

seeker of mystery wisdom

Acknowledgments

Many thanks to Jens Jensen, whose art has made my work beautiful. To Marsha Post for her transcriptions and to the staff of SteinerBooks.

Introduction

This story is quite profound. Years ago, I tried several times to read "The Chemical Wedding," but always ended up putting it down, often in despair. I had the feeling that there are lessons in it I couldn't understand but that are very important. I tried perhaps five different times to read it, but always reached a certain point where I would lose interest and just put it away.

Then, one summer, I decided I would actually try to "translate" it, even though I already had an English translation. That translation is in a Baroque style, and I hoped I could bring the highly symbolic story into the realm of contemporary consciousness. I spent a good part of a summer typing it out and teasing it, sentence by sentence. I kept asking myself: *What would be the practical lessons in this story for a contemporary person?* I sensed that there is something in it for today, even though the language can be difficult. I intuited that there is something profound in it—not just for today but also for the future. It points to something in the future that Rudolf Steiner characterized as the fundamental esoteric initiation challenge for contemporary souls—*uncertainty.* I was typing and typing and reached a certain point where I had a feeling of déjà vu: *I think this story has something to do with my own life at this time, but I also feel that it's more than I can handle.*

I couldn't finish the story and had agitated thoughts about it for two days. This was accompanied by strange dreams with deep feelings that I was a failure in life. I couldn't finish the book, because I felt in myself what I imagined was going to happen to Christian Rosenkreutz. Eventually I just forced myself to finish the book. Once I finished reading, it was clear to me that I was a failure in my initiation process. But the story reveals that these feelings were present for Christian Rosenkreutz throughout the whole story. That brought a kind of release for me. Rudolf Steiner says that Christian Rosenkreutz is the most highly initiated Western person. If Rosenkreutz could feel like a failure, I was in good company.

This realization was a turning point for me—a turning point for my life about how I could actually go into the world and try to represent Rudolf Steiner's teachings in my own way, even if that impulse failed. I felt like Christian Rosenkreutz gave me the ability to fail and still get up in the morning and continue to work. My understanding of that now is about how uncertainty is the mark of the new initiation taking place globally. So, I would like to show you how I understand this by pointing to certain alchemical motifs in the alchemical wedding. Those motifs have to do with an approach to the meditative life that requires reflection on the idea of marriage. We could ask: What is the marriage part of the alchemical marriage? What is the wedding? It's all about a wedding. What wedding? It mentions the bride and the bridegroom. Who is the bride? Who is the bridegroom?

Throughout the book are code words such as *Wedding, Bride, Bridegroom,* and *Virgin*—words that expand into many different meanings. In the process of working with these code words, I found similar code words in Rudolf Steiner's teachings, as well. They are not actually written words but more like symbols of alchemical ideas and processes. Esoterically, "marriage" has to do with bringing together two polarities in the human soul. The motif of marriage is the central theme of the Western alchemical tradition, which also includes esoteric traditions of ancient cultures. Gradually, I have come to see that alchemical symbolic language is the true basis of traditional medicine wherever it is practiced today. The soul alchemy of symbols that Steiner wrote into his mystery dramas is what Carl Jung did in *The Red Book* and Goethe did in his fairytale, *The Green Snake and the Beautiful Lily.* Alchemy is ecumenical in its reach.

Alchemical reasoning has to do with the marriage of the Bride, the soul, to Christ, the Bridegroom. The Bridegroom is Christ, and the Bride is the human soul. The plot is that they will eventually be married in the end times. Right now they might be engaged, but they will eventually become married; the universal issue is commitment. The Bridegroom is eager but the Bride needs time to feel things out and commit to the union. If the true "wedding" is to take place, the hopes and needs of both must first be balanced so that each is willing to commit to the other. A hesitant soul requires time to become willing to commit to anxiety-producing uncertainty, travail, and a whole lot of unknowing. Misunderstanding and the feeling of uncertainty that not knowing produces in the soul is exactly the challenge Christian Rosenkreutz faces again and again. This is the central motif in the book. Thus the subtitle of *The Alchemical Wedding:* "The Initiate of Misunderstanding."

This is the contemporary soul, faced with mountains of misunderstanding—continents of misunderstanding, worlds of misunderstanding. Yet, in this story, the compassionate healing force of patience arises somehow from misunderstanding.

> When I find myself in times of trouble,
> Mother Mary comes to me,
> speaking words of Wisdom,
> let it be.
> And in my hour of darkness,
> she is standing right in front of me,
> speaking words of wisdom,
> let it be. (Lennon–McCartney)

Patience is acknowledgment that any agenda, attitude, or perspective that I project onto others is essentially a misunderstanding of their true being ("I," or True Self). As a result, any judgment I make of another person's being is a misjudgment, a misunderstanding.

It is very useful to understand my role as a human being engaged in misunderstanding. I overcome misunderstanding by simply having patience to continue working toward understanding. This is true even when I am the one who feels misunderstood. Again and again, the motif of understanding based on uncertainty is what Christian Rosenkreutz faces. We could even say that this theme highlights the difference between *having knowledge* of something and *truly understanding* something. In the story, the Virgin mocks him many times for his alleged beliefs, and he cries because he has what is called the gift of tears. He cries, because her mockery makes him believe that she does not really see into him or understand his heart. He has no way of explaining to her the reality that underlies his inner life. He is at a loss to explain the intent of his will to her. He is caught in the dilemma of feeling that he is being misunderstood by the spiritual cosmos.

This is the posture of the contemporary soul and the problem of the future in the war of each against all. War is promoted through lies that create uncertainty. The war of each against all is healed when the individual human makes efforts to develop a patient understanding of one's own failings. This kind of difficult patience toward oneself eventually becomes patience for the failings of others. The key point is that, by recognizing my own misunderstandings, I see the danger of casting judgments about others. Casting judgments is a certain path to misunderstanding

A great danger to contemporary initiate wisdom is *inflation*, a kind of untruth. Inflation means that I think of myself as greater or more correct than I really am.* Self-monitoring this is a potent challenge for all esoteric students. Awareness of one's own misunderstanding diminishes inflation. In moments when we manage to diminish inflation, that experience is Pentecost. Although we say something from our own position, it is mysteriously capable of being heard by other

* This error is described in psychology as "The Dunning–Kruger Effect," a common cognitive bias and lack of self-awareness in which people believe they are smarter and more capable than they actually are. "Ignorance more frequently begets confidence than does knowledge" (Charles Darwin, *The Descent of Man*).

souls without causing turbulence. Without knowledge of our own misunderstandings, we can become immersed in the second Tower of Babel, represented by contemporary social media culture. This is one motif—*the great initiate of misunderstanding.*

The second motif in the story is linked to the first in a rather severe practice of patience. Everywhere in this work, Christian Rosenkreutz is being asked to wait—wait at the door, wait at the gate, wait to enter, wait to be recognized, wait, wait, wait. The way he deals with this is that his will is not idle while he waits; his will is turned inward in an effort to understand what his spirit is gaining by learning to wait patiently. External circumstances often prevent him from carrying through with his plans, but instead of reacting he waits and then cultivates an active inner spiritual kind of digestion. He frequently does this by going to sleep. Often, when he's faced with the dilemma he cannot solve, a kind of agitation arises—for instance, when the Virgin mocks him or when he gets pushed back or is stopped at a threshold. At such times, he is thrown back on himself, and instead of reacting or pushing he becomes inwardly active, asking himself if he understands. Frequently there will be a being, a wise person or guide who miraculously appears and acts as an agent of change.

As I understand it, this represents the wise person in us who understands patience and the laws of the higher will. Such a being is called *the witness* by Carl Jung and *the guardian* by Rudolf Steiner. The motif of the patient guardian is this: If you are spiritually active while you are waiting, a guardian will come and change roles, from initially being an adversary to becoming a confidant. Until the guardian becomes a confidant, we experience the guardian's admonitions as hindrances to our will. This is the role of the Virgin in this story. The only one who determines the difference in feelings about the guardian is the individual human. This is done by adopting a progressive posture toward what one learns by having to be patient. The Virgin is purifying Christian Rosenkreutz by poking him into reactions. She does this so that he will gain the capacity to perform the alchemical wedding without danger. This is the second great motif—*waiting, but being spiritually active while waiting.* This posture builds soul potential, so that the guardian will honor us with an insight or a visit, which then leads to the third motif—*deliverance and service.*

When the guardian comes to speak to Christian Rosenkreutz, it is always at a time when a serious judgment is about to occur. In these situations, Christian Rosenkreutz goes into deep uncertainty, which produces variations of either misunderstanding or being misunderstood. After his initial reaction, he becomes silent and patient inside. This opens the opportunity to interact with another being, after which he often goes to sleep. Because of the work he's done spiritually while learning patience, it frequently happens that he awakes in a higher state of consciousness. It is always an act of grace that somehow comes from another dimension (chance or fate). The pattern is this: Christian Rosenkreutz enters a sleep state so he will be open to receiving grace in response to the will he created by being spiritually active while waiting.

Christian Rosenkreutz is engaged in a beautiful kind of push–pull of emotional energy that moves delicately across the threshold and back. He learns to use the state of sleep and dream as a doorway into higher states of consciousness. As I understand it, this is what Rudolf Steiner encourages—that, as students of initiation science, we do the best work in our sleep. We have to structure our sleep so that we permeate it with the willingness to be open to the admonitions of the guardian. This means I have to put my own agenda in abeyance when I become fearful or agitated about having to be patient. The guardian's help allows us to begin to perceive and appreciate what is coming from the spiritual world clothed in the circumstances of the manifest world.

This is a direct picture of how our practice of patience leads to a kind of crisis that eventually creates a deliverance. Out of the grace of the deliverance comes the requirement of service based on what the grace has taught: *patience, deliverance, service.* Christian

Rosenkreutz is thwarted; he is thrown back on his own devices. What he wants to bring is not accepted; thus, he experiences uncertainty but works inwardly to not react. He then has a dialogue with another before going to sleep. When he wakes up, he suddenly sees in a higher state of consciousness. This happens again and again. Nevertheless, his learning task is not finished. Whereas he is able to see in a higher state of consciousness, this creates a kind of separation from the consciousness needed just to do the work. When faced with this polarity, he humbly perseveres and remains focused on the task at hand.

Accompanying Christian Rosenkreutz's humility is a sense of feeling inadequate to meet the demands of the service being requested by the gift of grace. He transforms this feeling by faithfully showing up to do the work, even when he knows that his effort is inadequate. In this, he is a model for dealing with the widespread social uncertainty of contemporary life. There is no guarantee that anything we do will bear fruit. This challenge is the basis of the idea that Christian Rosenkreutz can be called an initiate of misunderstanding. The poet Keats had a term he coined: *negative capability*. Keats felt that staying enthusiastically engaged in a problem that has no hope of a solution is a creative, magical tool for humans that can be cultivated. This capability allows patience to become a path toward deliverance.

Another motif is that of the Virgin. There are *virgins* and *Virgins*. Some are more powerful, some less; some are a little cranky, some lovey-dovey. They all have colors and various regalia, scepters, and costumes. The code word for the purified soul at the end of time is, according to Rudolf Steiner, the *Virgin Sophia*. At the end of time, human beings will have worked upon themselves to such a degree that their souls—their *collective* souls—will have been purified. All the souls of all the humans, taken together, will be known as Sophia, *Anthropos-Sophia*—the Sophia of human effort, the Virgin of humanity, our benefactor, our go-between, an advocate with the spiritual world for our ultimate stupidity and human failures. The Virgin in the story represents the future collective human soul.

Her great teaching is *do not judge.* If we really wish to entertain Sophia, our greatest error is judging others and ourselves, because we are too small to understand the world fully. To fortify this teaching to Christian Rosenkreutz, the Virgin of the chosen ten men continuously tests Christian Rosenkreutz with harsh judgments. She wants to purge any judgment of others from his soul, because she knows that, so long as he has that weakness in his soul, he will be unable to complete the wedding. He passes her tests, because his humility helps him understand how deeply he misunderstands the great laws she represents. When he is judged by her, he feels that it would be best to own the error, keep silent, and go to sleep. In times of uncertainty, people today are training as initiates of misunderstanding when being misunderstood by then casting judgments out of the anger at being misunderstood. The Virgin of the ten is the aggressive agent of this fierce soul battle that is the process of initiation.

So, the different kinds of virgins are merely showing different aspects of the Sophianic quest. We could say that the journey toward Sophia—and the attributes of patience, deliverance, and service—occur repeatedly as motifs in the seven days of this book. I've broken them down here to illustrate why I think these motifs are useful. When read symbolically, this story becomes a key esoteric teaching that leads toward a deeper understanding of useful soul postures for healing the social issues that permeate uncertain times.

Dennis Klocek,
Fair Oaks, California, March 2021

THE ALCHEMICAL WEDDING

Day One

Overview

The first day contains all the motifs—the leitmotif of the whole. Christian Rosenkreutz has dreamed of a coming wedding, and he hopes he will be invited.

It's Eastertide, and he is doing a ritual to break his fast; he is preparing a Eucharist. There is a great sound behind him in his meditation cell, and he becomes aware of a being's presence. He's afraid to look at the being, which he had actually summoned through his own attention. This is a large motif—you can wish and wish for the powers, but when they appear you wish you hadn't wished for them.

Christian Rosenkreutz is completely human. He's afraid to look, but when he turns around he sees an angel with large wings covered by hundreds of eyes, all looking at him. The angel has a handful of letters and gives one to him. On the letter is a sign, the hieroglyphic monad from the work of the alchemist John Dee. It is a combination of all the planetary symbols. Seeing this, Christian Rosenkreutz knows that this is a powerful summons. The letter feels heavy, like lead. He opens it and sees that it is an invitation to the wedding. It is upsetting to him because he said he wanted to go to the wedding, but now, in the face of so much power, he is not sure. Now the angel blows a trumpet and leaves. There is no do-over; it is done—he's been invited, but now he's not so sure.

Christian Rosenkreutz paces back and forth and thinks, *The only way I can get out of this is by going to sleep.* So, he goes to sleep and has a dream, and in the dream he finds himself in a dungeon with many other people. In the ceiling of the dungeon is a small opening, and every once in a while, the lid over the hole is opened and an old man looks down and says, "Be quiet down there!" And then he closes the lid. When the lid is open, Christian Rosenkreutz can see that there are many people crawling over and clawing at one another.

Then the old man says, "Well, my mother says we can let down a rope, and if you can grab onto it we can pull you up here. So, here's the rope." The rope descends, and all the people in the dungeon start clawing at one another.

Christian Rosenkreutz, being a person of misunderstanding, says, "I don't get it. Why is this the way it's supposed to happen?" He finds a rock to one side so he doesn't have to claw at people. He watches the rope coming down as all the others begin to grab at one another and knock the others away. Then the rope is pulled up with a couple of people hanging on it; they go to the surface above, and the lid closes over the opening. The old man says that they're going to let the rope down only a few more times, while below the people are becoming worse and worse, punching one another and clawing.

Christian Rosenkreutz stands to the side and watches, saying, "I don't get it—I just don't understand why it has to be this way." Then he realizes—because he has pulled away from the battle, the rope comes down in the middle of the dungeon and there he is on his rock at the edge of the dungeon. There's no hope, because he has removed himself from the battle in the dungeon over who gets on the rope.

He's the man of total misunderstanding, but at the last moment, he realizes, "Oh my God, I've put myself into a bad position here by not playing along." The rope is lowered again amid the battle at the bottom, and someone hits the rope so that it swings past his perch. Christian Rosenkreutz leaps onto the rope and is pulled upward. *Deliverance!* However, as he is pulled up toward freedom and reaches the top, the rim hits him in the neck and causes a large wound. This is his first wound.

He reaches the top, and they say to him, "We'll let the rope down one more time, and you must work to pull the rope up for the other people." *Deliverance and service.* After the rope comes up again, they close the dungeon lid. The old man is above with the people who have been saved. They are asking him about those who are still in the dungeon. The old man replies that he has asked his mother about it, and she, too, wants to change the way it is done, but she acknowledges that the directive from higher up states that if we don't do it this way, if we just let everyone come up, there won't be people left below to change themselves. When they change themselves they can change the Earth. The old man's mother says to Christian Rosenkreutz, "Look at you, you're bleeding. Bear your wounds for me." Then Christian Rosenkreutz loses the dream and enters a deep sleep.

THE ALCHEMICAL WEDDING, DAY ONE

It was an Easter Sunday and Christian Rosenkreutz, also known as CR, was preparing an unleavened cake for a ritual of thanksgiving. Suddenly, a terrible tempest arose in his small room. From out of the tempest a hand touched Christian Rosenkreutz on the back. At first, he was greatly afraid to turn around. When nothing happened, he eventually dared to look and there stood a woman dressed in sky-colored garments covered with golden stars. She had large wings filled with eyes. In one hand she held a trumpet, in the other a bundle of letters in all languages. Among them was a letter with a name on it that CR was forbidden to reveal. She sifted through her letters, laid one on the table, and then disappeared, giving a mighty blast on her trumpet. The letter was extremely heavy to lift, and on it was a mystic sign printed with the inscription "IN HOC SIGNO VINCES" (In this sign conquer). Christian Rosenkreutz recognized the sign as being free from the influence of the devil and opened the letter. It contained the following verses.

This day, this day, this
The Royal Wedding is.
Art thou thereto by Birth inclined,
And unto joy of God designed,
Then mayest thou to the mountain trend,
Whereupon three stately Temples stand,
And there see all from end to end.

Keep watch, and ward,
Thy self regard;
Unless with diligence thou bathe,
The Wedding can't thee harmless save
He will damage have,
That here delays;
Let him be ware, too,
Light that weighs.
Signed
Bridegroom and Bride

Christian Rosenkreutz recognized that this verse referred to a wedding that he had seen in a vision seven years previously. Since then, he had been following its progress by observing the motions of the planets. He had imagined that the wedding would be a pleasant affair when it finally happened, and he had been looking forward to it for a long time. Now, with the circumstances of the delivery of the letter and the verses in the invitation, he was aware of the divine import of the wedding, and he was troubled.

As he examined his soul he had the most extreme feelings of unworthiness and dullness regarding his ability to understand even the most rudimentary aspects of the Divine Mystery. He felt that his soul was filled with pride, pompousness, and carnal thoughts. He was particularly vexed by the references to the three Temples. He had no idea whatsoever what that could mean. The thought made him fear something dreadful. Altogether, he experienced deep anxiety over his frailty and impotence. He felt this so much that he sought to retire into his bed to escape the anxiety. He hoped that perhaps in sleep his angel would aid him in his understanding.

He was scarcely asleep when he saw that he was held in chains by his feet in a dark dungeon in the base of a tall tower. It was so dark in the dungeon that Christian Rosenkreutz could only gradually see that he was imprisoned there with multitudes of other humans, who were feverishly swarming over one another like crazed insects. Without warning, trumpets and drums announced the opening of the cover on top of the dungeon. Light poured in from above, and this caused all the others in the dungeon to struggle to heave themselves up over the others to be closer to the light. CR used this surge to struggle to one side of the group, where he found a large rock somewhat away from the crush to serve as a vantage place.

From far above, at the top of the Tower, a hoary-headed ancient man called down for them all to be silent. He then told them that because of the Wedding his mother would overlook their follies so that they might, as humans, keep in esteem things that would normally be considered false by the Gods. He said that, to enhance the goodness of his mother the Ancient Matron, she would allow a cord to be let down into the dungeon, and whoever could hang onto the cord would be released from the dungeon as the cord was pulled up. Then the ancient Matron commanded her servants to let down a cord seven times.

This instigated the most horrible struggle for the cord among the humans in the darkness below. After seven minutes a little bell rang, and the servants of the Matron pulled the cord up with four humans hanging on it. Christian Rosenkreutz ruefully realized that, since he was sitting on a stone in the wall of the dungeon, he had no chance to get near to the cord that was being let down in the center.

The cord was let down a second time to even more struggles among the prisoners. Fewer were able to hang on each time the cord was let down, owing to the increased ferocity of the struggle. The fifth time the cord was pulled up, the struggle was so bad that no one was able to hang on. The sixth time the cord was let down, the battle below was so fierce that someone hit the cord, and it started to swing back and forth. Just as it was being pulled up, it swung near to the perch of CR, and he jumped on and was pulled above the mass of struggling humans below. He hit the edge of the opening as he was pulled up and received a bloody gash on his neck. However, in his excitement at being set free he did not notice the blood running down his clothes, and he enthusiastically joined the other freed prisoners and the servants of the Matron in pulling on the cord for the seventh and last time.

After the last pull, the Ancient Matron ordered the cord to be put away, and the hoary-headed man addressed the prisoners still in the dungeon. He told them that the idea to release some prisoners had been long pondered by his Mother but that it was not really a cure for discontent among humans. He said that the joyful time is approaching when no persons will be wealthy and no persons in need. He cautioned that whoever has received great commands will have to work diligently to keep himself occupied, and whoever has been shown great trust by the Gods should be working incessantly to save his skin. He then told the struggling multitudes to stop complaining about their situation. He asked them to consider the question that, since they had already been waiting so long, what was it to them to wait for a while longer.

With this, the cover was closed and a great and piteous cry rose from below, bringing tears to the eyes of Christian Rosenkreutz. The Matron took the name of each one who had been redeemed and confided to her Son that she was sorely grieved over the ones still in the dungeon, and that if it were up to her, she would release them all. To this her Son replied that the process was given by God and cannot be otherwise, for if all were saved and in the higher realms, who would be left to do service for the world. The Mother was silent for a while and then replied with a sigh that it was as he had said. She then ordered the chains removed from the new arrivals. CR thanked her enthusiastically for his release. This pleased and comforted her.

Every one of the redeemed was given a piece of gold for a remembrance and to spend on the way. On one side of the gold piece was stamped the rising sun and on the other the letters *D,L,S.* They were bidden to go in peace and honor and to help their neighbors and not divulge to anyone else any secrets that had been given to them alone.

Suffering wounds from the chains on his feet, CR could not walk properly as he left the Matron. She saw this and called him to her and said that he should not let his condition afflict him, but that he should willingly call to mind his infirmities and thank God who has permitted him to be in such a high place with such imperfections. Then she asked him to bear his wounds for her sake.

Just then the trumpets sounded so loudly that he awoke and realized that this had all been a dream. Yet he could clearly see the wounds on his neck and feet. He pondered this and concluded that God had deemed he should be present at the Wedding. With childlike confidence, Christian Rosenkreutz thanked God for his blessings and asked for daily graces of Wisdom and Understanding. He further said that, if it be possible, he wished to be conducted to the very end of the Wedding. He then put on a white linen coat and pants and put a blood-red ribbon diagonally across his chest and shoulders. Into his hat he stuck four red roses. For food he took Bread, Salt, and Water. CR then fell to his knees and made a vow that, if God were to reveal anything through his grace, he would employ it not to his own honor or authority but only to be of service to his neighbor and to spread the glory of God's Holy Name.

Day One Commentary

My introduction to *The Alchemical Wedding* was a curious one. Thirty years ago I was the landscaper for the Sacramento Waldorf School. During my second week on the job, an arsonist set fire to the administration building that held the library. I was called at 3:00 a.m. by the fire department to shut off the water; the manifold for the campus was on the administration building and it had melted. So, I was there when the firemen left and I went into the library. There was a small part of a shelf left in the library that had about thirty books on it. The rest of the library had burned out. One of the books on that shelf was a book with the covers burned off: *A Christian Rosenkreutz Anthology*, by Paul Marshall Allen (1913–1998).* The outside of the book was completely destroyed but the inside survived. It became my introduction to *The Alchemical Wedding*.

Paul Marshall Allen was a remarkable anthroposophic scholar. He was familiar with or fluent in fifteen languages and traveled around the United States during the 1950s as an ambassador for Anthroposophy. Paul was a brilliant alchemist and scholar. He translated *The Alchemical Wedding* into English, but it has a kind of old-style English

* Rudolf Steiner Publications, 1968 (currently published by SteinerBooks). On Paul Allen, see Russell Pooler, *A Rosicrucian Soul: The Life Journey of Paul Marshall Allen* (Lindisfarne Books, 2009); also, Henry Barnes, *Into the Heart's Land: A Century of Rudolf Steiner's Work in North America* (SteinerBooks, 2005).

because he was such a scholar old texts. When you read it, the book makes little sense at first. I thought that was really a shame, because *The Alchemical Wedding* is a document for contemporary initiation problems, which are inflation and insecurity–the two great polarities. In times of the consciousness soul, the two great polarities of darkness in the soul are *inflation* and *insecurity*. Both arise from the same root—*anxiety*. The healer of this is *humility*.

The Alchemical Wedding involves the oscillation between inflation and insecurity. Inflation is the sin of our age. *Inflation* simply means I think I know more than I actually know, and tell everyone else about it. Inflation is well represented in today's online blogosphere and in the realm of politics. Basically, inflation operates by opinion—my opinion, right or wrong. The flip side of inflation is my opinion that you are wrong, while your opinion says that I am wrong; thus, we are both right about our opinions in that we are both wrong. That feeling is insecurity, characterized by Rudolf Steiner as the key quality of contemporary initiation.

The cycle of inflation and insecurity is like a dog chasing its tail if it is useless, or like a snake eating its own tail if it is esoterically significant. We can compare the oscillation between inflation and insecurity to modern news cycles, using opinions as suggestions is a charade of propaganda, or disinformation, which bypasses one's will to actually learn something. There is an old saying: "Only the true Master is self-limiting." The purpose of the propaganda avalanche of opinion is to make people so exasperated by suggesting unfounded opinions that they no longer want or recognize truth; this is the root purpose of propaganda. People reach the point where they are no longer able to recognize whether anything or anyone's opinion has any truth behind it. Steiner has called this the politics of suggestion, through which human moral capacity is diminished. This is why uncertainty and inflation rule in the realm of suggested unfounded opinion as a seedbed for what Rudolf Steiner calls *mass psychosis:* "I don't care what the truth is. Just let me have my personal point of view. Don't try to educate me and I'll be happy." Through propaganda, we can say whatever conflicting statement we like; it's just an opinion anyway.

To deal with soul oscillation, Christian Rosenkreutz's journey toward truth in *The Alchemical Wedding* presents a story for contemporary souls. It is a document about the initiation process of contemporary souls that oscillate between inflation and uncertainty, between thinking I know something and then discovering that I don't. Today, this leads to the position that we can say whatever we want. It doesn't matter whether it's true or not; I care only that a lot of people will hear me saying it. This is propaganda consciousness, which preceded the Third Reich in 1930s Germany. Eventually, people gave up thinking there was something to understand. This is a contemporary form of consciousness.

The Alchemical Wedding is about someone in the past who experienced an initiation in this realm for people of the distant future. It is a teaching from Christian Rosenkreutz about these questions: How can modern scientific consciousness use uncertainty in a constructive way? How can I transform knowledge into wisdom without inflation? How can I survive uncertainty simply by keeping my opinions to myself—at least until I discover something that I know is actually true? It might not be the ultimate truth, but I can set things out for myself and at least feel that I can begin a dialogue with reality. This is really what *The Alchemical Wedding* is about. It was written in a "hidden" language; its language is symbolic and metaphorical. To penetrate this language, it is useful to understand a few concepts that were widespread during the time of ancient alchemists, but today seem a bit odd.

My path to understanding these ideas went through the work of the scholar Paul Allen. I eventually met his widow, Joan deRis Allen (1931–2015). She was a lovely, bright woman and an anthroposophic architect. She allowed me to stay in her home while I was lecturing in Pennsylvania, and she allowed me to spend a day with Paul Allen's annotations outlining what he would change in his translation of *The*

*Alchemical Wedding.** That was a real treat for me— being able to talk to her about him and have access to his handwritten notes. I felt that, in bringing this work, now I could stand behind it as a document and consider it to be a core metaphorical, symbolic document of Anthroposophy on initiation practice for contemporary souls. To truly understand *The Alchemical Wedding*, we must understand that, when it was written in 1616, people had a very different worldview. Today, we might say it was channeled.

No one really knows who the real author was, because the one who wrote it down—a theologian— later disowned it. It came, intact, through unusual doorways and ended up as a unique document. To understand it, however, it is helpful to realize that it arose within a cultural context in which metaphor was a familiar language. People of that age understood metaphor as symbolic language that expresses higher meaning. Today, when we use symbolic language, it's presented merely as opinion. We don't understand that a higher world is behind symbols. We take most things at face value and then place them in context with scientific skepticism. However, when *The Alchemical Wedding* was written, it was widely understood that language had two levels: empirical language of the thing itself, with symbols and metaphor standing behind that empiricism as doors to higher understanding.

We held a conference some time ago on *The Flaming Door.*** It was about symbolic consciousness. Understanding symbolic consciousness has the potential to heal uncertainty. If we learn to think in symbols, we will have a feeling of having what could be called "collaborative will," from which synergy arises. When I am in symbolic consciousness, I have to understand that there is always something called the esoteric, or occult, law forming an organ, because much of

* Paul and Joan coauthored a few books, including *The Time Is at Hand! The Rosicrucian Nature of Goethe's Fairy Tale of the Green Snake and the Beautiful Lily and the Mystery Dramas of Rudolf Steiner* (SteinerBooks, 1996).

** See Eleanor C. Merry, *The Flaming Door: The Mission of the Celtic Folk-Soul* (Floris Books, 2008).

the language in *The Alchemical Wedding* comes from the alchemists who were physicians, chemists, and pharmacologists who understood that the substance they were working on was also a metaphor. It was a metaphor not just for a natural process, but a consciousness process. Salt is a substance, but also a process in nature; furthermore, it is a kind of consciousness. Alchemists understood that if someone makes a remedy, the consciousness of the one who made it is included in that substance.

Today, because machines make most of the substances we use as medicaments, we receive machine consciousness in those medicines, which does not include morality. Esotericists understand that the elemental world of machines is not a source of morality. Because it has no morality (like Caliban in Shakespeare's *Tempest*), the elemental world of machines can be used by any consciousness for positive or negative ends. There is no morality in the elemental world; there is morality only in human souls.

The great physician Paracelsus held a concept he called the *archeus*. In anthroposophic terms, we would call *archeus* the "life body," or ether body. Paracelsus called it the star body. He said that behind the physical body is an *archeus,* or star body, composed of forces held in the cosmos, which alchemists would call intelligence of the cosmos, or intelligence of a planet or a star. The consciousness of a pattern of form and rhythm that results in a substance we could call *archeus*. In other words, it is patterns of forces of attraction and repulsion, osmosis and diffusion, and convection cycles of rising warmth and descending cold. These elemental forces organize into cellular patterns.

Phenomena in the natural world in which forces move in a certain way create patterns that eventually become physical substances. Science imagines these forces as molecular bonding angles and electromagnetic forces, electrons, protons, and attraction–repulsion, all of which are elemental forces. To contemporary minds, these are merely interacting forces. In the ancient times, alchemists saw these forces as actual beings. The star body was considered a human vehicle that allowed people to incarnate and receive intelligent cosmic forces. The *archeus* was considered to be a kind of template. Flowing in or through that template was what Paracelsus called *mumia*, which we would call the flow of forces in the life body. The *archeus* is the structure of those forces of the life body. Thus, the structure and the flow are two sides of one coin, but they are not the same thing.

For Paracelsus, an organ is formed by the *archeus* and animated by the *mumia*. That is the occult, hidden law of organ formation. If I remove an organ from an animal or person, or if I find an analog to it in the natural world, the *munia* flowing through it congeals, but the *archeus* or formal principle remains present until the organ atrophies to the point where it's no longer useful. This was the basis of both healing and witchcraft in ancient times and the witchcraft side is why it had to go away. Nonetheless, this is the worldview on which *The Alchemical Wedding* is based, as well as the worldview of homeopathic medicine, Bach flower remedies, and other body–mind approaches to human wellbeing.

Body–mind systems today are resurrecting this whole way of thinking and what Paracelsus called the *spagyric process*. In spagyrics, it was understood that human beings contain forces given to them by nature. The symbolic word for this is *king*. A king represents the lawfulness of natural forces, the given. This is why the king was meant to be the dispenser of all wealth in the kingdom as the conduit of given forces, given by divine right to circulate that wealth as representative of the given. Symbolically, the king represents the *archeus*, the form through which the forces flow. We can call the forces of the given the etheric, life body, or the solar body in alchemy. These are the lawful forces given by nature. The code word for this is *king*. Understanding this makes reading *The Alchemical Wedding* much easier. Whenever "king" is mentioned this is what is meant.

The "Bridegroom" is the young king on his nuptial day, full of potential for plenitude. The Bridegroom is Christ (the future human true "I"), who on the first day invites Christian Rosenkreutz, as the initiate, to the wedding.

The wedding is between the king and queen. What is meant by "queen"? She is the soul that is not the given but whose destiny is to marry the given. We all know the king has his ideas, but the queen has "pillow talk." If the queen is unhappy, the king cannot be happy. In this coded language, *queen* is the soul, the eternal feminine. The eternal feminine is not given—the soul is free. The soul is where new life arises that has nothing to do with the king and his givenness. She is destined to unite with the king but brings to this marriage her own potential. In the soul, a new spirit embryo can be gestated that goes beyond the marriage; the king cannot do this by himself, but the queen can bring to birth the new human.

In *The Alchemical Wedding,* the marriage is between the given forces of nature that we must deal with and the not-given forces of freedom in the soul. They must marry each other. The Bridegroom as Christ is the new given that is about to be married to the soul. It hasn't happened yet, but there is great potential for it to happen if human beings can transform themselves through initiation science. The Bridegroom and the bride have to be brought together in a wedding ceremony, and when they do an embryo is created and gestated in the womb of the Great Sophia being, the virgin.

Our spirit embryo is gestated in the womb of Immaculate Conception. This is what the whole story is about—who we will be in the future. In most places today, speaking like this leads others to think we might be a few bricks short of a full load. Nevertheless, this was the worldview during the sixteenth century—the symbolic power of the king and queen and the virgin with the Christ as the Bridegroom. To alchemists, the reason we are on Earth is for us to transcend and become supra-human. This is a common idea among people who understand mystery wisdom. Among everyday people, such notions seem stupid, but for those who wish to accelerate the process of transformation, they must consciously marry the soul to the laws of nature.

In the ordinary world, this process of transformation often just means becoming ill. Getting sick is when your soul has to acknowledge, *I think I should listen to the king and wed my soul to my life forces.* We hope to gain wisdom from illness. In *The Alchemical Wedding,* healing occurs when the soul marries the given forces of nature, through which the "new" is born—the virgin, the virginal soul, the Sophia, the new embryo, the new human, the new Adam. These are all code words for those who have done the work of initiation. *The Alchemical Wedding* is a text of initiation. It is a symbolic text, called "The Great Work" in alchemy. The Great Work means bringing natural will, the forces of the natural world, into marriage, and integrating them into the soul. Carl Jung called it *integration*—integrating the eternal, True Self—our "I"—into the temporal self.

To alchemists, there are two forces that allow this marriage to take place—*solve* and *coagula.* A wedding always involves two polarities coming together. Here, the two greatest polarities are *solve* (dissolving) and *coagula* (coagulation). In solve, things that are formed become so dynamic that they start to dissolve and disappear, becoming increasingly rarified and force-like. In coagula, things that are rarified and more force-like begin to lose force and become more substantial. These are the two poles of becoming (manifestation) as one pole and going out of manifestation (dissolution) toward potential as the other pole. In the ancient world, dissolving into nothing was seen differently—not as "nothing" but as a void filled with the potential to give birth to something new.

Dissolving was seen as stronger and more enduring than manifestation. In the invisible world there is a stronger state of existence due to having a greater potential. When things manifest, they became "sorry guests upon this dark earth" (Goethe), because they no longer have potential. On a personal level, "I became me" in this incarnation rather than "who I could be." Looking into the eyes of a one-year-old child, we see potential; looking into the eyes of most of our contemporaries, we see lost or spent potential. The process of going from potential to manifestation is coagula. Quitting your job and doing crazy things is called solve. You don't know what's happening, but there you are, surfing the wave of potential. You are now open to more possibilities than when you said, "I've got to get up and go to my job." These are the soul's two poles. When an organ has formed from forces and becomes a physical organ, the forces that formed it become its function. The function of organs is to dissolve and to reconstruct. If my organs are healthy, they can do this breathing process between solve and coagula. This is the basis of most organic development. I either form something or move toward potential. In *The Alchemical Wedding*, the soul moves into coagula through cognition, facts, and words. Any word is the corpse of a living idea.

Solve always means I lose control of something when it returns to potential. We lose control over an idea expressed in words when we tell someone our idea. We have just said what we think, thus moving that potential idea into the manifest universe of another person. Then that person expresses the idea, and you realize it is now in the realm of solve since it is no longer under your control. In dialogue, expressing something as *coagula* and letting it go into the *solve* of another mind creates uncertainty. The rhythm of the back-and-forth of ideas in dialogue is the mercury that unites *solve* and *coagula*. We begin to see the nature of will when this rhythm works on our consciousness.

Throughout *The Alchemical Wedding* there are set points when Christian Rosenkreutz is engaged in dialogue with certain people or beings. *Solve* is listening to someone say something with which we totally disagree, but also allowing that person to say it without thinking unpleasant things. This is solve, and in this story Christian Rosenkreutz has to engage in a lot of solve in his dialogues with the beings that he meets.

Aristotle made a wonderful observation: "It is a wise person who can entertain a thought without believing it." This is the meaning of dialogue.

Let's turn now to a picture from the first day of *The Alchemical Wedding*. Christian Rosenkreutz is performing a ritual at Easter time and hears a sound behind him, but he is alone in his room. He becomes aware of a presence behind him, and he's afraid to turn around. When he finally turns, he sees an angel who has huge wings with eyes all over them, and all of them are looking at Christian Rosenkreutz. The angel hands him an invitation to a wedding. On the invitation is a sign called the "hieroglyphic monad," from the work of the alchemist John Dee. It is a combination of all the planetary symbols. Seeing this, Rosenkreutz realizes that he has actually been inwardly preparing for a long time for this wedding. Something like recognition is happening in him, which makes him both excited and very afraid. He is inflating, because he has been especially invited to the wedding, but he is inwardly conflicted. This introduces a motif of Christian Rosenkreutz and the Rosicrucian impulse that we could call the "witness" or "guardian" or "confidant Gatekeeper." The Gatekeeper is a being in the human soul that is in constant contact with the elements of destiny and desire playing out in every situation.

The Gatekeeper suggests that people are probably not as great as they or others might think they are. The Gatekeeper is the great reality check. Christian Rosenkreutz is in contact with the Confidant Gatekeeper in his reticence at being invited. The way he solves this conflict is to go to sleep. In *The Alchemical Wedding*, "going to sleep" refers to altered consciousness. When he says "I went to sleep," he is saying that he entered spiritual consciousness. In this case, he goes to sleep because he is dumbstruck by the sight of an angel with wings full eyes, who invites him to a wedding. However, this wedding is not a party, but more like a serious event for which he had better prepare.

The invitation is signed by the Bridegroom and the bride. Essentially, it says, "This is an official, personal invitation, and you'd better pay attention." The Alchemical Wedding is a marriage between the soul, with its appetites and passions, and the spirit, with its higher perspectives and demands. Christian Rosenkreutz is on edge and decides it would be best to go to sleep. When he does so, he has a dream.

In reading *The Alchemical Wedding*, it is worthwhile to pay attention to what Christian Rosenkreutz dreams, because dreaming is a Rosicrucian method for a spagyric, or alchemical, soul process. Such a process involves a laboratory procedure in which a plant is taken apart by distilling and burning and then rhythmically reassembled through alchemical art. A *soul spagyric process* is a systematic deconstruction of the thinking, feeling, and willing components of a belief to discover the motives behind it. Soul spagyric processes include cycles of dreaming and waking. Through a soul spagyric process, we can learn to purify our dreaming. We have to stabilize it and move dreams away from simple maintenance of the organism. We must move dreaming away from reaction against dialogue with higher beings. Only we are able to do this, and only we can know whether we have done it or not. And this, we could say, is the nature of the Great Work of *The Alchemical Wedding*. Christian Rosenkreutz is learning how to go into a dream and remain awake. In *The Alchemical Wedding*, when Christian Rosenkreutz enters a dream, he is doing an alchemical soul spagyric practice.

In the first day he dreams he's in a prison. This prison is his physical body. And in the prison, there are many inmates (other prisoners in bodies). There's a rope hanging down through a hole in the ceiling. The inmates are all clawing at each other to get the rope, because a door occasionally opens at the top and the rope is pulled up; whoever is hanging onto the rope is taken up and escapes the prison. Everyone else is left behind. This is his dream, and he realizes from it that the rope will soon go up and down. However, it bothers him to see all the others fighting with one another, causing him to lose interest in participating in the scuffle. He finds a small rock to one side and sits there watching the struggle. He soon realizes he has removed himself from the action of getting a hold of the rope. On his rock there is now no way for him to get out of this prison because he decided to avoid the conflict. He is caught between his moral vision and the struggle to escape.

During the fighting, someone hits the rope, which swings near his perch, allowing him to grab hold of it. As he is being pulled upward through the top opening, he receives a wound in his neck. Christian Rosenkreutz is bleeding, but he is so glad to have been pulled out of the dungeon that he grabs the rope to help the others up.

This introduces the motif of *blood* and *service,* which runs throughout the story. To alchemists, blood is a "very special fluid" that contains the light and warmth in which the spiritual part of the human being makes a dwelling in the body. Shedding blood in the service of others is also a significant symbolic element later in the story.

Once Christian Rosenkreutz is above, he finds himself in another world, where he meets a Great Mother and her ancient son. They represent this other world of dream, where we go to meet beings on the other side. In the language of the Hawaiian Kāhuna (*'Ōlelo Hawai'i*), such beings are known as *'aumākua,* a parental sort of person one trusts because they would never lie to you. They speak a language about the reality of the other side. It is not a personal matter that people are in the dungeon. The Great Mother says, "It pains me to have to do this, but it was written long before I arrived here. This is the way it's supposed to be; we are simply enacting the Great Will, and I am asking you to bear your wound for me." This is what she says to him. This is the end of the dream.

This waking-sleeping motif points to the shifting states of consciousness depicted throughout his journey. The distinction between waking and dreaming is often blurred, and yet the beings that Christian Rosenkreutz encounters on the other side of the awakened state are linked to events on this side of the abyss in profound and specific ways. This was a strange dream, but after working with this story for a long while, it is my experience that every time he dreams, he is actually going through his own body. He is penetrating the given, so to speak, to survey how his incarnation is coming along; his dream is really a question that asks how he can escape from the dungeon of the body in which he must suffer. In today's world, he might become somewhat "bionic" to ease his bodily suffering, but that is not the real answer. For example, the metal-on-metal contact of a hip replacement might release toxic cobalt into one's bodily systems, leading to heavy-metal poisoning. There are repercussions to everything we do; we could call it *karma*.

In the work of initiation, a key element is existence in the dungeon of our body. Dreaming is mostly about this issue. Initiation is the process of learning to be awake in our dream, so that during the day it becomes possible to differentiate between the dream and awake states. Eventually, that awareness plays over into waking life more fully, because in waking life it is possible to experience the onset of dream states.

Opposite that awareness is the experience of being awake within a dream. In life, most of our erroneous activities take place during the day, though in a dreamlike state. The chocolate-cake syndrome is a daytime dream state; all our appetites and desires are dreams. The goal of initiation is to be awake during the day, here, on this side, when I start to dream. When I am awake and begin to dream, if I am aware that I am beginning to dream I can place a symbol into my consciousness to monitor the dream. I need to do this, because negative beings on the other side want me to dream so that they can gain access to a human soul.

In waking life, substituting a dream impulse with a preordained symbol is the foundation of initiation science. To do this, however, I must separate my thinking, feeling, and willing spagyrically. I must set them "against" each other, which is called a *spagyric* process in alchemy. I have to *will* my thinking; I have to think into my will. Carl Jung called this process the *opus contra naturam*, or the work against nature (my unconscious bodily nature). If I want to make a spagyric medicine, I take a plant and distill out the oils. I ferment what is left and save the alcohol. Then I burn what comes from the ferment into ash, which I take from the plant and place into water. I let this set for a while as the water draws the salt out of the plant—salt that the plant used to attract water for its growth in the first place. I then purify the salt (a process called *sal*). Before I burn the plant, I remove the oil (a *sulf* process, named for the sulfurous oil). Now I have the oil; I have the salt; I have the alcohol. This is known as *mercury*. These three—mercury, salt, and sulfur of the plant—are broken apart chemically in a laboratory, and I purify each one in a long process, after which I bring them together again. This is *The Alchemical Wedding*. The plant arcana of spagyric laboratory work means separating the original form, purifying each individual substance, and then recombining them.

When I do a spagyric process with my soul, I have to break off the salt part of me from the sulfur part. I have to break away from habitual thinking (*sal*), where my will (*sulf*) is in lockstep with my thinking. I must separate habitual thinking from my unconscious life and *will* my thinking into the patterns that I choose. This is the function of inner-work practice. When I do this, I begin to see the difficulty of trying to separate will and thinking, which is called changing a habit. I can think *I don't want to do this anymore* and then watch myself do it. I go and do exactly what I just said I don't want to do. St. Paul said, "I do not do the good I want to do, but the evil I do not want to do" (Rom. 7:19). This is what we might call cognitive dissonance.

Whose will are we dealing with? Not ours! It's been grandfathered into another will structure. If we want to resurrect our own will from that other will structure, we have to make a spagyric of our own soul; we have to separate our thinking from our will. There are a couple of important ideas in this, and I have to ask myself: What in my soul is solve? What in my soul is the dissolving nature? We could call solve surrender. What can I afford to surrender to? How much of my life is surrender? On the opposite pole is coagula, which is, *No! I won't* go. *I think this, and this is just how it is*—it's coagula, whether in my thinking or in my will. I can be stubborn. I can have fixed ideas. All of this is coagula.

In alchemical soul work, I make an internal inventory of what is solve in my soul and what is coagula and try to solve my coagula and coagulate my solve. When I do this, what comes up? My feeling is in the middle, the mercury, and keeps things going. Christian Rosenkreutz moves in and out of spagyric processes as he makes his way toward the castle, even as work on the homonculus begins to unfold in the Tower. The mercury force in the spagyric process is rhythm. I am in mercury when I pay attention to the timing of my *sal* (thinking) and *sulf* (will) rather than to the outcomes of my thinking and will. I watch my *sal* and *sulf* as though I were watching the thinking and willing of someone else. I note the timing of a thought or will impulse—the hour, day, week, month, and year of my unconscious life of impulses. I look at the rhythms of unconscious impulses, because hidden in the rhythms of the unconscious is a thought or will impulse that prevents me from doing what I would will to do. If I want to unravel the stuck relationship of thinking and will, I must unravel it in time, in a rhythmic, mercurial way. Mercury is the healer.

Rudolf Steiner's great mantra is "Rhythm supplants power." I need to become a rhythm expert. The greatest rhythm—the most profound rhythmic changes in my daily life—is waking and going to sleep. The movement between daytime awake consciousness and sleeping consciousness is the largest shift in consciousness that human beings go through in life. Therefore, paying attention to the rhythm of sleeping and waking offers a doorway into dreaming. I can watch the tick-tock of my feelings as they happen, as I become aware of my tendency to dream during the day. If I pay attention to the content of my consciousness when going to sleep and awaking, I begin to recognize when do this during the day. I begin to become aware of my oscillation between these states of consciousness. To paraphrase an old saying: *It's ten o'clock; do you know where your head is?*

With the Rosicrucians and the work in alchemy, it was often said that it is more important to notice *when* you do something than *what* you are doing. We see a kind of rhythmic, mercurial structure in the manifestation of a perceptible object as it comes into being; this includes our own life issues. We have to see how an issue comes into being *in time*. Once we do this, we start to build a healing tolerance in our soul for our misunderstanding. We can observe ourselves misunderstand things without resorting to inflation or insecurity.

Is a mistake evil? We see such things in society today. If I kill someone or steal someone's life savings, I might go to prison and even become a celebrity. But if I have a sexual liaison with someone on the side, I am seen as morally corrupt. I don't want to be political, but as a society we seem to be confused about what is evil and what is just stupid. We treat what is stupid as evil and what is evil as being merely stupid. Parts of society even celebrate what is stupid without realizing it is evil. There are plenty of stupid things and only a few things that are truly evil.

When we work to enter dreaming more consciously, we can become aware of dreaming thresholds during the day. Certain bodily states such as low blood sugar can act as doorways to the stupid realm. I might suddenly find that I'm doing something I said I would never do. There are many such biological and soul rhythms. If I learn to pay attention to such rhythms, the art of rhythm replaces the power needed to plow through my stupidity. Our alternating states of consciousness become the foundation of the Rosicrucian–alchemical soul method of placing things consciously into sleep.

In *The Alchemical Wedding*, Christian Rosenkreutz is dreaming and waking, dreaming and waking in collaboration with beings on the other side (such as the Virgin), all of whom provide processes whereby he has to face the symbols of his own misunderstanding—lions and snakes, gatekeepers and kings. These are all images of inner states of consciousness that the beings who are trying to educate him in the initiation process provide as dream pictures and metaphors of what he needs to confront. This is what the story is about. When there is a lion, bird, or snake or someone being beheaded, these things are not happening in this world. Beheading someone in this world is murder; beheading over there symbolizes learning to stop our sensory processes so we can engage in pure thinking. Basically, in real meditation I am just chopping off my head. As Steiner puts it, I learn to think off of my brain. People who don't realize this might read about beheading here and think, *Ugh, is this disgusting!* In this world, it is disgusting; over there, it's a metaphor—a symbol of something happening within the soul during initiation.

What does blood symbolize? Blood is the dwelling in which the "I" lives, where one's "I"-being lives in the warmth (the will and enthusiasm) of the blood. Later, in the Tower, blood is warmed and fed to the dead ones so that their consciousness can awake fully and willfully on the other side. Essentially, this is what the work is about in the Tower on the sixth day. Through initiation, we can awake fully on the other side of the threshold between worlds.

How is this done? First, we have to chop off our head to stop thinking thoughts based only on a literal view of the sensory world. As our "I" incarnates into the warmth of our blood during the day and then excarnates into spirit during sleep, we have to disenchant sensory illusions and actively participate in the drama of developing "I"-consciousness. To find the doorway to do this, we have to place seed thoughts willfully and regularly on the other side. We separate certain thoughts (*sal*) and will them (*sulf*) through the dream portal as we go to sleep.

In Rudolf Steiner's work, this is the daily evening review exercise, which is based on the methods of Christian Rosenkreutz in the fifteenth century. My review thoughts go to the other side and become beings there that then help higher beings teach me about my life. Then I awake here, and I am led to things I had not realized I was dreaming. Nevertheless, they come to me on this side as insights and creative activities. The oscillation of day and night, day and night, is mercury.

When I learn to collaborate rhythmically across the threshold between worlds, I get synergy—a kind of afterburner for my thinking process, imagination, and will. I place things over there, and things return. Then, in daily life, I build another sense in my heart that becomes aware that what I am doing has more than one level. It is a kind of radar that I have to build from this side. If I wait for it to happen to me without the rhythmic work, it will happen, but ultimately there will be collateral damage.

The difference between collateral damage and self-inflicted damage is this: When I do the work myself, I am eating my own shadow instead of having someone serve it up on a plate to me. When this happens, I become aware. If I start working with my sleep–awake–sleep–awake rhythm, I start to experience collaborative will, and I can look for what we might call a self-adjusting process. I have faith that, when I begin a process and it starts to work, it will happen when it is time for it to happen, even though I don't know *how*. I know that I do not know, but I also know that I will know when I need to know. This is collaborative will, which leads to perception of a self-adjusting process. I understand that the other side is a coefficient of my activity here—a vector. I vector out and it vectors back. In our time, I recognize how the vector is moving in time. Time becomes plastic; I can stretch it and squish it to get things done that need to be done, because I am not feeling paralyzed by what is not being done, because maybe it really doesn't need to get done. In my case, when the download starts, I can usually feel a change in my heartbeat. I become clearly aware of my heartbeat. If this doesn't happen, I am left wondering.

This is a spagyric of taking the soul apart. If I am to take an idea into sleep, I must be able to form a picture, move it forward and backward, and then dissolve it. That will is very different from the kind needed to mow the lawn. When I mow the lawn, I expect that the lawn will be mowed; but when I do that, there is no download. When I take a picture into sleep and there's nothing left in my mind as I go to sleep, when I wake up and listen, it's silence; there's nothing there either. However, *letting go* allows the *letting come* of some form of symbol in my mind.

We can go even deeper. We can create a relationship between the *letting go* and the *letting come*—what we might call sacred sleeping. I take pictures into sleep that I want to work with, and they begin to speak to me. Over time, this spagyric process, this self-adjusting process, leads to keeping a journal and making observations about my inner life in the context of my outer life. I see the thread, and connections start to happen. Others might say, *You're crazy in the head.* However, if you learn how to do this, they are all moving in time with one another.

We all meet one another on the other side; you just have to keep the faith that you are being guided. Rudolf Steiner calls this *Inspiration*—forming and dissolving the picture he calls *Imagination.* I begin the process of Imagination, forming and dissolving a picture with which I want to work; I take it into sleep and start a rhythmic flow, back and forth between myself and some form of benefactor. In this rhythm, we cannot actually control the outcome. Steiner offers an indication about this work I am describing. The key is to *pay attention to small things.* It's not the big ticket items that help us make real progress, but the everyday little things we do that repeatedly reinforce our patterns. I want to start waking up to those little daily reinforcements.

In *The Alchemical Wedding,* the virgins continuously diminish Christian Rosenkreutz—*You don't get it,* or *You're just a horny old guy.* The Virgin continuously knocks him back a little, because she represents his purified soul. She is saying, *I'm going to knock you back so you can observe what happens.* She knocks him and he cries. This is the "gift of tears"; he realizes he does not understand. The greatest inflation is thinking our opinions are *our* opinions. Symbolically this why he had to give up his shoes after he enters the castle. Ownership and entitlement—even of his own shoes—are huge examples of inflation, because our shoes have been ensouled by us. We are afraid that if we lose them and someone else picks them up, they will no longer be our property.

Human beings attach to things naturally by uniting the soul with them. Hidden in our attachment to things is all the synergic energy we need to explore the soul processes. The potential for growth is locked up in immensely strong belief structures of proprietary ownership of things, including ideas.

A quality that always causes problems for Christian Rosenkreutz is his curiosity and deep attraction to knowledge. Books, little gizmos, and other fascinating things constitute the root causes of his mistakes. It's curiosity. In him, it's innocent, but each time he gives in to it, the Virgin kind of tweaks his nose, because she wants to alert him that he should look at this.

As human beings, one of our biggest inflationary issues is "my space." You are in my space. This is my space. It arises from having *my body*. I claim the stuff around me. Because my body is here, my space is here; I carry it around with me. When I am in my home, my space expands. When you enter my space, remember that this is *my* space. I might even have a more personal space that you should definitely not enter. A simple exercise is to notice how much space you need while talking with someone. I could talk in a loud voice. If I am giving a lecture, you will expect me to speak loudly. However, if I maintain my loud volume of speaking as I approach you, you will begin to feel like moving away because I am pushing my space into your space. This is fundamental. It's a small thing, but it happens again and again. When I wake up in the morning, before coffee my space is about ten feet out. After my coffee, maybe it's only a foot out. Coffee allows me to do a coagula. Once I am sufficiently coagulated, whatever you bring can bounce off my coagulation. This kind of feeling or issue is an example of the kind of little thing that we can take into sleep.

In *The Alchemical Wedding*, Christian Rosenkreutz dreams on the first day about escaping from the space in the dungeon. As an experiment tonight, choose a situation in your life when you experienced space as an issue. Maybe you live on a farm with thirty-seven relatives, and your space is affected by this until you are ten miles away from home. Find out where the edge of that family aura exists as a feeling in your locale. Picture yourself on this side of it, then go to the edge, and finally go inside of that. Maybe it's the front gate; maybe it's the pathway to the latrine—wherever it might be. However, there is a threshold someplace between your space and another. Think about it a little and then make this "movie": I am in my space and I have to enter another space. As I approach, I am back in my own space again. All my things are there. Now, play in and out of these spaces emotionally. Make a little movie in your head of moving in and out of these spaces. Perhaps you experienced a long-ago IRS audit, and each time you drive to work you pass the IRS building where you were audited. Your body and your feelings are stimulated to reexperience that.

Such inner-feeling pictures can create a compression, a soul coagulum. We will have to make a solve to loosen the compression, because it might transform into atherosclerosis, for instance, if it becomes chronic. Christian Rosenkreutz's dream about trying to escape from a dungeon filled with crazy people is also about today's people living modern lives and having to deal with inflation and uncertainty, lies and power—the uncertainty of life.

How can we find certainty in uncertainty? We can't, because it's not part of the given. We cannot create it from anything that already exists. The given is what the king knows. We must persuade the queen to marry the king. This means we have to get our soul to enter our life forces—our *archeus,* or solar body—to discover how this operates in us. This is especially true of the little things because, with them, we gain a doorway to perception of how our soul responds to uncertainty in a myriad of ways. This is not just a one-time matter, but little things that are maddeningly relentless.

The great value of *The Alchemical Wedding*, this teaching of initiation, is that it's okay to make a mistake. It's part of the learning process. It is not okay to inflate. The cardinal problem is inflation; the cardinal problem is believing that I am greater than I really am. The medicine for this is humility. This definitely does not mean becoming a doormat. Humility means understanding that I don't understand.

Athletes and musicians perform in the public eye and have to do amazing things on a regular basis, and they make mistakes. However, if they go inward and fret over missing a key shot or playing a wrong note, they're in trouble. A coach would tell a basketball player who missed fifteen shots to shoot more. Why would you want such a player to shoot more? Because no one wants an emotionally handicapped basketball player, but you don't call out your player and go over all the mistakes and think this will help.

In his later years, Rudolf Steiner experienced a similar situation. A group of young people came to him and said, "We don't like the way the older people are doing the rituals. We don't like all of the rules of the Anthroposophical Society branch. We don't like all the strange things that the older members are forcing us to do. They're always telling us to be quiet and not ask questions." Steiner advised them to create their own rituals if they didn't like what was given to them.

The story goes that Marie Steiner asked him, "What are you doing? These are young people; they don't know what they're doing esoterically!"

Steiner replied, "They will be corrected. The important thing is that they are enthusiastic enough to do the research." He took the position that we always receive tremendous forces from the spiritual world to correct things we don't understand. We usually blame those things on bad luck, a petty tyrant, or ignorant colleagues. All of this might be true but, alternatively, corrections are put into our begging bowl so we can gain the forces needed to reach the next level.

This is the picture that Christian Rosenkreutz has to experience continuously in *The Alchemical Wedding*, and he goes through these corrections with humility. For me, this is the message. As part of your daily review, find a feeling of space where you can actually say: *When this happens, I feel like I am in a different space emotionally.* Then run the scenario like a little movie about what happens before sensing the change in the emotional space, and about what happens in the emotional space, and about what happens after you have shifted. Make a little inner movie of that sequence. It will become a seed of coagula and solve that you can put into the rhythmic nature of your sleep. The collaborative will of your benefactor on the other side will take this and give you synergy tomorrow for the self-adjusting process that is the foundation of initiation science.

Day Two

Overview

Christian Rosenkreutz wakes in the morning of the second day and realizes that, although he dreads going to the wedding, he nevertheless has to go, because he has been preparing to go for the past seven years. This morning, he puts on a red sash and four roses in his hat and, in a happy mood, goes out to the road feeling as if he were going off on an excellent adventure.

As he approaches a crossroads, something occurs that we might call the mysterious act of grace. It's not like *grace has come to me, and I'm content.* This is fierce, modern grace. Modern grace is more in the mood of *Take up your bed and walk.* When he reaches the crossroads, Christian Rosenkreutz finds four signs hanging on cedar trees describing four different roads, all leading to the castle where the wedding is to take place. The first road is a short but dangerously rocky way. The second is a long and meandering path that will get you there if you go by the compass without turning either right or left off of the path. The third road is actually the royal way, which only one in a thousand can travel. And the fourth road is reserved for incorruptible bodies; all others will be consumed. He cannot decide which road he should take, so he waits. While he waits, he becomes spiritually active. Spiritual activity is known most fundamentally as *metanoia*—changing one's way of thinking. In alchemical works, as well as in myths and legends, changing your thinking is always accompanied by an image of some sort of bird. Alchemically, a bird represents a form of the thinking process.

While Christian Rosenkreutz is waiting (because he can't make a decision) he becomes spiritually active, and a dove appears. As he begins to engage the dove and feed it bread from his lunch, he develops an affection for it. Just when he feels he is connecting with the dove, a raven appears and steals the lunch and begins to harass the dove. This kind of harassment symbolizes the fact that his thinking is caught in cause and effect. His thinking remains based on causal chains of sensory experience. He must be cured of his black-and-white, cause-and-effect thinking.

As a raven initiate stuck on the path, he becomes angry at the raven for upsetting his peace. As he chases the raven away, he realizes that by chasing it he has made a commitment to a particular path. It is a rule that once you've committed to a particular path, you cannot turn around. In that moment, he realizes he left his bread behind near the cedar trees at the crossroads. But when he turns around to get the bread, a great wind arises and blows him back along his chosen direction. The question is this: *Has he chosen or has he not chosen?* This is the mysterious action of grace when a student can wait but be spiritually active. In this motif, Christian Rosenkreutz has the experience that something comes from the spirit as a source of ever-present help.

This is a profound motif in the story—the ever-present help of the spiritual world. Now, moving on beyond the crossroads, he encounters a secret magical garden. Its Gatekeeper is friendly but asks him to pay for a token. Christian Rosenkreutz pays with his water bottle and receives a token with the letters *S.C.* (*solve* and *coagula*). *Solve* means to dissolve, and *coagula* means to congeal, or precipitate. Christian Rosenkreutz is now at the water level. Water consciousness is awareness of the common element of flow in life and thinking. The water payment, the Gatekeeper, and the "*solve*" and "*coagula*" token all represent crossing a boundary in consciousness—from the flowing world of nature through the doorway to the silent inner world and the higher consciousness of light and air. The token allows him to continue on his journey. He will have to give the token to the second

Gatekeeper at the castle gate. He hastens on as it is growing dark. Near the castle, he encounters a virgin who is lighting lanterns in the fruit trees that line the road to the castle.

At the second gate he wakes another Gatekeeper, who stands guard with a fierce lion. Christian Rosenkreutz gives him the S.C. token and the remaining salt and receives another token to present at the door. This one has the letters S.M. (*sal mineralis*) on it. In *sal mineralis*, Christian Rosenkreutz has passed from the flow of *"solve"* into the precipitation of *"coagula,"* or salt. *Salt* refers to the intellect in alchemical terms. In this exchange with the second Gatekeeper, he has to leave his intellect behind and deal with the raging forces of his feelings depicted in the lion.

Thus, Christian Rosenkreutz enters even higher consciousness, whereby it is far more difficult to sustain focus. He is told by the Gatekeeper that the gate will be closed, so he must hurry. But the gate closes on his coattail, and he has to leave it there. Once inside he surrenders his S.M. token and receives another with the letters S.P.N. (salvation through being born), which is his true token for admittance to the wedding. He is then instructed to leave his shoes and give them to a beggar. He is given new shoes and a haircut like that of a monk and is escorted into the banquet hall by an invisible page.

Thus far, Christian Rosenkreutz has had several adventures and feels fine. However, at the banquet are rascal vagabonds (his term) from his own town, all of them drunk and hanging out with the nobles. As he enters, they all begin to mock him because he is late and slow. Again, Rosenkreutz is the person of misunderstanding. They say, "Hey, what took you so long? The old guy just went the wrong way as usual. Ha-ha! You don't get it, do you, old man?"

So, there he is, knowing he has actually done all of the right things and has had all the right tokens. Christian Rosenkreutz is met once again with misunderstanding, while watching as all the intoxicated people are picking the nobles' pockets while bragging about how important those nobles are and inflating their heroic deeds. In that moment, he feels a kind of rage arising in him. He has to ask himself: *Is my mood appropriate in this place?* The answer he comes up with is: *I am just misunderstanding. I don't understand why this banquet is filled with these people.*

Christian Rosenkreutz sits at the end of the table with an older man, and he says, "I don't get it. Why were all these strange people invited first, and why are they all seated next to the high table where the Bridegroom will be? Why are they all having such a good time while we try to be conscientious, yet we are seated down here?"

Then their mood is interrupted by trumpet flourishes and sounding drums as the Virgin makes her entrance into the hall. In a pleasant voice, she makes a proclamation:

> The Bridegroom wants all of you who think you were invited and deserve to be here to go with the pages. We have rooms set up for you with the best that the house has to offer. However, if you have searched your soul and think you might not be worthy enough to attend the wedding, then go to the table over here and we'll let you go tomorrow.

Most of the attendees feel they deserve the best and want to be cared for and have the nicest accommodations. Christian Rosenkreutz and eight men with whom he is sitting decide that they are probably unworthy, so they decide they will leave the castle the next morning. After the others have left, however, those who have decided to leave are tied up and thrown into a tiny room, piled one on top of the other, and then the lights are extinguished.

This is a picture of the initiation of misunderstanding. Those who searched their souls were bound up and cast into darkness. These nine persons who deemed themselves unworthy to continue the initiation process become those whom the Virgin champions to enact the alchemical marriage. Their real significance is that they are aware of their errors and human misunderstanding. This makes them most worthy of initiation.

The old man with whom Christian Rosenkreutz had been commiserating is tied up next to him. They begin to talk about the strange quality of it all. "I don't get it. Do you get it?"

"No, I don't get it."

"Well, there's not much real justice in the world, is there?"

It is in this mood that they go to sleep. Christian Rosenkreutz dreams that he is on a high mountain watching an ancient man cutting strings. The strings are attached to people's heads. Some people are high in the air, and some are close to the earth. When the old man cuts the string suspending those who are high in the air, they tumble and crash to earth. When the string is cut for someone who is close to the earth, they touch down gently. In this dream, Christian Rosenkreutz feels some satisfaction as he watches the people fall from their high place.

THE ALCHEMICAL WEDDING, DAY TWO

Christian Rosenkreutz left his cottage singing God's praises and soon entered a forest. He traveled through the forest until he saw a strange, green meadow. In the meadow stood three tall cedar trees that offered shade. Because the day was hot, he decided to sit under the trees and rest. As he approached the trees, under one of them he saw a tablet with curious letters on it:

> If you have heard about the wedding of the king, consider this. The Bridegroom allows you to choose one of four ways to reach the wedding, each of which (if you do not collapse on the path) will take you to the wedding.
>
> The first path is short but dangerous, with rocky places nearly impossible to get past. The second is longer and meanders, though it is plain and easy if you do not stray by trying to figure out the best way to go by using your compass. The third is truly the Royal Road, given by the king to afford you various pleasantries. Unfortunately, thus far this path has been traveled by only about one in a thousand. The fourth path is for only those who have incorruptible bodies. It is a fiery and consuming path not trodden by humans but only by immortals.
>
> Now choose which path you want of the three available to you. Whichever one you enter, know that it has been chosen for you by immutable destiny and once chosen cannot be forsaken except at great danger to your life. Beware, for you have no idea how much danger you are in by wanting to tread these paths. If you know yourself to be obnoxious in your ignorance of one small fault against the laws of the king, I implore you to turn back and return to your house while it is still possible.

Reading this, all the joy in CR's heart vanished. He looked and saw the four paths before him. He was unsure and waited a long time while pondering his possibilities and his unworthiness for his journey. Then he thought of his dream of being let out of the dungeon. He seemed to take some strength from it, and then he had the thought that if he were to consider his future based on a dream, he was sure to encounter ruin.

He was so overwrought at these thoughts that he decided to sit on the ground and have some food. As he took out his bread and cut a slice of it, a snow-white dove fluttered down in front of him. He broke off a piece of bread and put it down for her, and they sat eating together. A raven, the dove's enemy, was sitting in a tree and noticed the bread. The raven flew down and scared the dove, who dropped the bread. The raven picked up the bread and flew off to the south with the dove in pursuit.

Christian Rosenkreutz was so incensed at this that he stood and ran after them, shouting at the raven. He chased them the length of the meadow before he realized that, in his pursuit, he had traveled along the first steps of one of the paths. To his dismay, he realized he had left his bag and his bread back at the cedar tree. He tried to return along the path to retrieve them, but a great wind sprang up and would not let him return along the way he had chosen. He realized now that he must continue along this path that destiny had dictated to him.

He journeyed on and after a while spied a royal-looking gate far off on a high hill. He hurried toward it because it was late in the afternoon, and he was thinking of a place to stay. When he arrived, he saw an exceedingly beautiful Royal Portal covered with strange signs and symbols. From behind the portal stepped a man in a sky-blue porter's uniform. He was the Gatekeeper to the castle, and he demanded his letter of invitation. Once the Gatekeeper had read the letter, he joyously welcomed Christian Rosenkreutz as a brother. The Gatekeeper asked him for his name, which he gave and said that he was a brother of the Rosie Cross. The Gatekeeper then asked if he had any means to purchase a token. He had only his water bottle, so he gave that to the Gatekeeper, who gave him a golden token engraved with the letters S.C. (*Solve–coagula*). Then the man gave Christian Rosenkreutz a letter so that he could pass through the second portal closer to the castle on the other side of the hill.

By this time, it was getting dark, and a great beacon was lit on the first gate. Behind the gate, the road leading from the first gate to the second was enclosed by walls and planted with fruit trees. A lantern was hung on every third tree, and a beautiful virgin was going among the trees lighting the lanterns.

Aided by the light on the trees, Christian Rosenkreutz continued along the lantern path. Soon he reached the second gate, also adorned with images with mystic significance. An inscription in Latin was "Do! Dedicate yourself!" Under the gate stood a terrible lion chained to the portal. As soon as the lion spied him it began to roar and lunge at him, which woke a second Gatekeeper, who drove the lion back. He then read the letter from the first Gatekeeper that Christian Rosenkreutz had timidly handed to him.

The Gatekeeper addressed him with great respect, saying that he had been awaiting him for a long time. He took out a token and asked if Christian Rosenkreutz had anything with which to purchase it. CR had nothing left except his Salt, and with this he purchased the token. On the token were two letters: "S.M." (*Sal mineralis,* "mineral salt").

With this, a bell began to ring in the castle, and the porter told Christian Rosenkreutz to start running since the lights would all be extinguished soon. However, being eighty-one years of age, Christian Rosenkreutz could not run fast enough, and the lights that were being put out as the Virgin passed toward the castle were going out much too quickly.

The torch carried by the Virgin soon afforded the only light by which to see the path, and CR was forced to enter the narrow doorway at just the same time that the Virgin passed through. As they passed, the door suddenly clapped shut, catching his coattails. To get into the castle, he was forced to leave his coat in the door. The Gatekeeper locked the gate and gave the keys to the Virgin of the lamps, who took the keys with her as she ascended a spiral staircase into the court.

Left alone, Christian Rosenkreutz looked at the inside of the gate, which was rich with sculptures and signs. Two columns stood inside of the gate, each with a figure on it. The inscription on one column, which had a joyful statue on it, said, "Rejoice with others!" The inscription on the other, which held a statue with a sad countenance, said, "Feel the other's great pain."

Once inside the gate, he had to give the Gatekeeper his name again, which was recorded in a vellum book. After this, he was escorted to the court of the Lord Bridegroom, where he was given his last and truest token, which was inscribed with the letters "S.P.N." (*Salus per naturam*, "Salvation by nature"). He was then told to give his shoes to one of the poor who were stationed outside near the gate, and that he would be given a new pair. He gave his shoes to an old man, and two pages escorted him to a little room. They left their torches and went out, leaving him alone.

In the semi-darkness, he thought he heard two men enter the room. He could not see them but perceived that they were barbers because of their instruments. The invisibles treated him roughly as one of them shaved the crown of his head into a tonsure. The two invisible barbers then gathered up his shorn hair and left.

Two pages came in and laughed at Christian Rosenkreutz's new appearance, and then a bell rang and the pages took him through a series of passages and doors into a spacious hall, where there were many guests. Emperors, kings and beggars, noble and ignoble all sat together. He saw that he knew many of them, which caused CR to begin berating himself at how much time and effort it had taken him to get to the castle, whereas here were persons that he knew had no spiritual capacities whatsoever but had gotten here before him and were mingling with the noble spirit persons. He considered all of the time he had spent praying and supplicating God so that he would be worthy, and here were others who had gotten in before him and whom he knew to be of dubious character. Those persons mocked him, commenting that it was good that he had finally gotten to the wedding. They wanted to know what took him so long.

Christian Rosenkreutz answered that it was only by the grace of God that he was allowed to enter. The others all laughed at this, wondering why he was so fixed on the idea of giving credit to God in the midst of such a splendid wedding. Christian Rosenkreutz inquired of most of them as to which way, out of the three available, had they chosen to get there. They all said that they chose to come the short way, over the rocks. Then trumpets sounded, and his mockers immediately seated themselves at the head tables near the lords and ladies. CR, with a few sorry old fellows who were slow, found their way to the lowest table. Grace was said, but during grace there was much winking and joking among those at the head tables. Then meat appeared, brought by invisible attendants.

Once filled with meat and wine, those at the higher tables began to tell everyone tales of their greatest adventures and exploits, each tale becoming more grandiose than the last. Those fellows insinuated themselves among the nobles and wove such stories as to make your stomach revolt. Commonly, the sorriest idiots made the most noise.

The nobles and lords sat spellbound by the tall tales, while pickpockets and thieves began to work the crowd of nobles as the tales grew taller and taller. All the while, invisible waiters moved food and drink onto the tables and cleared the utensils when the diners were finished. One drunkard swore that he could see the invisible waiters with his special powers of clairvoyance. To the amusement of everyone, he was given a sound rap on his ear by an invisible server.

At the lowest table, Christian Rosenkreutz found himself in the company of a few quiet men. In conversing with them, he found that they all believed they did not understand, which prevented them from asserting themselves about their knowledge. CR began to rue the fact that he had even started on this journey, since it seemed that ignorance and boastfulness was the direction in which the wedding was proceeding.

One of the drunken rascals began to taunt CR as an old fool who was too timid to amount to anything. Christian Rosenkreutz thought that he had not done anything to deserve this scorn and ridicule. He was thinking of approaching the Bridegroom and telling him that he should have invited some other fool instead of him to this ridiculous event. As his anger grew, he realized that this feeling was a big part of his lameness. He remembered the dream of the Tower and the dungeon and how the chains had hurt his feet. He remembered the Ancient Matron asking him to bear his wounds for her sake. He thought, *Behold! To such impatience does the iniquity of the world reduce simple hearts.*

At the height of the chaos, Christian Rosenkreutz turned to an older man sitting at the lowest table, who commented, "Behold, my brother. If anyone came to instruct these blockheads in the right way, do you think he would be heard? I doubt it, since the world is resolved to be cheated by pretenders and cannot abide to give ear to those who intend its good."

All of a sudden, stately music began, sounding as if the harmony of the planetary spheres itself were playing. The music soothed the feelings of Christian Rosenkreutz and his older companion, since anyone who began speaking while the music was playing received a blow on the mouth from one of the invisible waiters.

After a half hour, the music ceased, and drums and trumpets sounded as the doors opened in the great hall. Thousands of small, lit tapers entered the hall, carried by invisible beings. This was followed by two pages with large torches who illuminated the self-propelled throne of a most beautiful Virgin. It seemed to Christian Rosenkreutz that she was the one who he had met in the orchard lighting the lanterns—the one who had squeezed through the gate at the same time as he. She had lost her sky-colored gown and was now arrayed in a snow-white glittering robe that sparkled of pure gold so radiant that he could not look at it.

As she reached the center of the hall, the throne stopped and all of the tapers bowed before her. The guests all rose from their seats. She spoke in a pleasant tone:

> The king, my Lord, is not far from us now, and he is with his lovely Bride. They have watched your arrival with great joy. You would do well to remember what was written in the invitation, that no one who was called here had not received God's greatest gifts long before they were invited. As a result, the Bridegroom and Bride consider that no one would be so desperate as to come here unprepared for this Wedding. So, they hope that in the following days things will go well with you all. Yet, humans have grown so bold and inept in their feelings that they thrust themselves into places where they were not called. Our hosts—resolving to celebrate the Wedding without the presence of cheaters, thieves, liars and rascals—have decreed that scales shall be set up tomorrow to weigh the participants, whereby each one will find what was left behind at home. If there be any here who think they have good cause to doubt themselves, let them quickly pack up and leave this place. Otherwise, they will feel forlorn and graceless tomorrow when they must run the gauntlet and be weighed. Those who have a bad conscience over this should know that you will all be left alone in this hall so that they should be gone by morning. But if anyone has confidence that he is prepared, he should go with his waiter to a room where he can wait in peace for morning. The others who aim above what's possible for them might find it better if they had gone away tonight, but we hope for the best of you all.

After she had spoken, she went to her throne as trumpets sounded loudly, covering the sighs from many in the hall. The Virgin was taken away on her throne, and the tapers accompanied each person. Most had chosen to take their chances with the scale.

Christian Rosenkreutz searched his conscience and concluded that he was most unworthy and ignorant, so he would wait in the hall with the rest and not seek a room. He decided that it was better to be content with the meal that he had already been given in the hall rather than to risk being repulsed when he tried to get something better. Nine persons, including Christian Rosenkreutz and the older man with whom he was speaking at the table, were led into a chamber and told to wait. After a short time, pages appeared with cords and asked if they had chosen to stay there. When they said that they had, they were bound and left in the darkness.

Thinking anguished thoughts, CR eventually fell asleep and had a dream in which he was on a high mountain and viewing a great valley. In the valley were a great multitude of people, each with a thread attached to their head. The threads went up to heaven. One person hung high, another person hung low, while some stood on the earth. In the air, an ancient man flew up and down. In his hands, he held a pair of scissors with which he cut the threads of the hanging persons. Those who hung near the earth were prepared when their thread was cut, and they landed silently and gently. But when the thread of a high-hanging person was cut, he fell to earth with a resounding thud so that the earth quaked. For some, it happened that their thread was so stretched that they touched the earth even before their thread was cut. CR enjoyed watching the higher ones tumble to earth. Those who had overly exalted themselves got a shameful fall as they came crashing to earth, sometimes taking out their neighbors. Christian Rosenkreutz also took pleasure in the fact that those who had kept themselves near the earth came down fine and gently. He enjoyed this so much that, when he was jogged by one of his fellow sleepers and awoke to find himself still among his fellow captives bound in the dark, he was very discontented. He shared his dream with the older man and they passed the night in conversation.

Day Two Commentary

Christian Rosenkreutz awoke in the morning after dreaming of the dungeon, and he resolved that he would attend the wedding; he would make the journey. In doing so, he took along provisions of water, salt, and bread. These three substances are symbolic. With the water, he is taking along his life body; with the salt, he is taking his intellect; with the bread, he takes his perception of the transformative, self-adjusting process. This is "I can do this" consciousness.

In life, we take things from the world in one form and transform them in such a way that they interact. This is a self-adjusting process we must monitor throughout life. In the end, we look at the results, and an image emerges of the whole: *Here's my salt. Here's my water. Here's my bread.* It's a perfect picture.

Christian Rosenkreutz packs these things for traveling on the road. Soon, he reaches an important crossroads, where a sign hangs on a cedar tree. Cedar is a tree that acts as a sentinel, guard, or protector. Because it repels moths and dampness, its wood is often used to make chests in which a dowry or other precious articles are kept. Cedar is a sacred tree whose leaves are used as smudges in rituals to drive away evil influences. In Christian iconography, cedar is linked to the protective and benevolent forces of the Christ. Later in this story, a cedar box is used to house the most precious substance.

The sign on the cedar tree indicates that there are four roads—a short rocky one, a long winding one, a royal one, and a road reserved solely for immortals. All four roads lead to the wedding, but the rule is this: Once you make a choice, you cannot go back. The crossroads is uncertainty, and he needs to decide, but of course he can't. So, he does something any good phlegmatic would do: He decides to have lunch.

He sits down to eat some bread, and he notices a white dove in the cedar tree. The dove is the Holy Spirit. The Holy Spirit is the future human, the teacher of the future human. The Holy Spirit is the spirit of healing, who understands that people do not understand reality when they do stupid things.

The dove flies down to Christian Rosenkreutz, and he feeds it pieces of his bread—his substance of I-can-do-this consciousness. Then a raven arrives, drives away the dove, and begins to eat his bread. The raven is a traditional alchemical symbol for the first stage of initiation. It was said that ravens eat the corpses on a battlefield. In alchemy, the corpse is a motif that refers to the dead aspects of matter that are present in sensory memories. To alchemists, the forces that animate the senses are gifts from higher realms, but what the senses behold in the world are not the animating forces but the residue, or corpses, of the sensory world. On the alchemical path, the first stage of information gathering in any study has the nature of a corpse being eaten by a raven. The first stage of initiation is always called *negredo* (blackness), which symbolizes all that we do not understand. Ravens, however, are among the most intelligent of birds and are the tricksters. This is a paradox.

Christian Rosenkreutz becomes angry that the raven has taken the bread from the dove. He starts to chase the raven but fails to notice that through this impulse he has chosen a path. When he realizes that he has made a choice, he also remembers that he has left his bread by the cedar tree. However, when he turns around to retrieve his supplies, a stiff wind arises and blows him along his chosen path.

This is a motif related to the idea of uncertainty and initiation. Do I make a choice based on my consideration of all the variables—a strategy that always leads to indecision as the result of more variables? Or do I learn how to make a choice in which fate comes into play? We have a polarity between waiting for an answer and the action of fate. This is a strong motif in *The Alchemical Wedding*. Can I afford to wait until I know? If I can afford to wait until I know and don't work while I'm waiting, I will go nowhere. If I can afford to wait and work while I'm waiting, I draw the necessary destiny to me; this is most effective. If I cannot afford to wait, I need to look at the reason I cannot afford to wait. If I can afford to wait while working diligently, I am assured of help from the spirit—that is, I receive something that stirs me into action.

Here we have a comment on the various levels of our will. Is the world structured so that my will be done, or is the world structured so that *thy Will* be done? Can I recognize the difference? Can I render unto Caesar what needs to be given to Caesar (*my will*) and render unto God the things that are God's (*your will*). Can my expectant will afford to wait until the Great Will (karma) is revealed? If I act and I feel I'm in accord with the Great Will, my will has synergy, because I am part of a self-adjusting process. My will becomes amplified when it comes into line with my karma; it becomes effective. Without it, I'm just on the "didn't I do this before" merry-go-round. This is a picture of waiting and fate.

"Waiting" means learning how to live in solve. Solve has soul, Sun, hidden in it. This is a condition of attentive will toward the potential of a situation—I create in my will the patience to attend without collapsing into believing that I know what must happen. I create a will-structure through my effort of finding and repeating a symbol to take into sleep so I can give it to the other side. Then I pay attention during my day to see what is returning from the other side. My attention here is on how this symbol is manifesting here—not what might be in it for me. It's a very different gesture toward solving a problem: *s-o-l-v-i-n-g—solve.*

The other side of this will-exchange is faith. *Do this now!* That's a coagulum of the potential. *You will do this now.* The way Christian Rosenkreutz decides which path to take is the result of his impulse to protect the dove from the raven. This gesture moves him toward decision, and it exemplifies the way he makes decisions throughout the story. It's useful to pay attention to this, because it is an esoteric technique with deep wisdom in it. If you are in a situation in which you cannot actually resolve something, and if you want to feel you are being supported, start a *self-adjusting* process.

On day two, Christian Rosenkreutz is on his journey when he is blown toward the castle. In esoteric terms, a castle is often seen as the head, the little box in which we live. It has little windows through which to fire arrows at the enemy and rooms in which to hoard treasured memories. This represents one's head. Christian Rosenkreutz is trying to enter his own head, and the motif is *thinking*. Because of the fact that he is entering his own head as he tries to approach the great castle where the wedding will happen, he must pass through various gates to get there.

This is where Christian Rosenkreutz meets the guardian, the "confidant Gatekeeper" as he is known to alchemists. This is the same guardian Rudolf Steiner describes in his book *How to Know Higher Worlds*.* The guardian's speech is always the same: Everything that you think is happening *to* you is actually coming *from* you and helping you to understand human life. This is probably the greatest paradox of all. If you understand this, it puts you between a rock and a hard place insofar as your will is concerned. In the presence of the guardian's consciousness you can no longer blame others for what you are going through in life. Blame merely adds insult to injury. The teaching of "no blame" does not appeal to everyone. It's like existential jet fuel—a drop of "no one is to blame, not even you" goes a long way toward liberation. This is the message behind the mocking and slurs aimed at Christian Rosenkreutz by the castle inhabitants. To get to the castle, I must meet the demands of the guardian, who asks us why we want to go there. *Do you know the secret sign? Do you have a token? Do you have something to prove you are capable of withstanding what you will find once you are inside the castle?*

The first token has "S.C." (*solve–coagula*) on it. He gives this to the Gatekeeper, along with his bottle of water—he gives the guardian

* See Rudolf Steiner, *How to Know Higher Worlds: A Modern Path of Initiation* (Anthroposophic Press, 1994), chaps. 10 and 11.

his life body. Remember, *solve* means to dissolve, and *coagula* means to congeal or precipitate. Christian Rosenkreutz is now at the water level of consciousness—awareness of the common element of flow in life and thought. The water payment, the Gatekeeper, and the token of solve and coagula all point to crossing a boundary in consciousness—from the flowing world of nature through the gate to the silent, flowing inner world of a higher consciousness of light and air. He enters his own life body. When his life body is accompanied by the S.C. token, Rosenkreutz understands that solve and coagula are the way that the life and soul bodies interact in forming thoughts. Thus, the guardian allows one to pass on and continue the work.

Then the guardian gives Christian Rosenkreutz a letter of introduction for the next Gatekeeper, so he continues on and reaches the next Gatekeeper, who asks him, "Where is your token?" On the token is written "S.M." (*Sal mineralis*). *Sal* is salt, and salt is code for thinking that produces thoughts. In the soul, thinking is a mysterious, fluid, creative force; it is *solve*. Thinking remains fluid, as potential, until it actually produces a thought, and then thinking becomes coagulated into the thought. This is alchemical salt.

The salt pole in the soul is the formation of thoughts, but in chemistry salt is both an acid and a base. When an acid is mixed with a base substance, they neutralize each other, and then the salt falls, or precipitates, out of the neutralized liquid. If I reintroduce acid or base to the liquid, the salt returns to a solution; salt alternates between states of solution and precipitation. Such processes are the bases of both our thinking and our digestive system. In fact, all of the chemical properties in the world are based on such a polarity of acid and base through the contemporary theory of electron donors or electron receptors (*redox*, or reduction–oxidation). This is the essential edifice of chemistry—solve and coagula of acids and bases.

Christian Rosenkreutz is asked, "Do you have a token for *Sal mineralis?*" Do you realize that your tendency to form sensory-based thoughts is mineralizing everything in the world around you into corpses? Mineralization of thinking is the creation of thoughts that are killing the world, which is in reality the fluid, creative activity of the hierarchies. Christian Rosenkreutz gives his *Sal mineralis* token and his salt to the Gatekeeper. Thus, he is able to move on to the next level. If you can actually connect with the way thinking falls into thoughts, this is the philosophy of freedom.* Christian Rosenkreutz has to show the guardian that he understands the difference between thinking as a creative spiritual activity and thinking that produces thoughts in which there is no further activity—no more will but only memory.

Christian Rosenkreutz reaches the castle. A virgin is moving around and lighting the lights before disappearing through a door. It's late, and he has to come up with the S.P.N. token. He has to show a letter, or token, with "S.P.N." on it to the next guardian. This is *Sal per naturam.* When he was studying alchemy, Carl Jung coined a well-known phrase in reference to the whole process of individuation and integration of the shadow. He called it *"opus contra naturam,"* or working against nature. *Naturam* refers to the formative processes of nature—the activity of nature, or nature as a verb. *S.P.N.* is salt by way of nature's activity, or what Paracelsus might have called the *archeus,* the structure of patterns behind the natural world. S.P.N. asks: Instead of just thinking dead thoughts, can you transform your thinking in order to participate collaboratively in the formative processes of the becoming of nature? *Sal per naturam* is the salt process portrayed in the physiological ontogeny of beings of the natural world.

The Gatekeeper asks:

> Do you think everything in nature is only sense-perceptible trees, bushes, dirt, and rocks, as well as your own flesh? If you think everything in nature is flesh, you cannot enter here. If you think nature includes only such corpses, you cannot enter. However, if you can harmonize your thinking, your *sal,* by

* See, Rudolf Steiner, *Intuitive Thinking as a Spiritual Path: A Philosophy of Freedom* (Anthroposophic Press, 1995).

> representing the processes of nature to yourself inwardly, then you have imaginative cognition, and the things you see inside this castle will not hurt you, and I can allow you inside.

Thus, Christian Rosenkreutz goes from "Do you understand solve and coagula" to "Do you understand that your intellect is salting everything? Now that you understand that your intellect is a force of death (as Steiner says), do you understand that you can actually control it to create a resurrection force in nature?" This is essentially what Christian Rosenkreutz has to acknowledge before he can enter the castle.

These are the alchemical steps that Christian Rosenkreutz has gone through thus far to arrive at the castle gates—the gates of his own head. At the gate, he has the right token. The Gatekeeper allows him in and says, "You must give your shoes to an old man." Basically, we have to give away everything we think we need. This is the castle's great teaching. The reason we have to give it away is that we believe it is exactly as it appears to us, but we have to learn that this is not the spiritual reality but only the way it appears under the influence of our senses.

This process of divesting of the familiar is like going to boot camp. When I went to Navy boot camp, they woke us up at three o'clock the first morning. They shaved off our hair and told us to remove our civilian clothes and place them in a box. Then they gave everyone a set of clothes smelling of mothballs. Finally, we were taken to the chow hall, which was arranged so we had to slide our trays along a rail to be served breakfast. At the end of the rail was a large mirror in which I appeared to myself as a bald man wearing ill-fitting, smelly clothes. After we all ate, they marched us to another building to pick up our boxes of civilian clothes before marching us to the old World War II barracks where we had slept. Everyone was given a label and told, "You need to address this box of clothes to your mother. Say, 'Goodbye, Mom!' *We* are now your mother, father, uncle, and sister;

we are everything. Say goodbye to who you were." Military people are good at getting a person to give away everything before entering the castle of military life.

Christian Rosenkreutz passes the Gatekeeper and goes through the door into the castle. Boot camp is over—head shaved, shoes given away, and coat gone. Now we're ready. We can go to the banquet. At the banquet Christian Rosenkreutz sees the town rascals who went the quick way, and they all make fun of him. This is a good picture. When you do this kind of work, people will say, "I don't think you understand things the correct way. Why not try getting up to speed with the real world?"

That's the picture of this initiation. Once you start to do this work, you appear rather stupid to the world. In esoteric language, we become "holy fools." This is the first of many times that Christian Rosenkreutz will be mocked and laughed at by people in the castle. Mockery and trickery are a favorite pastime of the beings in the castle. Christian Rosenkreutz shows a remarkable capacity for self-effacement, which will serve him well as the initiation proceeds.

Christian Rosenkreutz is now a holy fool. As such, he meets the Virgin who organizes the spiritual beings running the castle. She is the Virgin of the ten, as we will come to know her. Her task is to look after those who will attempt to enact the alchemical marriage. She is a highborn virgin and powerful, though she is linked to worldly events and not to cosmic ones, as are some of the more powerful virgins. In this tale, the virgins might also be called angels; they are evolved soul beings.

The Virgin says to Christian Rosenkreutz, "If you think you're going to fail this training, say so now and we'll have mercy on you and put you into that group over there." After being mocked so much by the town rascals, he replies, "I think I'm going to wash out of this training." At that , soldiers of the Virgin take hold of him, tie him up, and throw him into a dark room with a group of others who said they probably wouldn't measure up. Those nine people who admit they are unworthy to continue the initiation process will eventually become, with one addition, the ten who are championed by the Virgin to enact the alchemical marriage. Their real significance is that they are aware of their own errors and human misunderstanding. This makes them the worthiest candidates for initiation.

Day Three

Overview

Christian Rosenkreutz had gone to sleep and awakes to a higher experience. Grace came to him in the night. In the morning, the people who were tied up awake as those who had gone upstairs return from their rooms. The people upstairs had already eaten a nice breakfast and are all looking truly full of themselves, whereas the nine men who'd been tied up and slept on the floor look terrible. The invisible pages drag the tied-up men out in front of everyone, who ridicule them as stupid losers. Then the Virgin enters and turns to the men who were tied up, saying to the soldiers, "Release them from their bonds." Deliverance! The bonds are removed. Then all the men who had been upstairs overnight are surrounded, and each person is laid hold of by the men in armor.

Next, a large scale made of gold is brought into the room. The soldiers have seven weights for the scale. A person who is a moral "heavyweight" will not be moved when those seven weights are placed on the scale. The soldiers place each of the men Christian Rosenkreutz calls vagabond cheaters on the scale, and they cannot balance even a small weight. This weighing is meant to determine who is morally substantial and who is morally deficient. This is the judgment before the wedding.

The Virgin says to the men who have just been unbound, "Your task now is to judge the others who are being weighed." This is a very interesting picture. Christian Rosenkreutz says that he doesn't want to judge, but the Virgin says that someone must judge. Hearing this, tears come to his eyes, because he does not want to be the one to judge.

The freed nine who had been bound talk among themselves about having to judge others. About all of the vagabond cheaters, the Virgin is saying, "I think they should be stripped naked and whipped, and dogs should bite them. Then they should be flayed alive, driven out, and killed." Meanwhile, Christian Rosenkreutz is protesting to her that she doesn't understand—that they are only human. He's trying to be compassionate, and the Virgin seems to be ruthless. The Virgin tells them that they are too weak to judge and that she is only doing her spiritual task.

When the weighing is almost finished, it is decided that the nine men should also be weighed. Only Christian Rosenkreutz keeps the scales from lifting when all of the weights are used, and even when some of the soldiers hang on to the other end of the scale. From this it is recognized that he is the long-expected person.

"You are the One," everybody says. "He's here; he's the One!" Everyone is looking at him, saying, "Oh my goodness, you're the One." Christian Rosenkreutz tells them, "No, I'm not really the One. I don't understand how this has happened."

The Virgin tells Christian Rosenkreutz that, because he is the One, he is allowed to free one other person. An emperor has come up just short in the weighing, and Christian Rosenkreutz has compassion on him. He realizes that this emperor has a difficult job and a good heart and is not receiving his due, since he was missing only one weight. With this, the Virgin sees that Christian Rosenkreutz has the soul force of compassion. The emperor is pulled out of the group of the rejected and brought into the other group, which now numbers ten.

During the remainder of the banquet, Christian Rosenkreutz commits an error in protocol—a harbinger of future errors. He asks a waiter to deliver a choice bit of food to an acquaintance. However, no waiter is immediately available. Christian Rosenkreutz wants to let the recipient know it is an offering from him, so he rises to deliver the food himself. Immediately, one of the waiters is at his side and tells him to be seated and that, if one of the other waiters had seen him delivering the food himself, they would have told one of the pages, who in turn would have reported it to the Bridegroom. The waiter tells him that no one else had seen Christian Rosenkreutz stand up, and then asks him to have a higher regard for the order and not to mention this to anyone.

This is the first episode of this kind—one in which Christian Rosenkreutz is given a great honor. He begins to expand a little and relax into the mood of being honored, but is suddenly jerked back into a humble position through an unforeseen protocol. This happens several more times as Christian Rosenkreutz, this most archetypal human, strives to understand the subtle laws of the spiritual world.

As a relief from the intensity of the judgments, the ten are allowed to take a break in a garden, where there is a marvelous fountain nearby with a structure composed of four galleries with various symbolic features. On the first level is a white curtain that hides a mysterious person. The one above that is empty. The third and fourth levels are covered with red and blue cloths. Thus begins the motifs of galleries, towers, chambers, and winding stairs that continue throughout the story.

The four galleries in this image, as well as the marvelous fountain guarded by a lion, could symbolize the heart as an image. In many ways, the alchemical marriage is about the heart's transformation from selfishness to selflessness. The true human "I" lives in the warmth of the blood. Its castle is the circulatory system; the four chambers in the garden represent the atria and ventricles of the heart. Red and blue taffeta depict venous and arterial circulation. The most glorious gallery would be the left ventricle, from which oxygenated blood streams into the aorta. This phenomenon (which Rudolf Steiner calls etherization of the blood) is the central mystery of Rosicrucian practice.

The king waits here for judgment to be passed, which will lead to balancing karma so that the heart can become a crucible for the marriage of soul and spirit. When the time for judgment and punishment is over, a unicorn enters the garden to witness this transition from profane to sacred.

This part of the story introduces many images of Christ. *Bridegroom* has often been an appellation of Christ, who seeks to marry himself to the floundering human soul as the bride. The unicorn, a mythical magic beast, is also a Christ image in its meekness, willingness to sacrifice, sensitivity, and magical presence. Other motifs find the unicorn appearing when the old king is about to die and a new one ready to ascend to power. This is a powerful motif in the story at this point. Esoterically, a unicorn represents the purified and sacrificial nature of an initiate's will. As the ten wash their hands and heads, they are enacting the ritual purification practiced in many ancient mystery sites of the Old World. This says that they are now novices in the initiation ceremony.

Now that the banquet and the judging are finished, the chosen ten are free to explore the castle. Christian Rosenkreutz asks his page to show him some of the castle's wonders. The page obliges and has keys to many of the rooms. This page can be viewed as a symbol of Christian Rosenkreutz's curious intellect. The page knows many things and always seems to have the keys to the most wondrous rooms of the castle. He is present to satisfy every question that Rosenkreutz puts to him. The motif of the knowledgeable page as a representative of Rosenkreutz's curious intellect is an important thread in this story. It represents a complex yet all-too-human state of consciousness. The page takes Christian Rosenkreutz to see the royal library and the royal tomb. For a second time that day, he crosses a line in terms of protocol. Another page rushes up to him and his page and informs them that, if the Bridegroom knew they had entered the royal library and the royal tomb, matters would not go well for them. He pledges them to secrecy about the violation, but Christian Rosenkreutz has breached protocol for the second time.

Once all are assembled again, they are presented with what are called the "riddles of love"—complicated riddles on the nature of lower passionate love, as well as about higher moral love.

The Alchemical Wedding, Day Three

In the morning, those who were confident of their success on the scales and had opted to take rooms with comfortable beds awoke to find the nine men who had admitted to misunderstanding, bound hand and foot and looking rough. Comments passed among the nine, as well as the others that were not very nice. In their defense, the nine stated that they hoped to be released very soon.

Then trumpets and drums sounded, and the Virgin from the day before appeared again. She was dressed in red velvet with a white scarf. On her head, she wore a green laurel wreath. Her retinue consisted of two hundred men, each clothed in red and white. The Virgin came straight to the nine prisoners and saluted them. She said that because some of the assembled had been conscious of their wretched condition and unworthiness, this was greatly pleasing to her Lord the Bridegroom, and he resolved that they will fare all the better for it. The Virgin turned directly to Christian Rosenkreutz and said that she was surprised he had opted for the yoke of being burdened and bound. She imagined that he would try to make himself smug and haughty. With these harsh words, Christian Rosenkreutz began to cry.

She then commanded that the prisoners be unbound but herded together into a small group and put into a place where they could see the activity at the scales. She hinted to the assembly that it might fare better for the prisoners who had admitted to misunderstanding than for the presumptuous persons.

The scales were made of pure gold and hung at the center of the hall. There was a table covered with red velvet on which seven weights were placed. There was one moderate weight, four little ones, and two great ones. The weights were much heavier than they appeared to be. Two hundred men accompanied the scales, each with an unsheathed sword and a rope. The two hundred men were divided into seven groups, one group for each weight.

Once these preparations were completed, the Virgin mounted her throne and spoke in a shrill voice:

> One who goes into a painter's studio knowing nothing of painting but starts to expound on the art of painting in a prideful way will soon be derided by the world. And one who goes into the artist's guild without being asked to join, but enters anyway under the pretext of having skill in painting, will be derided by the world. One who appears at a wedding but was not intended to attend yet comes into the wedding in a prideful way will soon be derided by the world. One who ascends to this scale, with the weights proving to be unfriendly to his claim but instead causes the scales to bounce, shall be derided by the world.

When this speech was finished, the pages commanded each of the assembled persons to step up and onto the scales. One of the emperors immediately stepped forward, bowed a little toward the Virgin, and placed himself on the scales. Each captain of each group added his weight, which the emperor withstood to the wonder of all, until the last one was laid and caused the scale to bounce. The emperor left the scale with much anguish, so that even the Virgin pitied his state. She asked her people to hold their peace, and the emperor was bound and given over to the sixth band of men.

Next came another emperor who stepped haughtily onto the scale. He had a great, thick book hidden in his gown and thought that, with this weight, he couldn't fail. The third weight undid him, and he fell off the scale with book pages flying out of his gown. This sight made the soldiers laugh. He was delivered bound to the third group. Other emperors also stood the test and failed, much to the delight of the soldiers.

Then a short man who was also an emperor arose. He went to the scales and outlasted all of the weights. The Virgin arose and bowed before him and gave him a gown of red velvet and a laurel branch. Other kings and emperors also tried the scales, but few of those great personages held out against the weights. This process went through the learned, the unlearned, the gentry, and the common folks, and in each condition one or perhaps two were found perfect to match the weights.

Eventually the process came to the cheaters, vagabonds, and scoundrel pretenders. They were set upon the scale with such scorn that even the prisoners in the other groups were laughing. However, even among them there were persons of quality who were honored with velvet robes and laurel wreaths. After a while, the great multitude of persons was whittled down to only a few worthy individuals.

The captain of one of the weight groups asked for the group of nine prisoners who had acknowledged their misunderstanding and ignorance beforehand to be placed on the scale without danger of penalty, but solely for recreation and to see if anything right might be found among them.

Christian Rosenkreutz was thrown into confusion, because he understood that by admitting his misunderstanding he was not to stand being lashed out of the scale in a shameful way. The prisoners were led one by one to the scale, and when one of them failed, they were not ridiculed and lashed out of it but were led silently and peacefully to one side. The old man who was the companion of Christian Rosenkreutz held all of the weights and was afforded respect and recognition from the Virgin. Christian Rosenkreutz was eighth of the nine prisoners. As he stood on the scale the old man and the Virgin both smiled. Christian Rosenkreutz withstood all of the weights and even withstood the Virgin commanding three men to stand on the pile of weights on the scale.

One of the pages immediately stood up and cried out in a loud voice, "THAT IS HE!"

The other one cried out, "THEN LET HIM GAIN HIS LIBERTY!"

The choice was given to Christian Rosenkreutz to release one of the prisoners from one of the groups. He immediately chose the first emperor, who had aroused pity in him. The emperor was immediately set free and seated among the nine in the group. The last one was set up and failed to stand the weights. At the end of the judging, the Virgin spied the roses in CR's hat and graciously requested one of them. He was honored by this request. This first act was finished around ten in the morning.

The Virgin met with the seven captains and tried to work out how the prisoners in the seven groups would be handled. The first opinion was that they should all be put to death by degrees of severity in relation to their presumptuousness. This was not in agreement with all parties. Christian Rosenkreutz, the old man, and the newly freed first emperor came up with a solution. The principal lords should be led out of the castle with some degree of dignity. Others might be driven out more scornfully; they would be stripped and run out naked. Others would be hunted out with dogs or whips, with the worst and most presumptuous of them all to be punished in body and life according to each person's demerit. Those who willingly admitted misunderstanding were to be let out without punishment.

The group of nine plus the first emperor was led to a place where the execution of the sentences was to be carried out. Each of the seven groups of prisoners was led in and seated according to the qualities of each. Christian Rosenkreutz observed that persons of higher rank seemed to be more able to conduct themselves well in the face of unexpected fortune. The nine plus the emperor were seated at a table near the Virgin. On the table nearby, wine cups and food were available to them, much to the chagrin of the other groups of prisoners.

Pages entered and presented to each of the ten a golden fleece with the image of a flying lion on it. The pages asked the ten to wear these at the table. A page also possessed a schedule given by the Bridegroom to the ten concerning their duties in the sentencing of the prisoners. The ten asked the pages if it would be possible to send food and wine to some of the unfortunates. This request was taken to the Bridegroom and answered in the affirmative.

The invisible waiters began to take food to the others, who could see neither where it came from nor who sent it. Christian Rosenkreutz stood up to take food himself to one of his friends, and one of the waiters immediately came to him and said he was fortunate that no one had seen his move because, if they had, it would go straight to the ear of the Bridegroom, who would have certainly taken it amiss. The waiter proposed not to betray CR in this slight, but suggested that CR should have a higher regard for the dignity of the Order in the future. This so astonished Christian Rosenkreutz that he sat for a long time in his seat without moving for fear of doing something wrong.

Again, the Virgin made an entrance to the sound of drums and trumpets. She was preceded by a page who carried a tall, golden goblet. She took the goblet from the page and said that it had been sent by the Bridegroom and that all of the ten should drink from it. The cup was engraved with the word *Fortune,* which made CR sad since he was well acquainted with the fickleness of Fortune. The Virgin was also wearing a golden fleece with a lion insignia, similar to those worn by the ten men, who asked her the name of the Order. She answered that the time for knowing that would be after the prisoners had been dealt with.

The pages began to read out the offences of the higher group of prisoners from a small book. They were guilty of giving credit to fictitious books and had assumed too much of themselves. They came to the castle uninvited and tried to turn the Wedding into a market to make themselves wealthy. In this way, one had seduced another and plunged both into disgrace. The prisoners were forced to accept these charges with the utmost humility. Following this, a more severe check was given to the other, more villainous prisoners. They were guilty of consciously making deceptive books and of cheating and fooling others, diminishing the dignity of all human beings. They knew full well that they had made blasphemous and mocking images of holy things, which caused people throughout the country to lie and cheat. It was now clear that they willingly engaged in whoredom, adultery, gluttony, and other uncleanliness, all against the expressed orders of the kingdom. Therefore, they should confess to being vagabond cheaters, knaves, and rascals and should be driven from the kingdom and from the company of civil people everywhere and be killed.

Some of the ten had reservations about the severity of this sentence. The Virgin herself was in favor of it, and some of the others were raging that it should be carried out quickly. In this mood, the villainous prisoners readily confessed, but vigorously pointed out that the lords and those of high station tried to buy their way into the castle and the wedding with money and connections. They questioned why their sentences were not as harsh as those given to the prisoners of lower stations. The answer was that the Bridegroom intended to punish one and all, some more and some less severely and that, in fact, all of them should be preparing themselves for death. This caused most of the prisoners to weep and wail and prostrate themselves before the ten and the Virgin. The Virgin stood resolute in her position, while the ten began to cry in their extreme compassion for the suffering of the other groups of prisoners. The other prisoners were led to a great garden by the Virgin's soldiers. The ten were allowed to go into the garden unbound to witness the execution of the sentences.

In the garden was a marvelous fountain guarded by a lion. Near to the fountain was a scaffold, as well as four galleries built one over the other, the first of which was more glorious than all the rest. It was covered with a white taffeta curtain that hid a mysterious occupant in the gallery. The second gallery was empty and uncovered, and the third and fourth were covered with red and blue taffeta.

As soon as the company approached the first gallery, the Virgin bowed low to the ground. It terrified the ten to see such a powerful person bow so low before a mysterious other. The Virgin led the ten up the winding stairs to the second, empty and unadorned gallery, where the virgin who had first brought Christian Rosenkreutz the invitation on the first day entered and declared the sentence in a loud voice. She said that the Great Lord, the Bridegroom, had hoped from the depths of his heart that everyone assembled would have come to the Wedding in righteousness and with a good heart. This having proved not to be the case, he was forced not by his inclination but by the ancient and laudable constitution of the kingdom to exact the sentence. However, so that the whole world will recognize the clemency of the Great Bridegroom, he has decreed that the usual sentence shall be exacted in a more lenient manner. Therefore, in the first case he is willing to let the Lords and Potentates keep their lives and to dismiss them freely and frankly from the Wedding. They were admonished in the future never to covet entry to a Wedding, which would only end in a fall into disgrace.

Then followed the sentencing of those who could not balance out the weights on the scale. Those who could balance the first few weights were stripped naked and sent away. Those who could balance only two of the light weights were stripped and branded and then sent out. Those who could balance the heavier weights but not all of them were dealt with more gently. Those who admitted to misunderstandings on their own accord were given liberty without blame. Those who could not balance any weights—the convicted vagabond cheaters—were punished in body and in life with sword, halter, water, and rods as an example to others. Those who failed in the weighing were many, and those who drew all of the weights from the ground were few. Among the 126 of those who weighed anything, there were none who weighed the same because of the different combinations of weights.

After this, the Virgin of the ten broke her wand, and the virgin who had delivered CR's invitation blew her trumpet as they stepped with utmost reverence toward whoever stood behind the taffeta curtains. The lords were the first to leave, and each redeemed himself with jewels, gold, money, and other things they left for the Lord Bridegroom. Each was given a *draft of forgetfulness,* so they would have no memory of the proceedings. After they had left, the willing volunteers also departed, followed by those who had been stripped, followed by those who had been scourged. The beheading and hanging of the truly wicked then took place.

Christian Rosenkreutz contemplated the human blindness that keeps human beings continuously busy with what has been forbidden since the Fall of humankind—that is, entry into Paradise. With this, the garden was empty and silent for a period of five minutes. Then a snow-white unicorn with a golden collar came into the garden. The unicorn bowed low to the lion on the fountain. The lion broke a sword he held in his paw into two pieces and cast them into the fountain as he roared loud and long. Soon a white dove brought an olive branch to him, which he devoured immediately, and this quieted him. The unicorn then returned to his place.

The Virgin led the ten down the winding stairs of the scaffold, where they all showed reverence toward the curtain. They washed their heads and hands in the fountain and waited there in silence until the king returned to the hall through a secret passage. The ten returned to their previous lodgings, each with a learned page who could discourse on any subject they wished. The Virgin took leave, promising to return in the evening for the ritual of the hanging up of the weights. She said that the ten would be presented to the king in the morning.

Christian Rosenkreutz began a tour of the castle with his page and his old companion and saw many wonderful things, including the royal sepulcher, from which he learned more than was contained in all books. In the same place, the glorious Phoenix also stood. His page explained it all as each of the ten was guided by their respective pages into the most effective subject for the particular genius of each. In the royal library was a great book with all of the figures, rooms, portals, writings, signs, riddles, and so on concerning the castle.

With this, another page approached their page and whispered something. CR's page immediately handed over the keys to the royal sepulcher and royal library to the other page, who took them out of the room. He said to CR that the king had decreed no man should gain entrance into the royal sepulcher and the royal library. He entreated the two men not to reveal this transgression in any way to anyone else. Both CR and his aged companion hovered between joy and fear. They left the rooms in silence, and no man inquired further about it. They were led by their page into a marvelous market place where all manner of arts were displayed. In the center of the area stood a remarkable clock on a turret that showed the time as the motion of the planets. In a great room there stood a terrestrial globe whose diameter was thirty feet, half of which was in a depression in the ground. Two men could turn this globe easily. On the globe were golden rings that, on close inspection, marked the birthplace of Christian Rosenkreutz, his aged companion, and all of the others. The page led the two into the center of the globe, where they contemplated the stars until supper was nearly finished.

Christian Rosenkreutz was the last to be served. When he arrived at the table, the waiters showed him the utmost reverence and recognition. He lowered his eyes in embarrassment, and this allowed the Virgin of the ten to steal close to him, grab him by the gown, and lead him personally to a place of honor at the table.

Once the company was warmed and merry with wine, the Virgin stood and said that she had a great contention with one of her sisters. An eagle was living in the chamber of the virgins, and the two virgins vied with each other over who was beloved most by the bird. One day, they approached the eagle to settle the dispute, resolving that the one to whom the bird showed the greatest friendliness was the most beloved. The Virgin of the ten held a laurel branch in her hand, and the other virgin had nothing. As soon as the eagle spied them, he immediately gave to the other virgin a laurel branch, which he'd been holding in his beak, and then gestured that he should receive the laurel branch from the Virgin of the ten. Owing to these gestures, each of the two virgins imagined that she was the most beloved. All of the others looked to Christian Rosenkreutz for the answer, since it was obvious from the demeanor of the Virgin toward him that he should be considered a special person.

Christian Rosenkreutz suddenly found himself unable to answer. Instead, he offered another riddle as a reply. He said:

> I had two companions, both of whom loved me. They wished to know who I loved the most, so they agreed to come to me together, and the one I embraced would be the most beloved. They did this, but one of them could not keep pace with the other, so he remained behind weeping. The other one came to me and I embraced him, but I was confused about what was happening. Later the two disclosed the ruse to me. I was unable to resolve this in myself and decided to let it rest until I found someone who could help me come to peace with this event.

Christian Rosenkreutz turned to the assembled guests, and none of them could provide an answer.

With this evasive riddle, the others had seen how CR avoided answering the Virgins challenge, and another of the ten immediately proposed another riddle.

> In the city where I lived, a virgin had recently been condemned to death, but the judge took pity on her situation and said that if anyone was willing to become the virgin's champion, he would be free to do so. The virgin had two lovers, one of whom immediately prepared to become her champion. He arrived on the battleground completely prepared and expecting to meet the other lover. He chose his place for the fight and awaited the time for battle. The second lover also resolved to fight but arrived late, thus gaining the less advantageous position for battle. Although he knew he was the underdog and in the more challenging position, he decided to fight anyway for the sake of his love. He was vanquished by the other, and the virgin's life was saved. However, both the victor and the vanquished asked for the heart of the virgin.

The person telling this tale asked the others to tell him which of the two loved her the more? No one could answer. The Virgin of the ten interrupted, saying that she was looking for answers to her riddle, but now she could see that she herself had gotten caught the net, so she asked if there were any more riddles. In answer, the third riddle was presented. It went as follows.

> In my youth I was in love with a worthy maid. To plead my case to her and to get a chance to meet with her, I employed the help of a matron familiar with her. Although the matron, the maid, and I as the suitor were together in a secret place, the relatives of the maid broke in on us unexpectedly. The relatives were in a rage and wanted to kill me. I pleaded for my life, and the relatives met together to see what might be done. They decided that I would marry either the matron or the maid for the period of a year, and for the next year I would marry the one left unmarried by the first choice. I would then choose my wife. Tell me, friends, whom should I marry first, the matron or the maid?

Everyone assembled laughed at this riddle, with some muttering which one should be chosen, and yet none wanted to give an answer.

With this, the fourth riddle began.

> In a certain city lived a noble married lady who was beloved by all, especially by a certain young nobleman who wished to plead his case with her. She was virtuous and did not want to hurt him, but she also did not want to yield to him, so she gave him a condition she considered impossible. She said, "If during the winter you can take me to a green garden in which the roses are blooming, I will go with you. If you cannot do this, you must resolve never to see me again." The young nobleman traveled to many foreign countries, sparing no expense to see if he could find someone capable of performing such magic. In time he found a little old man who promised to do this if the young nobleman would give him half of the estate he owned. This being agreed upon, the young nobleman returned home in the dead of winter. He invited the noblewoman to his green garden, where the roses were blooming. Seeing this the noblewoman asked the young nobleman if she could return one time to her husband. She met her husband with tears and sighs, lamenting her situation. The husband, perceiving her faithfulness and out of great love for her, told her that she must honor her bargain and return to her lover, who had gone to such great lengths to procure her. The husband's integrity impressed the young nobleman so greatly that he thought

> himself incapable of touching such an honest and noble wife. Thus, he sent her home again with honor to her husband. The little man who agreed to do the magic perceived the nobility of all of this and could not be a lesser being than those involved, so he restored to the young nobleman his properties.

The riddler then asked, "Please, my lords, which of these persons showed the greater nobility of spirit?" No one, not even the Virgin, could reply except to ask if there was another tale.

Without delay another started. "My lords I have a quick one. Who has the greater joy, he who beholds what he loves or he who is thinking of what he loves?" The Virgin answered immediately, "The one who *beholds* the beloved!"

"No," CR answered. "It is the other."

Thus, a contest began, but before it could proceed further, a sixth called out, "My lords, I am to take a wife. I have before me a maid, a married wife, and a widow. Who should I take as my wife?"

Immediately, a seventh replied:

> Things go well when there is a choice, but I have no choice in my situation. In my youth I loved a fair and virtuous virgin, and she loved me in the same way. Because of her friends, the relationship ended and we could not be together. She was married to another, who was an honest and loyal person who kept her with love and affection.
>
> During childbirth, her pains were so great that she fainted as if she were dead, and she was interred with great lamenting by her husband. I thought to myself: *Since I cannot be with her in life, in her death I might hold her in an embrace for one last time.* So, my servant and I went at night to her fresh grave and dug it up. Upon opening her coffin, I found her heart beating and a slight breath. Due to my warmth, her heartbeat increased as I held her until she finally awoke, alive in my arms.
>
> I took her to my home and bathed her chilled body in a bath of herbs and committed her to the devoted care of my mother. After a short time, she came to term and brought forth a son.

> After two days, I told her of all that had happened. I asked her to live with me so that the suffering of her husband would not be increased at that time. She replied that she was as much in love with me as she was with her husband and would need time to consider this whole unusual turn of events.
>
> The next day I left on a journey for two months, during which she lived with my mother and her son while recovering from her struggles. Upon returning home I invited the husband as a guest, and during dinner I asked him, "If your deceased wife were to come home, would you receive her?" With tears and laments he affirmed that he would. With that, I brought his wife to him and their new son, along with an account of all that had transpired. I asked him to ratify my claim to her love, since he had buried her while she was still alive. After a long dispute, he saw that I had a legitimate claim to her hand and was obliged to free her from their relationship, though he felt that the son was still his heir.

The Virgin interrupted here and asked how it was possible that the man was willing to double the husband's grief in a time of great sorrow. He answered that the man felt he was acting in a concerned manner toward the husband and all involved. A dispute arose among the assembled guests on this point, but in the end most agreed that he had done what was right by the husband. The man answered, "I returned both the son and the wife to the husband." He then addressed the guests, asking, "Which was greater, my honesty or the husband's joy?"

These words so cheered the Virgin that she had a round of drinks given to all. After that round, the rest of the riddles were a bit perplexing, but Christian Rosenkreutz remembered a tale that someone had brought. "A certain physician bought a parcel of wood for the winter and warmed himself with it all winter long and in the spring sold the same wood. He thus had the use of it for nothing."

The Virgin asserted, "Here we must have some skill," and all agreed as they said thanks for the meal and rose from the table.

The Virgin asked all if they wished to begin the wedding. "Yes," replied a virtuous lady. Christian Rosenkreutz asked the Virgin what her name was, but the Virgin just smiled and gave this riddle: "My name contains five and fifty and yet has only eight letters; the third is the third part of the fifth, which when added to the sixth will produce a number whose root shall exceed the third itself by just the first, and it is the half of the fourth. Now the fifth and the seventh are equal; the last and the first are also equal and make with the second as much as the sixth has, which contains just four more than the third tripled. Now tell me, what is my name?"

Christian Rosenkreutz understood, but he asked her if she would tell him just one letter. He asked, "What does the seventh contain?" She replied that it contains as many as there were lords present there. Christian Rosenkreutz said her name, and all were very pleased.

Meanwhile, other virgins had made themselves ready and entered, accompanied by two pages, one jovial and mirthful and the other angry and aggressive. Following them were four virgins. One humbly gazed downward at the ground. The second was bashful. The third seemed amazed and could not abide very much levity. The fourth brought small wreathes with her with which to manifest her kindness. After these, two more virgins entered, one in a sky-color gown with golden stars and the other in green with red and white stripes. The last one entered alone with a coronet on her head. She gazed upward toward heaven, not the earth.

The ten thought she was the Bride, since she was so powerful in her presence, but they were mistaken. Afterward, she ruled over the whole Wedding. The Virgin of the ten showed extreme humility to this ruling Virgin, who had entered last. Passionately, the ruling Virgin told them all to lift their eyes to their Creator and learn to acknowledge his omnipotence.

Next to the admonitions of this Virgin, Christian Rosenkreutz thought that their own Virgin of the ten seemed more worldly. The words of the ruling Virgin pierced him to his very bones and marrow. The ruling Virgin addressed him specifically, telling him that he had received more than the others, and that he must be sure to make a greater return. This command puzzled him.

In the hall was an unnamed queen who presided, it appeared, over this part of the wedding. The queen quietly told the assembled virgins to lift the weights that had been stored after the sentencing. Each virgin received one weight, some lighter than others. She gave the last and heaviest weight to the Virgin of the ten. In this, Christian Rosenkreutz perceived that their Virgin was protecting them as human beings.

So, the ten followed humbly behind her in procession to the scaffold as she approached the first chamber with the curtain, where the Virgin of the ten hung the heaviest weight. At the center of this room was a pulpit. The unnamed queen knelt at this pulpit with the ten around her, while the Virgin of the ten read the prayers. She asked that this wedding might honor God and be of benefit for all. After this, they all went into the second chamber, where the first virgin hung up her weight, and so on until all the weights were hung.

The unnamed queen departed with her Virgin. The Virgin of the ten remained for a few hours with them after the departure of the unnamed queen, and then she herself bid everyone a good night. Christian Rosenkreutz slept a deep sleep but was bothered by a bad dream of a door he was struggling to open until, after a long time, it finally opened.

Day Three Commentary

In the banquet hall, the town ne'er-do-wells—the drunks, pickpockets, and con artists—are all shown to the plush, upstairs suites, while the ten are shown to dismal, unpleasant rooms. Christian Rosenkreutz awoke in the morning after commiserating most of the night with an older man who could be thought of as his personal guardian of the threshold. The ten are tied up and led to the banquet room, just as the ne'er-do-wells are coming down from a nice breakfast. Spying the ten bound men, everyone begins to laugh and mock them. The Virgin enters and frees the nine, while the rascals are surrounded by armed soldiers.

Each of the rascals are placed on one side of the golden scale and weights on the other side. When the weights lift a rascal, he is deemed too light morally to attend the wedding. Alchemically, the number *seven* usually refers to the activity of the planets, and the various smaller weights would represent the inner planets—Mercury, Venus, Moon, and Mars. The largest weight is the Sun, while the other larger weights represent Saturn and Jupiter. This scheme would accord with an older system with Earth in the center. This system (which is correct perceptually, though not astronomically) is most commonly used in alchemical thought. The seven planets in this arrangement constitute the human astral, desire body. The people are being weighed to determine the worth they have developed in their soul life. In this context, Rudolf Steiner assigned seven virtues to the weights in this story. This judgment, a turning point in the story, must take place before anyone can attend the wedding.

The question of human freedom and liberty is also an important theme of *The Alchemical Wedding*. During the judgment, Christian Rosenkreutz gives the Virgin a rose from his hat, which she had been admiring. This implies that the connection between the Virgin and Christian Rosenkreutz as an initiate is a subtle, underlying motif related to the issue of human freedom in the context of initiation. We could ask: Who is the Virgin? What aspect of human consciousness does she represent? We might answer, with Meister Eckhardt, that an unredeemed soul is the Virgin seeking to be at the wedding with the Bridegroom to fulfill her destiny. For Meister Eckhardt, *Nous patheticos* is the soul in pathos, the dramatic soul. The picture in this idea shows a young Virgin spending her time wondering what it will be like when she and her Bridegroom are finally together. She is filled with expectation and longing and lives only to be recognized by her prince charming. In the context of initiation, the expectant virgin soul expects spiritual practice to lead to various powers, insights, and spiritual experiences. The *patheticos* virgin soul expects to be recognized by the spirit for efforts to develop a practice.

The other side of this for Meister Eckhardt is the married, wifely soul—*Nous poieticos,* the poietic, productive soul. This soul has solved the riddle of being married and now just works on the practice, because she knows that the real meaning of life is to be occupied with the productive work of self transformation. This is the central motif of the alchemical marriage as an idea. The marriage between soul and spirit is not the final goal but a productive path. It is not a cause for recognition but for doing the work without recognition—simply because it needs to be done.

The riddles given to the men being weighed represent a transformation of the relationship between the Virgin to the ten men. Until now, she has been somewhat of an adversary, but after the judgment she admires a rose in Christian Rosenkreutz's hat, which he gives to her as a sign of affection. The rose symbolizes the alchemist's struggle to overcome the lower earthly forces in the soul and transmute them into fragrances of heaven. Giving a rose to the Virgin is a step toward higher insight, but the Virgin of the ten is not the only virgin in the castle. There are many degrees of "virgin" in this story. Some resemble angels, some are more exalted divine beings, and still others are servants and attendants. The Virgin of the ten is intimately linked to human destiny and initiation. She accompanies the ten men throughout the entire alchemical marriage and is their support in the land beyond normal understanding.

Owing to the weighing process, it is recognized that Christian Rosenkreutz is a moral heavyweight and the expected one in the castle. In other words, he is the one who can complete the alchemy of transforming death into new life. The Virgin asks him for a rose. This more intimate mood is present in the passage about the mysteries of love. What begins as a simple riddle posed by the Virgin to Christian Rosenkreutz becomes a complex tapestry of moral questions about various implications of love and morality.

The Virgin poses a conundrum to Christian Rosenkreutz about the virgins' pet eagle, and how that eagle interacted with two virgins who agreed that the virgin favored most by the eagle would be the most loved by it. The eagle actually interacts in a loving way with both. The Virgin asks Christian Rosenkreutz to solve this riddle.

The virgins are clever; they already know what our issues are and how to ask embarrassing questions. You have to come clean about things with them. She asks him a question that is difficult for him to answer without revealing his own values. Not to be outdone, Christian Rosenkreutz asks the Virgin a riddle in which two people who loved him agreed that the first one to embrace him when they meet would be the most beloved. However, one person is unable to keep up with the other, who thus becomes the first to embrace him. Christian Rosenkreutz asks the Virgin if the result is true love.

This question leads to a cascade of unanswerable riddles about love and affection from the other men. This motif illustrates an esoteric principle: *Answer a question with a better question.* When Christian Rosenkreutz is asked a question, he answers with a better question, and the other men with him get it. This is the way they interact with the Virgin. Their questions about love and affection become deeper and deeper. Who loves whom more, or who does not? There are deep moral issues, questions, riddles about various degrees of love. They are a truly remarkable series of conundrums about love and marriage and use terms that have symbolic alchemical meaning.

The first few riddles deal with infatuation and first meeting in young love, whereas the Virgin and the lover are concerned with how much the lover loves them, which is *Nous patheticos*. Another riddle introduces a third variation of love—the matronly soul. A man loves three women: a virgin, a wife, and a matron. All three are free to be married. He asks which one he should marry. These three women are symbolic examples of the triple goddess, a concept that stretches back to early Greek mythology. Persephone, Demeter, and Hecate are names for the virgin, the wife, and the crone of Greek mysteries. They represent the life cycle of potential, production, and decay. In this alchemical marriage, the riddles focus on these three stages of the soul: the expectant soul, the productive soul, and now the soul facing decay. The men ask, "Which stage is the best for the alchemical marriage?"

The plot thickens with the seventh riddle, which introduces the subject of love passing thorough death and resurrection. This is the motif of the alchemical work to take place in the Tower later in the story. Here it is given in the context of two lovers and one woman who survives death to enter another relationship.

After the riddles, the ten are free to explore the castle. Christian Rosenkreutz and his page inadvertently violate castle protocols and are sharply rebuked. This is a motif we will meet again on the fifth day.

Day Four

Overview

A turning point in mood occurs on the fourth day. Thus far, Christian Rosenkreutz has been tied up, thrown into a dungeon, faced judgment, and more. It hasn't been easy, but it hasn't been sinister either. On the fourth day, a drama darkens the tone. First, the ten men are given golden fleeces to wear, bearing this inscription:

> *The light of the Moon shall be as the light of the Sun, and the light of the Sun shall be seven times lighter than at present.*

Alchemically, these words point to the fundamental issue in initiation—the transformation of intellectual thinking into spiritual perception. The Moon represents intellectual understanding, or reflective thought. The Sun represents original, creative thinking, which is akin to God and reason. Because the light of the Moon is to become like that of the Sun, the intellect will be transformed into reason, which will cause human creative thinking to become Godlike. When this happens, the Sun will become a much more powerful star. The golden fleeces symbolize the esoteric order into which Christian Rosenkreutz is being initiated. The original golden fleece was a device used by gold miners in the Middle East. They would submerge a fleece in a stream coming from gold veins in the mountains. The fleece would collect the gold flakes, which are heavier than rocks. As a symbol, it represents consciousness that can capture spiritual gold from across the threshold, where day consciousness is submerged in the unconscious.

On the fourth day, the story takes a strong turn toward complicated symbolic imagery of alchemy. The ten men are taken for the first time into the presence of the king and queen. Led by the Virgin, they must climb a flight of 365 stairs to the royal chamber. These 365 stairs symbolize the expansion of consciousness to higher states of awareness, whereby, according to Rudolf Steiner, an event takes a whole year (365 days) to emerge fully into conscious understanding. Ascending a flight of stairs symbolizes the gradual development of higher states of consciousness, and the ten are on the verge of higher insight. In this state, they finally see the king and queen—spirit and soul.

On the previous day, Christian Rosenkreutz had seen the queen, who is not named, in one of the chambers. Symbolically, he had recognized the non-cognized aspects of the soul. His memory of this experience enables him to endure the sight of the soul in its glorious, transcendent vestments of higher development in the vision of the king and queen together. Strangely, the ten men encounter not only one king and queen in the upper chamber, but also three royal couples—an old king and a very young queen; a dark king and dainty aged matron; and a young couple, characterized by Christian Rosenkreutz as less comely than he had expected.

These three royal couples are images of the three human soul forces—thinking, willing, and feeling. Alchemists would refer to thinking as *salt,* willing as *sulfur,* and feeling as *mercury.* The ancient king and the young queen represent the dual capacity of salt for thinking—the old faculty of its male intellect aspect and knowledge of cause and effect. This is the precipitation side of salt. The dissolving side of salt in the natural world serves organisms by giving them the abilities of the most fecund creative forces. This is represented by the beautiful young queen. The dark king and the dainty old matron, whose head is covered by a veil, represent forces of the will—dark in its cognitive capacity, because will impulses in the human soul are hidden from one's thinking. Will is considered the origin of all other soul forces; therefore, it is old. It is obscured (covered) in the soul by sleeping unconsciousness, which characterizes its primary nature. The third pair represents the familiar, everyday aspects of sensory experience in their common (uncomely) appearance. The dreamlike feeling that arises from sensory experience has great potential to be lifted into the dynamic force of creative imagination. This transformation is accomplished in the marriage of opposites in an alchemical process of death and transfiguration. The large, costly crown above them represents this tremendous potential.

After their audience with the Royals, the ten are led to a hall where they become objects of a game played by the virgins. It is a numbers game that determines which of the virgins will sleep with each of the ten men. In the end, the virgins play a trick on the men, making them the butts of the joke as the virgins leave the room laughing.

The ten are then led back to the upper room, where they and the Royals are to view a drama—the story of a young girl who is kidnapped by a dark king and taken away to foreign lands—that includes subplots of betrayal and corrupted innocence. The young princess walks on the wild side for a while and eventually becomes a concubine of the man who kidnapped her. Thus, she betrays her father and her prince, leading to jealousy and anger and eventually to redemption through true love.

Between these scenes of great moral failings are strange little vignettes with comic elements, and commentaries on the circumstances of betrayal related in the Bible. The drama is a symbolic prelude to the wedding event. The kidnapped baby princess is the infant soul floating in the womb of nature. The dark king, who could be called the adversary, represents the retarding forces set against the progress of the infant soul. An ancient, benevolent king who is the father of the princess represents the human potential to become a world creator, given the gift of freedom by God the Father.

In the drama, these potentially creative forces are set against the retarding, degrading forces in a continuous state of tension. The soul is born into nature, and the ancient king, followed by the prince, swears to protect the soul against the spiritual adversaries of humanity. In the third act, for instance, the young princess is rescued by a knight hired by the king.

After her rescue, the princess is given materials to study to become suitable one day for marriage to a prince. This points to the eventual marriage of soul to spirit. The knight who rescues the young girl warns the king that the princess might prove to be a difficult student, since she finds it difficult to behave herself in the world. Nevertheless, the princess agrees to the provisions set out by the king. She is meant to study Daniel's vision in the Bible, which concerns the end times, when the three soul forces will manifest as beasts, along with a fourth beast more terrible than the other three, which rises against God the Father. This fourth beast is the Antichrist. This motif at the beginning of the next act points to the significance of the soul turning against the ancient king, who had been its protector, and making an alliance with the dark king, the Lord of the Earth.

The story of Nebuchadnezzar is depicted during the interlude. He was the king of Babylon who conquered Jerusalem and engaged Daniel as his soothsayer, because he was having troubling dreams. Nebuchadnezzar had already asked his astrologers and sages to explain a dream he'd had, and they gave him an answer, saying it was impossible to know the dream unless the king described it. Nebuchadnezzar was furious with them and commanded that all the sages and astrologers of Babylon be destroyed. However, God had revealed the king's dream to Daniel. He said that King Nebuchadnezzar had seen a great metal idol with a head of gold, a breast of silver, a belly of brass, and feet of clay. A great stone smashed the feet of the idol and scattered the pieces until no one could recognize them. Daniel explained that the king was the head of gold, and the other metals were the kingdoms that would follow his, each more inferior than the previous until all is broken.

The final scene introduces the motif of a tower, which will dominate days five and six. The Tower is depicted on the back of a mechanical elephant. This is an interesting image. The elephant—the will of the body—is sometimes shown carrying the world on its back. We see in this image of the mechanical elephant that the mechanical will of the physical body supports the Tower. The Tower, where the alchemical creation of the new human will take place, has seven floors. A different stage of the work takes place on each level. Those seven stages can be seen as the system of seven chakras in the subtle bodies of the adept. During the following days, the Tower and its seven stages and strange devices will become significant.

At the ceremony, the Royals (the three kings and three queens) are all dressed in white. They are at the banquet table, along with the ten who are with the Virgin. At a certain cue, the three kings and queens stand and remove their white garments, under which they are dressed all in black. Pages enter and remove the white wedding decorations from the wall, and suddenly everything is black.

The ten men sit and watch silently, as does the virgin. Then a coal-black man enters with a huge axe. He approaches one of the kings and cuts off his head. The king's head is then wrapped and placed in a coffin, while the blood is collected in a golden chalice and also placed in the coffin. Then the coal-black man walks toward the second Royal, the queen, and cuts off her head. He does this to all six Royals, one after the other. Christian Rosenkreutz says, "Oh, this is the bloodiest wedding I've ever attended."

Then out of nowhere, someone appears with an axe and lops off the head of the executioner, which is likewise placed in a small chest. The men are all deeply disturbed by this, and they are led down into the castle to their rooms. Christian Rosenkreutz enters his room in a condition of profound misunderstanding. He thought he had partially understood what the marriage was about, what was going to happen, and what the king and queen were doing. What started as a marriage suddenly became a murder.

Christian Rosenkreutz sits in his room and decides to sleep. He falls asleep, but we don't know what sort of sleep; the story is vague about what really happens. While pretending to be asleep in bed, he notices on the wall a kind of flickering light. The castle is by the sea, and looking out the window he sees seven ships on the water, each of which has a flame coming from its mast. He understands in that moment that the Royals are not dead; they have been beheaded for a good reason, though he doesn't know what it is, and recognizes that he does not know. However, he does know what he is looking at. This is a poignant moment, and he's in an altered state. He wakes his page to view the event. In this spectacle, he sees that the souls of the Royals are still connected to their vehicles, even though they have been terminated.

This beheading of the kings and queens can be seen as an analogy of the meditative life. One cuts off the head so that sensory activity no longer interferes with thinking, feeling, and willing as spiritual perception. By beheading the Royals, higher sight allows us to see, but we might not understand what we see. Still, we know that we see.

Once again, this is the initiate of misunderstanding. Christian Rosenkreutz then went to sleep.

THE ALCHEMICAL WEDDING, DAY FOUR

Observing the paintings and tapestries that adorned his room, CR was still in his bed. Suddenly he heard coronet music, as if a procession was underway. His page jumped out of bed and said in anxious tones, "The rest are already presented to the king!"

In a panic, Christian Rosenkreutz rushed to get dressed and ran out of his room to meet his page, returning with joyful news that the coronets had announced the end of breakfast, and the others did not want to wake him because of his advanced age.

It was now time for all to assemble at the fountain. On the fountain, the lion had exchanged his sword for a large tablet, on which was the script of ancient monuments, reading:

> Hermes, our leader who is behind everything,
> Son-in-law of lost humanity,
> Counselor to God,
> Source of learning,
> Knowing's healing medicine,
> Streambed of the flowing stream of wisdom.
> Drink a toast from myself, who wishes for you much
> more power:
> Please bathe everyone who is willing,
> Agitate those who dare to have courage,
> Drink brothers, and live!

The ten bathed themselves in the fountain and drank drafts from golden cups. They followed the Virgin into the hall and put on new clothes made of gold and set with flowers. Each was also given a golden fleece set with precious stones. On each fleece was a golden medallion with a figure of the Sun and Moon in opposition on one side. On the other side was this verse:

> The light of the Moon shall be as the light of the Sun;
> The light of the Sun shall be seven times lighter than present.

The ten were led by the Virgin to a door that had never been apparent before. It led to the royal winding stairs, and the door was unlocked. The Virgin led the ten up three hundred sixty-five stairs. The higher they climbed the more artistic and precious were the furniture and accessories. At the top, they passed under a painted arch where sixty virgins bowed to them. After this, a little bell was rung, and a beautiful virgin entered, bringing them each a laurel wreath. As this happened, a curtain was raised, and Christian Rosenkreutz saw the king and the queen together for the first time. The sight was overwhelmingly heavenly and glorious.

The whole room glistened with precious stones and gold. The queen's robes were so rich and splendid that it was impossible to look at them. CR remembered the unnamed queen he had seen the day before, and this enabled him to maintain self-consciousness in the presence of such overwhelming power and majesty.

Individually designated virgins took each of the ten by the hand and presented them to the king. Now the Virgin of the ten began to speak:

> To honor your majesties, these lords have traveled here at great peril to life and body. Your majesties have reason to rejoice, since the greater part of these adventurers serve to further your majesties' estates and empire. I have desired to present them to your majesties so I might discharge my commission. Please take from them information concerning my actions and omissions.

With this she laid her branch on the ground. At this moment, each of the ten desired to speak on behalf of the Virgin of the ten, but none of them were able to speak at all. At length, the king's astronomer Atlas spoke on behalf of the king.

> Their royal majesties rejoice at your arrival and will that their royal grace be issued to each and all. With your administrations, Gentle Virgin, they are most satisfied, and accordingly a royal reward shall be provided for you. Yet it is their intention that you

shall this day accompany them, inasmuch as they have no reason to distrust you.

With this, the Virgin humbly took up the branch again. Then, the ten stepped aside with their Virgin.

At one end of the broad room stood a semicircle with three glorious royal thrones, the middle one being higher than the others. In each throne sat two persons. In the first sat an ancient king with a gray beard. His queen was extraordinarily young and beautiful. In the third throne sat a black king of middle age, whose queen was a dainty old matron, not crowned but covered with a veil. In the middle sat two young people wearing laurel wreaths on their heads. They appeared to be lovers, but they were not remarkably handsome. Over them hung a large and costly crown, and behind them sat a group of ancient men, none of whom was armed, and no other guards were present for the couple. Cupid flew about above the lovers, making gestures as if to shoot an arrow at them or at the assembled company. He tormented everyone assembled, threatening to shoot arrows at them. The designated virgins made a game of trying to catch the little rascal.

Standing before the queen was a small but curious altar with a book covered in black velvet and a small taper in an ivory candlestick. Next to this was a celestial sphere that turned of its own accord, a small watch, and a little crystal siphon fountain from which a clear blood-red liquor continuously flowed.

Last of all was a death's head, and in its eye sockets a small white serpent passed continuously in and out in a circular fashion. She was such a length that just her tail remained in one of the eye holes as her head entered the other—that is, unless Cupid startled her and made her disappear altogether into the skull. Along the sides of the room were wonderful images that moved of themselves as if alive, all accompanied by the most wondrous vocal music.

After seeing these wonders, the ten all returned with their Virgin down the winding stairs, but the door at the bottom had been securely locked and bolted. When it was opened, they entered the hall, and one of the other virgins asked the Virgin of the ten why she spent so much time in the company of these men. The Virgin of the ten replied that she was not afraid of any of them except Christian Rosenkreutz. This statement went to the heart of CR, and he felt that she was mocking his old age. However, the Virgin of the ten comforted him, saying that if he behaved well toward her she could release him from his burden of old age. After this, a lively conversation on the arts developed among the group, but the thoughts of CR were now turned to the idea of becoming young again.

These thoughts eventually put him in a sad mood. The Virgin of the ten saw this and remarked that if Christian Rosenkreutz were to lie with her that evening he would be in a more pleasant mood in the morning. This brought great laughter from the others, and CR blushed all over and eventually had to laugh at his embarrassment. One among the men sought to turn the embarrassment against the Virgin, asking that the group bear witness to the fact that the Virgin had offered to spend the night with CR. The Virgin replied that she would be content to do just that if she were not afraid the other virgins would be resentful that, against their will, she had picked the best for herself. The other virgins replied that the high office of the Virgin of the ten did not make her proud, and that they would not be resentful if she gave consent for the other virgins also to spend the night with men of their choice. The Virgin of the ten turned to the men and asked them if they would consent to allowing chance to determine who would sleep with whom. It was proposed that this would take place after they had something to eat.

Then they all arose, and each walked up and down the hall with the virgin of his choice, but the Virgin of the ten said that chance would determine who will be partnered. At this the men and the virgins separated. The virgins acted as if there was a dispute but soon had the idea of mixing the company in a ring. The Virgin of the ten proposed that she should count herself as one, and that she be paired to the seventh person, whether a man or a virgin. All agreed to this proposal. The virgins had mixed so subtly that the men did not suspect a trick, but each knew her station beforehand. The counting started, and the first seventh person was a virgin, as well as the second seventh, and likewise the third until all of the virgins were chosen and none of the men. The virgins began to laugh at the poor men, who'd been tricked and stood alone. The men had to be satisfied with the virgins' humor.

During these proceedings, the little cupid entered the room. His purpose was to bring a round of toasts from the king and queen and to call the virgins into the presence of the king. The virgins went to the king, but they soon returned and initiated a dance as the prelude to a comedy production.

The ten began a procession back to the house of the Sun to await the arrival of the young king and his Bride. The procession was led by the unnamed queen, whom they had met the previous day. She was dressed in white, wore a small but precious coronet, and carried a small pearl crucifix. The crucifix had been fashioned that morning by the young king and his Bride. Then the unnamed queen left, followed by the six virgins who had led the procession the previous day. They carried the king's jewels, which belonged on a little altar.

Next, the three kings came from the three thrones in the Tower. The Bridegroom was in their midst, plainly dressed in black—a small black hat with a small, black, pointed feather. The Bridegroom tipped his hat to the ten as he passed as a token of favor toward them. The ten bowed courteously to him and to the other kings. Following the kings were the three queens from the throne room in the top of the Tower. Two were richly attired, but one in their midst was also dressed in plain, black clothes, with Cupid holding up her train. The ten then followed the queens, and after them the virgins, who accompanied them until Atlas, the court astronomer, finally followed them all.

After proceeding along many paths, they arrived at the house of the Sun. The procession was seated next to the king and queen to watch the comedy. Although separated from the king and queen, the ten sat to their right and the virgins to their left.

In the first act of the comedy, an ancient king sat on a throne accompanied by servants. A small chest was placed before the king. It had been found floating in the water. When opened, out came a little baby girl, jewels, and a letter addressed to the king. When the king read the letter, he wept. The letter informed him that a strange king had overtaken the country of his aunt and killed everyone in the royal family except for this infant, the Royal Daughter, to whom the strange king wished to wed his son once she had grown up. The king swore that, because of this deed, he would maintain perpetual enmity toward the strange king. He commanded that the child be tenderly nursed as he began to plan his revenge against the strange king.

The interlude consisted of a fight between a lion and a griffon, with the lion claiming victory.

In the second act, the strange king, a lying, treacherous fellow, was troubled that his murder of the royal family had become known abroad, and that the little girl had been taken from him through his own servants' cunning and betrayal. He sought information about the king and his court from fugitives fleeing a famine. With this information, he was again able to steal away the now-young Royal Daughter, to whom he wished to wed his son. His anger was so great that he wished to kill her himself; instead, however, he was deceived again by his servants through various plot devices, and her life was spared. Act two concluded with a triumphant address by the strange king.

In the third act, a great army of the king was raised against the strange king. This army was put into the command of an ancient and valiant knight, who entered the country of the strange king and rescued the Royal Daughter from a tower. Soon after her return, a glorious scaffold was erected, and she was placed high upon it in a place of honor. Then twelve Royal Ambassadors arrived at the court of the king, and the ancient knight who had rescued the young woman gave a speech. He praised the king, who had initially rescued the young woman as an infant, gave her a good education, and provided for her. As an aside, he also mentioned that she had proved to be a difficult student regarding proper behavior. The old knight then confirmed that, in doing so, the king had intended for his son to wed the young woman when they were of age. The king had a document drawn up describing in detail the provisions to be observed by the young woman so that the eventual royal marriage to his son might occur. She signed the document in agreement to all of its provisions and thanked the king for his good graces.

In another interlude, the four beasts of Daniel from the Bible were brought before the assembly, and their signification was described in a wondrous way for all to behold.

In the opening of the fourth act, the young lady was shown restored in her kingdom, where she was crowned. She ruled her domain for a short time with joy. Many ambassadors visited her to wish her prosperity and to gaze at her radiance. Soon, however, she began to cast her eyes wantonly at all who approached her, flirting with the ambassadors and the Lords of her own king. In this, she was truly revealing her role in life.

Her behavior was soon brought to the attention of the strange king, who moved quickly on such an opportunity. He arranged for counselors under his influence to turn the heart of the young woman against her king and benefactor. Her own steward, provided by the ancient king, was powerless to change her misdeeds. She was easily blinded by great promises of the strange king and submitted herself wholeheartedly to his advances. She was taken once again by the strange king, and her whole kingdom gradually came under his dominion through this influence. Once this was accomplished, the strange king caused her to be shamed. He put her on a scaffold, tied her to a post, caused her to be scourged, and ultimately condemned her to death by poison. She was cast into prison, expecting that each day would be her last. The poison did not kill her but made her leprous, and she suffered unheard-of torments. The fourth act closed with these sorry scenes.

During this interlude, an image of Nebuchadnezzar was displayed. All manner of arms adorned the head, belly, breasts, legs, and feet of the image.

In the fifth act, it was revealed that the young king was informed of all of the events that had passed between the strange king and his future spouse. He entreated his father, the ancient king, to send help to her. The ancient king dispatched ambassadors and healers to comfort her in her sorrows and to teach her about her transgressions and inconsiderate behavior. However, she would not receive these teachers. Instead, she consented to become the concubine of the strange king. This was done and the young king was informed of the events. At this point a band of fools entered the play, each armed with a cudgel. They quickly formed a globe of the whole world, which they quickly destroyed completely with their cudgels. It was a fine comedic interlude.

In the sixth act, the young king resolved to do battle with the strange king, which was done at great expense to the young king, who was left for dead. Eventually, the young king was able to overcome his wounds and gain the release of his spouse. On returning to his own kingdom, the young king placed his future spouse in the care of his steward and his chaplain, who tormented her further. At last, when matters had become almost unbearable, the actions of those two reached the ear of the young king, who dismissed the steward and sent someone who could break the neck of the priest's power. This being done the young king began the process of adorning his beloved for their future marriage.

After this act, as an interlude, an enormous artificial elephant was brought in to carry a great tower holding musicians who played the most wondrous music.

In the seventh and final act, the Bridegroom and Bride appeared in unbelievably solemn and high splendor. All the people cried out, "Long live the Bridegroom, Long live the Bride!" This magnificence ended the last act to the great pleasure of the king and queen and everyone assembled.

As a curtain call, the players promenaded through the hall singing:

> This time full of love
> Does our joy much improve
> Because of the Royal nuptial.
> Therefore, let us sing
> That from all parts it may ring:
> Blest be he that granted us all.
>
> The Bride most exquisitely fair,
> Whom we attend with long care
> To him in truth's now plighted;
> At long length we've obtained
> What she'd strived to contend.
> He is happy; that is so foresighted.
>
> Now the parents kind and good
> By entreaties are subdued.
> Long enough in cage was she contained;
> In honor increase,
> Till thousands arise
> And spring from your proper blood.

After this song, thanks were given and received, and the comedy was finished joyfully. All the nobles then departed, save for the ten, who were to accompany the royal persons up the winding stairs and into the royal throne room. This was the first time that the ten were to sit near to the king. A little altar was placed in the middle of the room. The young king was gracious toward the ten, but his manner betrayed sadness as he often sighed. The old king and queen were serious, except for the young wife of one of the ancient kings.

All of the Royals sat at the first table, with the ten sitting at the second. Some of the principal virgins sat at the third table. The rest of the virgins were obliged to wait. All of this was accomplished with such solemn stillness and silence that it was almost frightening. The Royals were dressed in glittering snow-white garments. Above the king's table hung the large crown, its precious stones softly illuminating the tables below. The other lights in the room were all kindled from the single taper on the little altar at the center of the room.

The young king frequently sent meat to the white serpent in the skull on the little altar. This caused Christian Rosenkreutz to muse silently on its significance. The stillness was broken only by the prattle of the little cupid, who tormented CR almost unceasingly. Still, despite his jokes and tricks, there was no mirth in the room, giving those gathered a mood of peril. Everything was so strange that Christian Rosenkreutz broke into a sweat.

Supper ended in this way as the young king asked for the book on the little altar to be brought to him. He opened the book and asked the aged astronomer Atlas to read from it. The old man asked if the assembled would abide with his words in both prosperity and adversity. This question sent a chill through CR. The old man then asked in a sad tone if they would give him their signatures on his request. No one could see any way to avoid this, so they all agreed to it. Then each one rose and wrote his name in the book.

After this, the little crystal fountain with the small crystal glass was brought forth. The Royal persons drank from the glass and passed it along until all had done the same. This was the draft of Silence. All of the Royals then presented their hands to the ten, saying that henceforth the men had to stick to them or they would never more see them again. This brought tears to all of the ten and even the virgins. The Virgin of the ten then spoke for the outstanding character of the ten men, and the Royals seemed to gain great satisfaction from this. Then a little bell was rung, which caused all of the Royals to withdraw into brooding silence. The Royals quickly removed their white garments, under which they wore entirely black ones.

With this, Christian Rosenkreutz suddenly noticed that the whole hall was hung entirely in black velvet, as were the floor and ceiling. The tables were removed, and the ten men were given black habits to wear. The Virgin of the ten entered the room, bringing six black scarves that she wrapped around the eyes of the six Royals as blindfolds. When they could no longer see, servants brought in six coffins, and a low black seat was placed in their midst. Finally, a very tall, Dark Axeman entered, bearing a well-sharpened axe.

The old king was first to be brought to the low seat, and his head was instantly whipped off by the Dark Axeman. It was wrapped in a black cloth, with the blood being received in a great golden goblet. These things, along with his body, were immediately placed in one of the coffins. The same happened to the other five Royals. CR feared that after them it would be his turn, but as soon as the six had been beheaded the Dark Axeman turned to leave. He was instantly beheaded by another person at the door, and his head and the axe were brought to the center of the room and placed in a small chest. CR thought that this must surely be the bloodiest wedding ever, but since he had no idea what was happening, he told himself just to pay attention and surely these matters would eventually be revealed. It helped him that the Virgin of the ten kept telling them to remain calm and to pay attention.

She said, "The lives of those who were just beheaded are in the hands of the ten men." She added, "You men should follow me so that the death of these six will make it possible for many to live. Now go to sleep and do not trouble yourselves over the proceedings." She herself would have to stand watch over the dead corpses during the night.

The men did as the Virgin requested, and they each retired with their pages. Christian Rosenkreutz spent a long time conversing with his page but soon realized that the purpose of the conversation was to lull him to sleep. CR pretended to sleep but could not get the images of the beheading out of his mind.

Around midnight Christian Rosenkreutz got out of bed and went to the window, which afforded a beautiful view of the lake surrounding the castle. As soon as the clock struck midnight, he saw a great fire arise on the lake. Fearing that a ship was on fire he opened the window. On the horizon were seven ships making their way toward the castle. A flame hovered above each ship, moving back and forth, and sometimes coming to rest on the decks, only to return aloft again.

In his heart, Christian Rosenkreutz knew that the flames were the spirits of those who'd been beheaded that evening. As the ships gently touched the shore, Christian Rosenkreutz saw the Virgin of the ten walking toward them with a torch. Behind her, the six coffins and the little chest were carried onto their respective ships.

Christian Rosenkreutz woke his page so that he could also see the event. As soon as the six coffins were laid in the ships, the ships with their flames passed back over the lake together. He saw that hundreds of watchmen were stationed along the shoreline and the rocks around it. They attended to the needs of the Virgin and stood watch over the proceedings until, at last, she bolted down the doors of the castle once again.

Assessing that nothing more would happen that night, Christian Rosenkreutz and his page went to sleep. In the morning, through conversation it became clear that he was the only one who could have seen the proceedings, since his window was the only place from which the boats could be seen.

Day Four Commentary

This document uses obscure references from a time when people received a classical education and were familiar with literature such as the Bible and the classics. Today, most people have little idea of who Nebuchadnezzar was.* A standard practice in alchemy was this: Any image or formula from an alchemist always contains an error or needs to be translated, because it is never as it appears. In ancient times, it was considered an alchemical insult to people's intelligence to give them a formula without an error or an image that didn't need to be pondered to understand it. Alchemists wanted intelligent individuals to understand that they need to participate in the formula so as not to violate the hidden laws between the worlds.

This recalls *The Sorcerer's Apprentice.*** The apprentice used a magic spell he'd found in the master's book of spells to make a broom do his work of hauling water. The spell allowed him to begin the activity, but it didn't explain how to stop it—a good analogy for many of our problems today. We live in a "Sorcerer's Apprentice" period. Ancient wisdom understood that whatever one does eventually tends to move toward its opposite condition. Thus, an error or conundrum was always included in any teaching, formula, or image. It was understood that one had to work with it to find the error. Once the error was found, a person could understand the whole context of what was being studied. That worldview concerning truth and error, intelligence and learning was different from what is prevalent in reductionist machine-driven research today. Alchemists teach their students by using symbols that are purposely ambiguous; the greater the ambiguity, the greater the potential.

* Nebuchadnezzar II (ca. 605–562 BC) is identified in the Bible as the king responsible for destroying Solomon's Temple and for orchestrating the "Babylonian Exile" of the Hebrews. He is a significant character in the book of Daniel.

** Paul Dukas (1865–1935) composed *L'Apprenti Sorcier* in 1897, a symphonic poem inspired by Goethe's ballad "Der Zauberlehrling" (1797).

The methodology is to use an image (the corpse of a living idea) and return it to potential in the mind. The intent is to take what has been formed back to its unformed state, *solve,* so that we can participate in a self-adjusting process. An ambiguous image is built inwardly as a series of events. It is then dissolved and placed where we no longer have contact with it, so that when it comes back it requires us to observe how it has changed. This practice eventually allows us to do that kind of participatory observation with the feelings we wish to modify.

Working with ambiguous figures such as "The Rebis" is a technique whereby feelings can be trained by our intelligence; this is the alchemical worldview. Feelings need to be trained, honed, and stabilized by consciously dealing with ambiguity. One's sense of self-worth and self-image feels threatened in ambiguous situations. *The Alchemical Wedding* is about how alchemy allows us to separate our personal, instinctual feelings in response to ambiguity from the feelings that are integral to the world's ambiguity—feelings of the world soul that exist as the fundament of reality. In the world soul, ambiguity is the process whereby *everything* moves toward its opposite, a method that requires unpredictability and uncertainty. If I say where a subatomic particle is, I cannot say how fast it's moving. If I say how fast it's moving, I can't say where it is. This is another ambiguity, or paradox. Science is replete with paradoxes such as Werner Heisenberg's uncertainty principle and the inability to reconcile gravity with quantum theory, a fundamental paradox. The biggest force in the world and the smallest force won't come together with the way we perceive and think.

Welcome to alchemy and to paradox and ambiguity. One trains to view a symbol, hold and form it inwardly, dissolve it, let it go, and then retrieve it. When I retrieve it, I don't consider it finished but just part of the self-adjusting process. I want to withhold judgment of what I retrieve until the self-adjusting process reveals an archetypical reality of the symbol in place of my belief du jour,

The Rebis

based perhaps on reports of scandals and dysfunction in the world today. These things keep people off balance and unable to entertain creative social thoughts. When we are worried about a scandal, we don't have time to deal with the factual, paradoxical realities of our existence as human spirits in physical bodies. This is why I say, *The Alchemical Wedding* is a story about today. Alchemists understand that a social malaise is a kind of yeast that is always bound to occur if things are to get better. Alchemists call this social malaise a *simulacrum,* or simulated culture. It's not really a culture, but a *simulation* of culture, based on imagery meant to beguile and confuse. In education today, we don't have training to work within paradox and ambiguity, because our training deals only with "the right answer." Like lab rats, when the light comes on and the food pellet drops, you know you did the "right" thing by giving the accepted answer to a question.

In contrast to this, Christian Rosenkreutz experiences the symbolic dimension of his consciousness under the influence of benefactors on the other side, such as the Virgin and the king. They speak to him continuously about the real need to marry the individualized soul with the given patterns in the cosmos. When the soul marries the given patterns in the cosmos, freedom marries necessity and a new human is born. This is the new Adam, the new soul, the new spirit embryo, the new true human, the True Self, the transcendent "I"-being (as Rudolf Steiner calls it), spirit human. This has been the goal from the beginning—the spirit human.

Alchemists teach a symbolic path and journey by using highly ambiguous symbols. They teach this way to develop capacity, so that when one's feelings encounter ambiguity, they don't polarize or befuddle the will. One simply says: *There's another paradox. How can I work with this one?* This path builds resilience and capacity. Christian Rosenkreutz is being taught to build capacity, even though he was, according to Steiner, the most highly initiated Western individual. He still has to go through the essential initiation school and through dialogues with those trying to help him. They help by telling him: *We don't think you get it.* To help him see this, they confront him with paradox after paradox. It's the Virgin's—the Sophia's—school of tough love. The others believe they already understand everything, but Christian Rosenkreutz says: *I don't understand.* That's the secret key.

I've been studying *The Alchemical Wedding* for a long while, trying to make sense of it. This is the closest I have gotten to making sense out of it. Christian Rosenkreutz appears in this story as "the initiate of misunderstanding." He has made a career of misunderstanding, which made him the beloved of the benefactors, because he's pliable. He has a receptive, creative will that those who are teaching him appreciate. When we look at a symbol such as the "Rebis," we can see that this is a riddle. *Rebis* means a riddle.

On day three, we saw scales and riddles. Everything was a riddle to those in the castle. A riddle means taking ambiguity and understanding that there are two worlds that intersect in it. There is the world "here" and the world of metaphor or symbol, sometimes called the *imaginal realm*. The world of symbol cannot be understood literally. If it is taken literally, we get social malaise. Today's image of this is the autistic spectrum. People on the autistic spectrum have a difficult time with metaphor, because they take everything literally. They do not understand metaphor; it makes no sense to them because it lacks a logical structure. (We will revisit this issue later.) Because autism has become an epidemic, the technique of working with symbols is appropriate for today. Symbols are not intended to be taken literally but as paradoxes, which means we have to expand rather than restrict their meaning.

Any symbol I present is always paradoxical. That's the basic idea. There needs to be room for an error in a symbol, simply because we are human. Moreover, if you present your view of the symbol back to me, there is also an error in it because you are human, too. If we can tolerate this and work with it, we build shared meanings that go beyond literal interpretations; we enter the realm of symbolic images.

When we take a symbol into sleep, it allows us to dream and retrieve pictures of our own biography from the imaginal dream realm. On the other side, whatever we put into sleep is immediately adjusted for our karma and put into the language of our operating system—our life. Everything that goes into the other side comes back in the context of what we need to do. No matter what it is, we cannot escape it. This is the value of relying on dreams after we learn how to filter them.

This image of the Rebis is a dream filter—one we can run a dream through. We see a king and a queen, both in the same body but with two heads. The term for this being in alchemical language is *the great hermaphrodite*. It is predicted that human beings in the future will not have sexuality once the king and the queen marry—when the soul and the given forces of nature marry. Our inner life will become procreative. Rudolf Steiner stated that our larynx will have become a womb and that our inner life will be procreative. The images we make through speech will create beings. This is the future, because it's the way the hierarchies created us.

Every indigenous culture says that the world was sung into existence by high, spiritual beings. When we become the tenth hierarchy, we will sing into existence another world of beings; we will be procreative. We will be both the king and the queen and will have self-procreative capacities. Today, what we call "creative thinking" is a dim image of that future capacity. We can be self-procreative. The Rebis image (page 104) shows a two-headed person that represents the king and the queen. In the king's right hand is a compass; it makes circles, which represent the Sun. Above the right hand is the Sun. The king, the Sun, the ether body, the given—these represent the great circle of established existence. They are forces from the periphery. In the left hand of the queen is a square—Earth, houses, architecture, constructed things. The cube represents Earth, or what falls out of the Sun. The code for this is *Moon*—everything that is not originally creative but sort of "conjunctionally" creative—anything that is a consequence of the original creation is called *Moon*.

In the Rebis image, above the square in the left hand is the Moon; this is basic Rebis language. Below the figure is a dragon, which always represents wisdom received from Earth. In the ancient world, especially in the East, this was vital; people received vital and energetic wisdom from the Earth. They lived close to the seasons and the life of the Earth, and through time such earthly wisdom came to be codified as the dragon.

The original dragon represented the procreative and creative forces of life. Then there is the dragon as an image of the fallen dragon, cast down onto earth, where he began to eat people. In Japan, the culture of the dragon led to Godzilla, the shadow dragon. Thus, we have the dragon as the procreative force, and the shadow dragon, destroying the Earth, as the earth dragon. The king and queen have come together in the Rebis and stand on the dragon. This means they have the foundation of Earth wisdom, but it has been transcended.

Then we have Earth itself, with Jupiter and Saturn, and squares and triangles and the orbit of stars around the outside. The stars are the crystal heavens, the source of all geometries. In the alchemical world, that's the place we always go when we dream. We go to Saturn and Mars and Venus and so on in our soul body, because that astral realm is the source of the soul. So the royal couple have this as a kind of accompaniment.

At the very top, the big star in the center has Mercury, the healer; it is the one that resolves all the paradoxes—not by having an answer but by having a dialogue and communication. This is all contained in the egg. The egg is the great symbol of the astral body in all traditions. If you go to Mexico and you go to the *curandera*, or healer, she takes an egg, runs it up and down your back and tells you to leave it under your bed for three days. She then takes the egg after three days and drops it into a glass of saltwater. According to the form in which the albumin congeals, she can say if dead Uncle Chico is upset with you; then you might have to take a chicken to a volcano and throw it in, along with a blessing for him. You do this, and you are better.

The egg symbolizes the whole realm of the astral body, the soul. All the drama of the Rebis, the dragon, and the earth takes place in the context of the soul; this is all a reading of the Rebis symbol. If we want to work with it, we could take it into sleep in little bits and wait for dream insights to return from the spiritual world. Then we take it into sleep again, and it comes back again. Then we might encounter something—perhaps in a book or something we see—and a part of the symbol would light up in our consciousness as an understanding. This is the technique.

According to Rudolf Steiner, this is a fundamental method for educating adults. Teach them how to take symbols connected to daily life into sleep and retrieve them again. This is a Rosicrucian impulse in Steiner's work. This description I just gave is just one example of how to understand the Rebis. Actually, we could understand it in numerous ways; the idea is that it is paradoxical and can lead to freedom. In *The Alchemical Wedding,* it is understood that Christian Rosenkreutz is *the initiate.* He is eighty-one years old and has spent a lifetime studying these matters. Nonetheless, he still needs finishing school—he needs to be polished because he has to deal with human issues, the karma of just being human. The irony of the story is that he falls short with his Venus adventure, yet he remains part of the work and the game.

The spiritual world is asking: *What do you not understand about your humanity and your vulnerability?* He actually becomes Guardian of the Threshold but wishes otherwise. This is a picture of initiation. Christian Rosenkreutz is the most highly initiated individual of the West. It's not about getting into heaven and being served peeled grapes by twenty-one virgins. Rather, it's the modern person's "pick up your bed and walk" consciousness. The virgins at the castle are not there to peel grapes. There is no way to fully understand these matters, but only a question: *Who are you?*

Finding out who we are is a large part of the solution—but it is a solution only for each of us as individuals, not for everyone. It is solely for me because *I am the problem.* If we are not part of the solution...this is the modern consciousness. It's never solved forever, and it's not solved for everybody. In the future, the political structure will look very different (one hopes) once we understand who we really are. We will not look to leaders for solutions, because we will be on the path of initiation. By contrast, if someone makes the grade as an initiate, it makes the task of initiation better for everyone. It's a paradox.

Peering through the veil

The image of the person crawling on the ground and peeking at the stars beyond represents the theme of day four of the wedding.* Day two was thinking; day three was feeling; day four, the will; day five is a turning point. Five in numerology is known as *Malum*, meaning "bad" in Latin. Five is the number of the human being, because the human condition is always the place where the drama between the cosmos and the Fall plays out. Being human is the condition of the cosmic scapegoat; the human hierarchy is designated to carry the burden of dysfunction for the whole cosmos.

On ancient Saturn, the archai were in their human condition; they carried the burden of experiencing the senses as something that set them apart from the progressive cosmos.** On ancient Sun, the arch-

* The image first appeared in 1888 and was probably commissioned by Camille Flammarion for *L'atmosphère: Météorologie populaire*. The image shown here is a colorized version of the wood engraving by an unknown artist.

** On the "planetary" stages of evolution, see Rudolf Steiner, *An Outline of Esoteric*

angels lived in the human condition; they carried the burden further, having a sensory life that made it clear that they could feel separate from the creation. On ancient Moon, the angels were in their human condition; they carried the burden further and could begin to interact with the separated sensory world through pictures they carried within, which no one else could experience. As human beings, we believe that the world of senses is totally separate from us and that our inner life is completely hidden from everyone else. Our sensory experience feels completely separate from creation. In the next round, animals will be in the human condition; they will carry the burden to even greater lengths, and we will be their guardians, just as the progressive angels are for us in this round.

Malum, or bad, has the cosmic meaning of the place where the action is—where rascals meet the evolutionary road, a strange place where strange things happen. This text is a kind of initiation for those with challenges—initiation for those who understand that freedom is the most precious thing we have, even when we abuse it by cheating and lying. The better freedom is to live and let live without lying or blaming. Freedom is even more perfect when we give our freedom to someone else. This is the great paradox, but it is the nature of this book. It is Rudolf Steiner's books *The Philosophy of Freedom, How to Know Higher Worlds*, and *Theosophy* all rolled into one. Once we've been given freedom, what is the best thing we can do with it? We can give it away to serve another person. This is the highest thing we can do with our freedom. When we do this, *freedom becomes love.* This is the theme on day four.

Day four is about altered consciousness when I finally penetrate the veil of appearances. The task of initiation is to use symbolic and metaphorical imagery, so that the imagery leads us to a perception—that behind the image is an archetype so powerful that it makes our insides quake. This is the theme of *The Matrix* movies. We think the

---

Science (Anthroposophic Press, 1997), chapter 6, "Cosmic and Human Evolution Now and in the Future."

world is a certain way but find that behind the world of appearances is another, far vaster world that is somehow more real than the one in which we live. We are Neo—Adam, the new Adam, the new human. What does the new human have to do? Like the archetypes of Christ and Christian Rosenkreutz, the new human is under attack.

The great work is to penetrate the symbol's appearance to see the force of the being *behind* the symbol. Behind the phenomenal forms of things is the power of true being. Behind the form of a triangle is a geometric consciousness or power, the being of a particular form of awareness. And behind the circle is the power of the consciousness of a being with another form of awareness. All the little circles and triangles we have in the world, as well as Grail cups, trees, lions, or whatever—behind every phenomenon in the world, when we penetrate through we can see the genuine force that exists; we see another world behind the world of appearances.

The first task of initiates is to learn that we are living in two worlds simultaneously. The second task is to learn equanimity when confronted by the uncertainty that comes from that discovery. The third task is to learn to navigate within that other world. Thus, our first realization is that there are two worlds. *I think I'm losing my mind.*

The corollary to that realization is: *Oh, I have to die.* Yes, we do. Here we have to die, because we see our self here as separate from everything else. Over there, we don't have to die. There, our consciousness is continuous; there one is a player among players. Here we are worried about our bank accounts. The hierarchies living there are the source of all the energy of the archetypes, and they know we are beguiled by worrying about our bank accounts all the time. They continuously try to help us see that a bank account and money are just spiritual beings among other spiritual entities. They are "shapeshifters" and can become anything we want them to be.

In this sense, money is pure spirit. It is our beliefs in connection with money that leads to the drama of winners and losers. In itself, money is pure spiritual activity of transformation—pure alchemy. It is a spirit being that has force and a specific consciousness. When we learn to view phenomena such as money in this way, what we do on this side and what we do on the other side come closer to touching each other. Steiner says that the veils become thin.

On day four, Christian Rosenkreutz is crashing through the boundary between worlds and wakes up on the other side. In his waking state, he realizes he is the one intended to complete the great deed. He says, "I think you've got the wrong guy." But there he is at the wedding, because he realizes his humanity. He begins to understand as he sees the Royals beheaded. He starts to see. Like St. Paul he is blinded, but then the scales fall away, and he can see the reality. This is an ancient and ubiquitous theme. It's everywhere. It's what happens when we see God and are unprepared. This is the dialogue with the lower Guardian at the Threshold: *If you come in here unprepared, you are going to be upset and uncertain. So, I'm telling you, maybe step back a little bit. If you can't stand the heat, stay out of the kitchen.* That's the gist of what the guardian has to say.

Christian Rosenkreutz has been given a similar message by the virgins: *If you can't do this, just say so, and we'll tie you up and throw you into a dark room.* Yet, because he *does* say this, they realize he has the capacity to stand the heat. This is the exquisite paradox—he knows he can't do it, but this is why he is chosen to do the great alchemy of the homunculus. Humility gives him the strength needed to be an initiate. That is contemporary initiation in a sea of inflated consciousness, where anything is said and then immediately splayed out into the world. True, false, lies, absolutely stunning stellar truth, and bald-faced lies—all mashed together and flowing through our body in waves of electronic pulses.

In this story, the healing that Christian Rosenkreutz brings is the fact that *he knows he doesn't know.* This gives him an insurance policy when he is confronted by people who tell him that he doesn't know. Initiation means learning to put up with double-talk, simulacrum, and lying, always with the humility of understanding that

I don't understand. This capacity is the greatest aid to sanity. With this, we can get things done in life that we've come to do in keeping with our karma and destiny. This is why this book is a tremendously contemporary text. This is a particular teaching of how to stick your head out beyond this physical reality and into the next world and be in two places at the same time

This well-known image symbolizes an alchemist doing the great work. One's body is in this world of trees, rivers, and villages, as well as the Sun, Moon, and stars. Everything inside the stars, Sun, Moon, trees, and nature is *the given;* it is the realm of the king. We open our eyes and look out, and we see the stars. The stars we see are the *given* stars. The stars we don't see are where we live in freedom from the given. It is the only real freedom possible, because everything else is given. When it is given, we owe. This is the transactional politics of economics. You do this for me, I'll do that for you. It is lobbying. Everyone is trying to get around the logic of laws to find loopholes, because we all want freedom.

We have the picture of the alchemist half in and half out of the given (page 112). Pushing through from the landscape to the other side is reminiscent of an old hymn:

> *Ezekiel saw the wheel*
> *way up in the middle of the air.*
> *And the little wheel runs by faith,*
> *and the big wheel runs by the grace of God,*
> *A wheel in a wheel*
> *Way up in the middle of the air.**

The wheels are the hierarchies and the realm of the great movements of time and the cosmology of the eternal reality of human souls—the human being as an eternal reality. That's what this being in the picture is experiencing—a reality in which, while here, we can also be there. The two worlds interpenetrate and connect when we do the work.

* Song by William L. Dawson, inspired by the first chapter of Ezekiel.

In books on alchemy, they call the figure on the ground the artist or worker. The artist knows something lies behind the veil of appearances and works to stabilize the soul to avoid being upset by that, and then learns how to navigate within it—how to create a self-adjusting process in the other world, because there is a self-adjusting process on which the human archetype is based: *Christ.* But if I am inflated, I can't get access to Christ.

Thus, the core message of this book is this: *Do not inflate yourself.* The image is a meditation on the reality of alchemical work once we have trained a part of our consciousness to know how our higher self operates simultaneously in that other context. When we do something, we can have a kind of failsafe, or little flag, in the program that says: *This is what's happening now.* That failsafe voice is the guardian who says: *I think somebody's phishing for your soul. Maybe you should pay attention. I wouldn't open this email if I were you.*

We have this kind of language today, because most technological devices are shadows of the archetypal reality on the other side. All of our communication devices are shadows of esoteric capacities—clairaudience (phones) and clairvoyance (videos). Televisions and cell phones use instant communication remotely, something that took people a long time to master in esoteric schools. We are living at a critical time for the rise of alchemical wisdom in people who are rascals but designated to carry the thread of the mystery schools. It is my understanding that this is why Rudolf Steiner incarnated—to teach us rascals that we have to carry the thread of initiation through the reef of great stupidity and the reign of the great being of mocking, lying, denial, and an antipathetic agenda. So, like the sign in the mall says, "YOU ARE HERE."

Christian Rosenkreutz goes through these challenges in this story. He must understand how to live on two sides of the threshold simultaneously. How do I work with being misunderstood without inflating? If I inflate myself, how do I face the music when the authorities call and say: *We'd like you to come down, because we'd like to talk with you. We are disappointed in what you have sent us?* That's what happens to him in the castle. Culturally, we are now coming to the great IRS correction in the sky, so this story is very timely. The theme of day four is the *Will.* Christian Rosenkreutz is entering his own will impulses. Moreover, there is a theme here of what Rudolf Steiner calls aging and juvenilizing.

There is one pole of the aging process in the natural world, whereby all organisms grow old and lose their vital forces. Simultaneously, in human beings there is a juvenilization of potential for higher consciousness as life forces diminish. These two poles work into each other. We could even say that the purpose of diminishing life forces for humans is to lift our consciousness. We can actually say this, because the reciprocal of that is my life forces are diminished as I raise my consciousness. That's the foundation of occult physiology: *Consciousness diminishes life.* It is also the foundation of the biological principle. The reciprocity is there: *As life is diminished, consciousness is enhanced.* The quality of raising consciousness higher is done at the expense of the organism's life force.

On day four, the ten men are led by the Virgin into a room decked out for a wedding. In the banquet room, three sets of kings and queens sit on a dais. They will be part of the marriage ceremony. To understand this, it is useful to see how royalty was viewed in the past. The queen is potential, and the king is the given, the one who manifests. The true purpose of the king is to be an image of the divine world and to distribute the forces of wealth and wellbeing throughout the kingdom.

The Golden Bough by Sir James Frazer is an interesting book on the relationship between power and monarchy, kings and queens, and the science of royalty in the ancient world. It's a classic in the field of how magic flowed in the ancient world. Frazer was opinionated, so we have to discount that part, but his research is amazing. In past times, the king was not meant to be of this Earth. This is why we see pictures of kings and queens being carried around in a little chair. According to Frazer's research, if the king's foot were to touch the ground, the people would have to kill him. First, they would kill the ones who dropped the litter, and then they would kill the king. After they killed the king, they had to say, "The king is dead. Long live the king." This is because they understood that the king was meant to be in another world, as a kind of advocate, bringing the forces of procreation and wealth down to the kingdom.

The crown was a kind of antenna—not jewelry, but made to receive cosmic forces and tuned specifically to the king's physicality. Actually, it was intended to get the king's physicality out of the way so the cosmos could enter his head. The design of the crown—the weight and form, as well as the jewels in it—was supposed to balance everything, allowing his higher self to enter his thinking more easily. There was a whole science involved in this. Thus, the king was meant to be in the next world and to send down the latest news to the people. If his foot touched the ground, he was dead, while there was another one waiting in the wings. This was the idea of divine lineage. Kings were given free rein to do whatever they wanted, but they were never to touch the ground or even grow old. As soon as they began to feel their life forces weakening, they had to abdicate by being beheaded. They were immediately replaced by a new king in the blood line. The people needed a king who was fit to lead so that everything would go rightly in the kingdom.

Early on, this is what a person was trained to do as king. Over time, however, kings not only touched the ground, but also owned the ground. They could dole it out to whomever they liked and take it away from anyone they disliked. This is the shadow side of the king's power over the given. On one side, the king has divine right, based on being a benign channel of divine forces. On the other side is the shadow: *This is my kingdom. Also, by the way, what land do you have over there that I can add to my kingdom?* As lore goes, as a king grew older he could sense the limits of his vitality and just want a bigger bank account so he could go to the storeroom and run his fingers through the gold and jewels.

This is the shadow of the given: *What is given is held tightly and not circulated.* There's a grand monetary image in this. If we sequester wealth, we create scarcity. This is alchemical *coagula*—the shadow side of the king. The coagula has to be redeemed through sacrifice on the part of the king. The queen is *solve,* or cosmic potential. The potential is revived when the king sacrifices his absolute power. This is done in the nuptial chamber as a teaching. Alchemically, this is the famous king and queen in the bath.

In the first royal couple, we have a young queen and an old king, the "Royals." The young queen is full of potential and matched with an old king; his life forces are diminishing—he is a shadowy king married to a young queen. In this iconography, the queen is the Moon, procreating and giving birth from the invisible realm. The great gift is that the queen of the kingdom actually kept the king in balance. Without her, he might become a tyrant and abuse his awesome power. Without the touch of the eternal feminine, the solar force of the given begins to turn toward the shadow side, because the feminine is the creative, and the masculine is the legislative, deciding where to place creativity. The king proclaims how the issue will go. Later, in the bedroom, the queen asks: *Are you sure you want to do it that way, honey?* The queen maintains the creative force to temper the king's impulsive temptation to sequester power. Creative potential is her great gift. Now we have a young queen who represents this creative force. The shadow side of the queen is the creative becoming personally fantastical, with stratagems, spoils, and subterfuges, devolving into the need to control everything and question every impulse, no matter what it is. *Why are you doing this? Why don't you do that?* This is the queen's shadow side. The shadow side of the creative creates from personal fantasy rather than from archetypal reality. Both king and queen have the gift and the shadow; the gift and the shadow are linked. In the first royal couple we have an old king and a young queen.

In the third couple is a dark king. Here, *dark* usually refers to the will—or better, to being personally willful. In Rudolf Steiner's language, *the human will is dark*. It is dark because one's will is generally not penetrated by consciousness. We are not normally in contact with our motives for doing things. *Dark* means obscured; it means I cannot penetrate an impulse with an understanding of my motive. When I scratch my nose, I cannot penetrate all the will forces in my body with which I do that. I could read all the anatomy and physiology available, and what happens during the moment of scratching my nose is more or less automatic. I could write fourteen books about it, trying to understand what takes place. I could get down to the way mitochondria metabolize sugars through the Krebs cycle or some such thing, but it would still not explain the impulse to discharge my will. I can know what happens physiologically, but I do not experience it cognitively in the execution of the will. That's where the will is, but it is dark, which means I don't cognize it as a soul force. The third couple is a dark king accompanied by a dainty, veiled matron. Being veiled, she is the feminine side of the dark will, representing creative forces that don't interact with the will. As a result they have become obsolete. She is not procreative and full of potential, but matronly.

Thus, the story has an old king and a beautiful, young, and vigorous queen. There is also a dark king accompanied by a dainty matron who, instead of a crown, wears a veil. Between these two royal couples are two individuals of average age and, as Christian Rosenkreutz describes them, unremarkable in appearance. A large crown is suspended above them, and they are lifted onto the royal dais because they are lovers. They are "Royals," but not *completely* royal. They are common people whose crown remains above them and who, as the story tells us, are lovers.

Behind this couple stands a circle of ancient men. The two Royals represent the given on the male side and potential on the female side, whose destiny is to meet because they are lovers. However, they have not consummated their marriage, which would allow the forces of potential and the manifest to give birth to a new creation. Alchemists would say that the king and queen have not yet been united in the bath. The task of uniting them is the alchemical wedding that Christian Rosenkreutz must accomplish.

These six individuals who constitute the three couples are known as the Royals. These are powerful pictures of the relationship between the *given* part of the human being and the *potential,* representing stages of the given (what must be done) and the freer, *solve* side of the queen, which is limitless potential. However, this polarity in these three pairs of Royals has already reached a certain kind of anticlimax that must be fully completed by humans. These are the beings in *The Alchemical Wedding* who will be married, who *must* be married.

The three royal couples are images of the three human soul forces: thinking, willing, and feeling. Alchemists would call thinking *salt*; willing is *sulfur;* feeling is *mercury,* the great healing. The ancient king and the young queen represent the dual salt capacity for thinking—an old faculty in its male aspect of intellect and knowledge of cause and effect. This is the precipitation side of salt. The dissolving side of salt in the natural world serves organisms by making them capable of the most fecund creative forces. This is represented by the beautiful young queen.

The dark king and the dainty old matron whose head is covered with a veil represent the forces of the will, dark in its cognitive capacity, as will impulses in the human soul are hidden from our thinking. The will is considered the origin of all other soul forces; it is old. It is obscured (hidden) in the soul by sleeping unconsciousness, characterizing its primary nature.

The third pair represents everyday familiar aspects of sensory experience in their common appearance. There is great potential for the dreamlike feeling life arising from sensory experience to be lifted into a dynamic force of creative imagination. This transformation is accomplished though the marriage of opposites in an alchemical process of death and transfiguration. The large and costly crown above them represents this tremendous potential.

There is a little altar near to the Royals, with a black book and a small taper in an ivory candle holder. A celestial sphere and a small watch rest on the altar, along with a small crystal fountain, from which a blood-red fluid flows. A death's head, or skull, completes the implements, with a small white serpent circling the skull and going in one eye socket and out of the other. As it enters one eye socket, its tail moves out of the other, making a complete circuit of the skull.

The little altar is a small representation of the three soul forces. The book and the candle are images of the quest for knowledge, a key aspect of the alchemical marriage. The celestial sphere and the watch indicate the need to link the marriage ceremonies to the correct planetary movements. The time element is the will. The little crystal fountain with the blood-red liquid can be seen as the higher capacities of a heart purified of base desires, blaming, and anger. Freed of these forces, the heart can be transformed into a vessel for distilling the delicate perceptions of the spiritual world.

Prior to the wedding ceremony, the Royals will all drink from the fountain. The skull, with the serpent passing in and out of the eyeholes, portrays the earthly sensory life that continuously sends impulses into and out of the skull. It is this continuous flow of sensory impressions that makes the task of purifying the impulses of the heart so difficult and is the main obstruction to accomplishing the alchemical marriage.

The room is set up for the ceremony; the ten men meet and greet the Royals and then the ten leave with the Virgin to return down the stairs. Back in their own area, the Virgin suggests to the men that they each choose sleeping partners from among the other virgins. This turns out to be a ruse, but it is an important element in this story.

Rosicrucians were under oath not to undertake occult efforts to prolong their lives beyond a normal lifespan. The oath arose to deal with the widespread practice of making magical potions, elixirs, rituals, and talismans intended to prolong life. In this passage, this idea is linked to the offer of the Virgin to sleep with Christian Rosenkreutz.

In the magical practices of the day, it was thought that an old man could renew his vigor by sleeping with a virgin.

The force of sexual desire is an important theme in the development of this story; the marriage of the king and queen involves conjoining the two principles of male and female into what alchemists call *the hermaphrodite*. In this case, the Virgin offers the men the great temptation of sleeping with the other virgins to test the purity of heart of the chosen adepts. Sleeping with a virgin to prolong life is "sex magic," a shadow of the Great Alchemical Marriage. Here, this theme follows the contest of riddles from the previous day, and the virgins cleverly escape the task of sleeping with humans.

Having passed this test, the ten men accompany the Virgin back to the upper chamber to join the Royals. There, they all watch a seven-act play as a prelude to the marriage ceremony. The Royals watch the play with the ten. The play shows why the marriage needs to be performed—that is, the soul needs to experience the Fall and the estrangement from Creation in order to be resurrected in a new life. This play addresses the soul's Fall and redemption.

Following the drama, all the Royals suddenly stand on the dais and remove their white wedding dresses, under which they are all wearing black. Christian Rosenkreutz then notices that everything connected with the wedding things has somehow also become black, which gives him an uneasy feeling. Next, a coal-black man appears with an axe, and proceeds to chop off the Royals' heads. Christian Rosenkreutz comments that this is the bloodiest wedding he has ever attended. As the Axeman turns to leave, someone strikes him dead by taking off his head, too.

In esoteric language, the coal-black man is an image of the human double—not the shadow, a retarding element that represents barely conscious fragments of personality in the human soul. Shadow elements are often qualities that we don't like about ourselves and lurk in the subconscious, just below ordinary consciousness. Those elements occasionally boil up into awareness during moments of weakness.

When human shadow beings connect with each other in a human soul, they become more deeply seated and even less conscious. They become a kind of composite of shadows known esoterically as a *double*. There are many kinds of doubles, but they all share a profoundly disabling hindrance to human progress. Being chronic composites of shadows they are not easily recognized and thus difficult to confront.

The only way to deal with a double is to develop soul forces consciously so that they no longer rely on the body's sensory experiences. Because our head is the primary source of sensory impressions, beheading the sensory-inspired soul forces is necessary for the initial stages of the alchemical wedding. For our soul, this means experiencing a death process whereby the sensory world is abandoned and our sensory life is beheaded and placed in a coffin. This is an image of sense-free thinking.

In this story, the double performs the beheading, because it lives deeply in one's unconscious life behind sensory experience. The double is also beheaded, because its role in the eventual redemption of the senses is to perform a sacrificial act. The transformed double becomes the New Adam, the potential state to which Christian Rosenkreutz aspires as an adept. Redemption of the senses is the central mystery of *The Alchemical Wedding*, and beheading the Royals is the first step toward redemption. When this happens, the stimulus–response patterns linked to the senses are placed in the hands of the newly independent, conscious human being. Beheading symbolizes the act of turning off our sense impressions, since our head is the main stage of most sensory experiences.

Essentially, when meditating we are trying to cut off our head. We shut down sensory experiences so that our consciousness stops processing sensory input. Why is this important? Sensory input is the result of the soul's "Fall" from Saturn to Jupiter to Sun and to Earth; it is the story of our incarnation. According to Rudolf Steiner, the sensory activity we experience is the seed event of that Fall: "Then their eyes were opened, and they saw they were naked" (Gen. 3:7). It is our sensory experience that creates turbulence in the cosmos.

Our sensory experience is not a part of how the given is structured. According to Rudolf Steiner's spiritual research, our sense organs are simply meant to be "mirrors." He represents this as the human phantom's question. The phantom and sense impressions have become coagulated into the organism; the life forces, stimulated by sense impressions, have become chronically personalized. This chronic condition underlies autism, addiction, and the general need for therapy. All of this has to do with the fact that the senses in our heads keep us informed about the mirror world, but not about the real world behind the mirror. The senses relay a constant barrage of experiences that lead us to believe that the mirror world we experience is the real world, and that the real world and its spiritual forces are merely imaginary. This is precisely what Ahriman would have us believe. Materialism rules our consciousness, because for materialistic consciousness the only reality is the realm of matter. Ahriman's great power is belief in the supremacy of matter in contrast to believing that the important thing is what happens in our soul–spirit. These two beliefs are at war in the world today. Between these is the understanding that these two belief structures must be made to relate to each other: *There is no matter without spirit, and no spirit without matter.* We must penetrate matter with our senses and then turn them off and go inward with our experience. Essentially, we have to cut off our head.

Cutting off of the heads of the Royals by the Axeman is the beginning of the marriage; beheading separates thinking based on sense experience from the will and feelings; this is the realm of initiation. This picture in the context of a wedding can be experienced as a kind of murder. It is disturbing if we try to understand it in materialistic terms, but if we understand it from an esoteric perspective, we realize that this is what happens every time we silence our thoughts in meditation. Fundamentally, we kill and decapitate the Royals.

Christian Rosenkreutz wonders what all this has to do with marriage. After the beheading, he goes with his page to his room. In this story, we must pay attention to the page, because he is always present when Christian Rosenkreutz is about to become a rascal. The page represents intellectual curiosity and intellectually getting to the bottom of things. The page is the source of Christian Rosenkreutz's notion that he can do things and go places that no one else can. This is a temptation of initiates on a path of knowledge. The great temptation is *knowledge,* and the remedy is to give up knowledge for wisdom. Unfortunately (and fortunately), wisdom is always won the hard way. You cannot gain wisdom by reading a book, but only through experience.

Thus, gathering information is the first step on the path. Understanding that information is the second. Realizing that the information does not give me understanding is the third. And learning to get rid of the information so we can absorb the lessons of experience leads to wisdom.

Christian Rosenkreutz's page tries to lull him to sleep with interesting conversation, but he fakes sleep until the page goes to sleep. He is still awake at midnight. Suddenly, Christian Rosenkreutz sees a light flickering through the window of his room. He gets up and looks out onto the lake and sees seven ships approaching the castle. Each ship has a flame arising from its mast. This flame is known to sailors as *St. Elmo's fire.* Under certain conditions, a ship's rigging collects static electricity and a flame will shoot up and from the mast. Sailors consider it a portent of the need to pay attention. In *The Alchemical Wedding*, this is a warning to Christian Rosenkreutz that something is about to change.

Through the window, he sees the Virgin with a torch, leaving the castle with the six caskets of the Royals. Each casket is loaded onto a different ship, while a little cedar chest containing the head of the coal-black man is placed on the seventh ship. Seeing this, Christian Rosenkreutz understands that, although the Royals were beheaded, they were not actually dead. This is the great teaching of initiation—when we die, we are not really dead.

Christian Rosenkreutz calls his page, and they watch the scene together. With this understanding, he can now go to sleep.

Day Five

Overview

Christian Rosenkreutz awakes early on the fifth day, and it suddenly feels like a different world. No one else is awake in the castle. He leaves his room and meets his page in the castle. His page had told him earlier, during the banquet, to go into the library, where a different page arrived and said, "You know you're not supposed to be in here. If the Bridegroom finds you in here there will be trouble, so don't mention that you were here." Christian Rosenkreutz's flaw (if we can call it that) is that he knows he doesn't understand but really wants to and is willing to go to great lengths to make that happen. He's willing to go into places where he probably shouldn't go. This is a pattern throughout the story, but his misunderstanding leads to higher sight.

Having awakened early while everyone else is still asleep, Christian Rosenkreutz goes down into the castle. There he meets his page, who says, "I think there's something interesting that you might like to see."

Rosenkreutz responds, "Really?"

"Yes, do you see that door over there in the floor?"

Suddenly a door appears in the floor. The page walks over to it and pulls on a little hidden ring and lifts it, revealing steps, which the two descend. The page is Christian Rosenkreutz's intellect, his servant, curious and knowledgeable. His intellect leads him through the opening and down the steps.

Below is a strange fountain in the form of a great copper kettle. In the kettle an angel stands holding a strange tree in his arms. Both the angel and the tree are made of gold. The tree continually drops fruit into the kettle, where the fruit turns into water. The water spills over and through channels into three smaller kettles, which form a little altar supported by an eagle, an ox, and a lion made of jewels on its base.

Now Christian Rosenkreutz has higher vision, meaning that he is able to see the activity of beings living in higher worlds, represented in the forms of things in the mundane world. From that perspective, the altar symbolizes an aspect of human life. An angel guides the transformation of the fruits of knowledge gained from the tree of knowledge. Physiologically, the nervous system is known to alchemists as the tree of knowledge. The glands were considered to be the fruits of that tree. When an adept transforms sensory activity, it affects secretions of the glandular system, resulting in the production of a higher substance that resembles pure soul force without the darkness of the passions. The glands secrete a response to sensation, which is analogous to fruit dissolving into water. The three soul forces of thinking (eagle), feeling (lion), and willing (ox) form a base of precious jewels to receive these transformed substances from the copper distilling vessel on the altar of love. From the perspective of an alchemical analog, the little altar could be considered the pituitary gland. Once Christian Rosenkreutz sees this altar, the page suggests another level to explore.

There is another door in the floor that opens to steps leading down into darkness. With the permission of Christian Rosenkreutz, the page leads the way down to another chamber, where there is a bed with a curtain around it. The page asks him, "Would you like to see behind the curtain?" He is of two minds; on the one hand, Christian Rosenkreutz has a bad feeling about doing this," but on the other hand he is curious, so he decides to continue on.

The page opens the curtain, and there on the bed is Venus, the goddess of love, naked. When Christian Rosenkreutz sees Venus, he realizes the truth of ultimate reality but also realizes he is in real trouble. He has seen the sacred vision that we will all see at the end of time, but he has seen it prematurely and realizes its importance.

The page closes the curtain and they return up the steps. They close the little door with a clang, and now Cupid, the son of Venus, suddenly appears. Cupid asks, "Old Man, what are you doing here?" Christian Rosenkreutz explains that he was lost and that the page had found him wandering about.

Cupid responds sternly, "It is a good thing you didn't open that door in the floor, Old Man."

The wheel of karma is turning. Cupid takes his arrow, but rather than shooting it he grabs Christian Rosenkreutz's finger and nicks it with the arrow. Instead of being shot with the love arrow, he is only wounded by it because of his curiosity and his belief in the primacy of the intellect. Love is going to wound you one way or another, and that's what Christian Rosenkreutz has to learn. You might have been following the advice of your page, but you were ignoring love. You were a little premature, and now there are serious implications. "I've made this little wound in you, and now get out of here, Old Man."

When the senses have been transformed by humanity, love will bring forth the new Adam, the higher transformed subtle bodies of the human being. It is the lower body that is formed from the activity of the senses. When Christian Rosenkreutz is able to see in a higher way, the force of love forms a spiritual embryo within his soul. This spiritual embryo will be brought to term in the womb of Venus–Sophia, as wisdom becomes love and human beings become world creators. For now, this vision is withheld from humans due to the dangers of inflation. As Cupid says, there would be trouble for everyone if he were to see love nakedly with his spiritual sight. So the page and Christian Rosenkreutz leave the chamber.

They find out that day that they have to take a journey to the island. They must take a circuitous journey, a symbolic journey, and now Christian Rosenkreutz has his second wound. The second wound is again deliverance and service. He was delivered from the bottom of the dungeon, but he was wounded. Now he is wounded by his curiosity. Eventually, these wounds of service will provide a motif for the culmination of the work.

THE ALCHEMICAL WEDDING, DAY FIVE

At daybreak, Christian Rosenkreutz could not sleep, so he dressed early and went down to the great hall. No one else was awake. He asked his page to tell him more about the castle and the proceedings. His page was willing and led him down some steps to an underground chamber. There was a great iron door with strange inscriptions on it, which he copied. Behind this door was a dark passageway leading to a very small door that was open slightly. The page said that it was opened just once to let the coffins pass through and had not been shut since. CR and the page stepped through the threshold. This chamber was the king's treasury and had only the light that came from enormous jewels. However, the most glorious thing in the chamber was a magnificent, ornate sepulcher. It was so rich that CR wondered why it was not guarded more closely. He thanked his lucky stars that he was permitted to see something no person had ever seen.

The sepulcher was triangular in shape and had a great copper kettle in its center. The rest was made of pure gold and precious stones. An Angel stood in the great kettle holding a strange tree in his arms. The tree continuously dropped fruit into the kettle. As the soft fruit fell into the kettle, it turned into water, which ran over through channels into three small kettles. The four kettles and the Angel thus formed a little altar. The little altar was in turn supported by an eagle, an ox, and a lion on a base made of jewels.

Christian Rosenkreutz asked his page what this meant. The page replied, "This is the tomb of Lady Venus, whose beauty has undone many men in fortune, honor, blessing. and prosperity." The page then showed him a copper door in the pavement. He said, "We can go farther down through this door." It was extremely dark and the page immediately opened a small casket in which there was an ever-burning taper. With this he kindled one of the many torches that lined the walls. CR became uneasy about going so deeply into hidden areas of the castle. The page told him that it was fine to do this so long as the Royal Persons were still resting, and that CR had nothing to fear.

They then encountered a strange bed with curtains all around. The page drew one curtain, and there was Lady Venus, stark naked in the bed. In the dim light Christian Rosenkreutz could not tell whether this was a statue or a person, but it moved him inwardly since it was so sumptuous in the flesh. The page drew the curtain closed, but the image of Lady Venus remained imbedded in the mind of CR. Behind the bed stood a tablet with other curious writing. Christian Rosenkreutz asked his page about the writing, but he laughed and said that someday he would know what it meant.

The page put out the torch, and the two ascended. In the upper chamber, Christian Rosenkreutz noticed that the tapers he originally thought to be candles were actually pyrite that gave off flames like stones. The heat from the pyrite continuously caused the tree to melt, yet it continued to produce new fruits. The page stated he had overheard Atlas telling the king that, when the tree has melted, Lady Venus will awake and become the mother of a king. With this, little cupid flew in and demanded to know what spirit had led them to this place. CR replied that he had lost his way in the castle and happened upon this place, and that the page had found him there just as Cupid arrived. Cupid answered, "It would be well for old busybody Grandpa to mind his own business, because if he had been aware of the door in the floor it would be trouble for everyone." With this, cupid placed a strong lock on the door in the floor. CR thanked God that Cupid had not arrived while they were still in the lower chamber. "Nevertheless," said Cupid, "I can't let go of the fact that you came so close to my sacred Mother without redress." Thus, Cupid put one of his little darts into one of the flames and pricked CR on the hand with it. CR was glad that this episode was so quickly finished

Meanwhile, the others had gotten out of bed and entered the great hall. Cupid came into the hall seeking out CR. He looked at the drop of blood where he had pricked CR and laughed, warning all the others to deal carefully with CR, since he would soon be ending his days. With this, the Virgin of the ten entered the hall. She had prepared herself for a journey and was dressed all in black velvet. She carried her laurel branch with her, as did the other virgins. She asked the men to form a procession and follow her into the place where the coffins were kept. Christian Rosenkreutz thought his companions must think that the Royals who were beheaded yesterday were still in the coffins, although he knew they were elsewhere because of his vision during the night.

Standing close to each of the coffins were eight men wrapped in scarves as against a strong, cold wind. They were pallbearers. The ten men followed the coffins out into the garden, where there was a wooden building with a roof, upon which was a glorious crown supported by seven columns. Within the building were six sepulchers, each with a large stone standing nearby, with a round, hollow stone standing in the center. With great reverence, the coffins were laid in the graves, and the stones were placed over them. The little chest was to lie in the middle.

Christian Rosenkreutz thought his companions were deceived by this, since they thought the coffins contained the corpses of the Royals. On top of the building was a flag with a phoenix on it. Christian Rosenkreutz thanked God that he was permitted to see more than the others could. Once everything was finished, the Virgin of the ten spoke: "I hope that everyone assembled will be constant in your engagements and not regret the pains you will undergo in the future, but with good hearts be helpful in restoring the present buried royal persons to life again, and without delay let them rise again with me to make the journey to the Tower of Olympus." She wished to travel with the men to obtain medicines there that would be useful in this process of restoration. All present agreed to undertake this task.

The men all followed her through a small door leading out of the garden to the lake shore. There, the seven ships that Christian Rosenkreutz had seen the previous night stood empty, moored to the shore. Each virgin placed a laurel branch in each ship. The ten men were distributed among six of the ships and bid farewell by the virgins. The ships set sail, and soon the castle vanished from sight.

Each of the ships were operated by two persons. The ten men found that five of the ships each had several regular bodies, or platonic forms, aboard them as a device. The ship carrying Christian Rosenkreutz and the Virgin of the ten had a globe on it instead of a platonic form. In the first ship lay the Dark Axeman. On that ship were also twelve musicians, and its device was a pyramid. Next followed three ships abreast, *Mars Earth,* and *Mercury.* CR sat in the center, on *Earth.* Behind these came the fairest ships, *Sun* and *Moon.* In the rear there was only one ship, *Venus,* on which were forty virgins.

The ships passed across the lake and into a fjord, and then out to sea, where numerous nymphs, sirens, and sea goddesses surrounded their flotilla. The sea goddesses gave a great pearl to the Virgin as a gift for the wedding of the Bridegroom and the Bride. The sea goddesses entreated the Virgin to make a little form with the ships, so that they might provide some music. The Virgin then had the two great ships, *Sun* and *Moon,* stand in the center, with the other five arranged to form a pentagon around them. The nymphs and sea goddesses surrounded the ships and began in delicate sweet voices to sing a long song about the virtues of love. When their song ended, the Virgin soon dispatched them, presenting them with a long, red scarf and thanking them for their song.

Christian Rosenkreutz was becoming aware that the injury from Cupid's prick on the hand was being aroused by the siren song. He realized that the wound on his hand was similar in nature to the wound he received on his neck during his dream on the first day, when he was dragged through the roof of the dungeon.

They reached the Tower of Olympus after some hours of sailing, and they shot pistols to signal their approach. This was recognized by a large, white flag raised on the island. A small, gilded boat was launched and moved toward them. In the boat was an ancient man who was the Tower warden. The Virgin was with us, so we were received in a friendly way and conducted to the Tower. The Tower was set exactly square on the island, surrounded by a thick wall and a meadow dense with flowers and with many gardens with unusual fruits. Near the Tower was another, inner wall. The Tower itself was composed of seven round Towers grouped together, the midmost being the tallest, with seven stories.

The men were led off to the side, as Christian Rosenkreutz saw the coffins being removed from the ships and brought into the Tower without the others noticing. Once the coffins were out of sight, the ten men were led into the Tower at the very bottom, where they found a laboratory in which they were obliged to beat and boil plants and precious stones to extract their essences and put them into glasses.

The Virgin directed this activity in a careful and knowledgeable way. The task was extremely laborious. Meanwhile, without the knowledge of the other men, Christian Rosenkreutz perceived that three virgins were diligently washing the corpses in another apartment. After working for a long period of time, broth and a little wine were brought to the men, and they each received a thin mattress on the ground.

CR was not sleepy, so he went for a walk in the garden. After a while, he came to the great wall. The sky was clear and the stars were out, so he thought he would pass the time contemplating the stars. By chance, he discovered a set of old stone stairs leading to the top of the wall. The moon was shining brightly and aided his climb up the stairs. While climbing, he realized that a major and rare conjunction was to occur that night. He was watching the heavens for the conjunction at midnight when he spied a fire out at sea. He saw that it was the seven flames making their way across the ocean toward the Tower, where they climbed to the very top and settled themselves. As soon as they did this, the wind began to pick up and the seas began to groan and thrash. CR grew afraid and hurried down the stairs to his mattress on the hard ground. He carried his bed to a gently falling fountain and used its soothing sounds to help him into sleep.

Day Five Commentary

On the fifth day, Christian Rosenkreutz is in an altered state of consciousness, because he has seen the Royals beheaded and now knows that they are still alive in some form. However, he is only just beginning his adventure in altered consciousness. In this section, the symbolism of each event becomes even more profound. We could say that the symbols represent a journey that, through higher vision, Christian Rosenkreutz is actually taking through his own organism. Christian Rosenkreutz had awakened early; no one else was up and about in the castle. He experienced the bloody wedding yesterday, after which he had a vision at midnight before going to sleep.

Through his inner work, Christian Rosenkreutz has been given the gift of second sight. Now he can see the actual reality behind the appearance of events; in a word he is clairvoyant. Christian Rosenkreutz goes down into the castle with the page, who says, "I know where there is something that would really interest you—it's a secret room. Are you interested?" Christian Rosenkreutz now has second sight, but he hasn't yet developed the "I" of the heart, which could have warned him, "If you do this, it'll create a problem." He has reached the stage of initiation where he can "see," but it is the level called *imagination.* He has not yet experienced *inspiration* and *intuition.* Imagination is good, but it is just the beginning stage of initiation. Imagination is not completely penetrated by sacrifice, which is the issue about holding on to personal beliefs that gets us all in trouble. He has imagination; he has seen, and now his appetite is whetted for more. The page mentions a small, secret room that is actually the sepulcher for the Royals.

The page opens a secret door in the floor, and inside there is a tomb with a kind of altar—a fountain and a tree in a cauldron, guarded by an angel. The fruits on the tree are melting and dropping into the cauldron, which causes it to overflow into three cups supported by small sculptures in the form of three animals—a bull, a lion, and an eagle (will, feeling, and thinking). This is a metaphor for the archetypal journey through the consciousness of the soul of a seer, or initiate. As a metaphor for Christian Rosenkreutz's journey through the body, this little altar might represent the guardian angel who guides the transformation of the fruits of knowledge gained from the Tree of Knowledge.

Physiologically, glands are like fruits on the tree of the nervous system. The nervous system is known to alchemists as the Tree of Knowledge. The glands linked to the nerves are stimulated by sense impressions. They then melt or "sweat" secretions of their neurotransmitters into the bloodstream. These secretions are hormones that activate the soul as impulses of thinking, feeling, and willing. Thus transformed, the sensory activity of an adept renders the secretions of the glandular system into conscious images that are workable symbols of the sensations. The forces of the hormones are experienced in a higher way. This means they produce effects available to consciousness resembling pure soul forces, minus the darkness of passions resulting from habituated sensations. In the sculpture in the tomb, the symbolic soul forces of thinking (eagle), feeling (lion), and willing (ox) hold cups to receive these transformed fruit-like substances from the copper distilling vessel on the altar of Love. The little altar could be thought of as the pituitary gland receiving sense stimulation and secreting thyroid stimulating hormone to be carried throughout the body.

Within the tomb is a door in the floor that is open just a little. The page says it was never shut after they carried the Royals' coffins through it. Christian Rosenkreutz and the page go down through the opening in the floor; in other words, he is going down into his own body-consciousness. He is entering his unconscious, but he has the capacity to see. He is a seer, but he has to go into his own unconscious. Carl Jung, in his alchemical work, calls it "eating the shadow." With our capacity to see, we have to eat our own unsavory beliefs. As seers, we have to go into our own psyche and look at our own flaws symbolically, so that we can make a medicine from the poison preventing us from serving the whole.

Christian Rosenkreutz is a seer; he has imaginative cognition. Now he has to return into his unconscious soul and penetrate it. When he does so, he sees a large curtain. The page draws the curtain aside, and Christian Rosenkreutz sees Venus, or Love, naked on the bed. Suddenly, he realizes he has crossed a line and they should get out of there. He has seen Love naked on a bed, which is highly transformative but also a problem cosmically, because it's premature. The task of the initiate is to experience prematurely what everyone else will experience later. He has made an error, but he is not evil; he will just have to suffer the consequences of being ahead of the culture in his consciousness. Christian Rosenkreutz has witnessed the central mystery of human existence—the mystery of Love in its naked state. His curious intellect, symbolized by the always-ready page, led him into this central mystery, but he cannot fathom the mystery itself. The page closes the curtain, and they both quickly leave.

Once they are out and the door is closed, Venus's son Cupid arrives. He says to Christian Rosenkreutz, "What are you doing here, old man? Did you go down through that door?" Christian Rosenkreutz replies that he had gotten lost—he was just walking around when the page found him. His action is a transgression of the initiate and the second time his page led him to a place where he was not supposed to be. The first time was when he first entered the castle and was led into the royal library by the page. He was warned then that he should not be there. This time, however, he went deeper and caused Cupid to show up. Cupid cannot ignore it this time, since Christian Rosenkreutz was so close to violating Venus by seeing her. Because he was found there, Cupid takes one of his arrows and, instead of shooting Christian Rosenkreutz with it, nicks him on the finger, drawing blood.

Christian Rosenkreutz considers this to be a close call and hurries to join the other men at breakfast.

After breakfast, they are reintroduced to the king of the castle in preparation for a journey to the island where the Great Work will take place. Cupid arrives and points out to everyone that Christian Rosenkreutz was nicked on his finger by Cupid's arrow. However, they all made a joke of it. They know that Cupid is the biggest rascal of them all, because he loves to shoot arrows at someone who shouldn't be somewhere. Actually, he just likes to shoot his arrows, but in this instance he was upset about his mother Venus.

Having finished breakfast, the ten men escort the Virgin into the garden, where there is a wooden building with a glorious roof supported by seven pillars. Eight men serving as pallbearers have wrapped their necks with scarves and stand by each coffin, each of which is also next to a hollow stone. At the center of the building stands a great hollow stone, around which all the coffins are arranged. The little chest with the head of the coal-black man is placed at the center of the arrangement, while a flag with a phoenix flies on the glorious roof. This arrangement is supposed to serve as the burial of the Royals, but Christian Rosenkreutz, having second sight, knows that the Royals are actually on the ships and not in the coffins.

As a metaphor for an inner journey into one's own body, this scene can describe the anatomy of the human skull itself, which is the focus of most sensory input into the organism. Eight men in scarves, serving as pallbearers, can be seen as the teeth wrapped in gums—eight on each side of the mouth. Alchemists would say that humans are carried to their graves by their own mouths, owing to what goes into them and what comes out. The wooden building with the glorious roof could be the dome of the cranium, which is supported by seven pillars—the occiput, the sphenoid, the two zygomatic bones, the two nasal bones, and the maxilla of the upper jaw. Moreover, there are six venous sinuses, equivalent to six coffins; two cavernous sinuses, or the combined sigmoid; and transverse sinuses (with the sigmoid as a curve of the vessels); the straight sinus; and the great sagittal sinus. These six major sinuses are coffins for the cranial venous blood as it makes its way out of the cranium. At the very center of the brain is the great "hollow stone"—the ventricular system of the combined two lateral and the third ventricles.

The second-century surgeon Galen thought of this area as the seat of imagination and the place where inner pictures are formed in human beings because of the intimate interaction of cerebral spinal fluid within the ventricles, with the nerve impulses that stream into the midbrain just below the ventricles. Most of our sensory nerves are focused in this area. Here, the head of the coal-black man is buried in a chest. We could also view the six coffins as the six openings of the sensory organs in the head—two nostrils, two ears, and two eyes. The chest with the head of the coal-black in it at the center might represent the mouth and the tongue.

Again, the motif of transforming the senses is revealed as the alchemical path. We must cut off our sensory input if we wish to take the path of self-transformation. At this point, we could ask: What is the significance for this initiation to see Venus naked? There is a rich history of this kind of thing in the world. This is what we would call the error of the initiate. The error is that, through knowledge, the initiate knows or does something prematurely. There is always this gesture of bringing something into the world prematurely. It needs to happen, but when it does it inflames things and gets out ahead of them. This is the initiate's error–trial. It's not simply that Christian Rosenkreutz saw Venus naked, but that he saw it too early in a cosmic sense. Nevertheless, it is the destiny of an initiate to do this. This is a curious thing, but it is the karma of his initiation. There are many examples of this. There is a well-known book titled the *Golden Ass*, written by a Roman named Apuleius. It is a classic in the field of psychology.* It tells the story of a young man who becomes estranged

* See for example, Marie-Louise von Franz, *Golden Ass of Apuleius: The Liberation of the Feminine in Man* (Boston: Shambhala, 1992).

from his birth family and is taken in by a coven of witches. They teach him witchcraft—what we call sex magic. Within this story is another story called "Cupid and Psyche," "Amour and Psyche, love and soul, or love and consciousness. C. S. Lewis retells this story within a story in his book, *Till We Have Faces*.* The protagonist is an ugly princess who is told by her father that she has to wear a veil over her face because she is so ugly. She has a beautiful sister who falls in love with Cupid (Amour) and leaves the father's castle to live in a strange one, where Amour comes at night to visit her but does not allow her to see him. Other beings living there tell her, "He's really very beautiful, and you really should ask him to reveal himself to you."

So, she asks him to reveal himself, but he says, "Oh no, that would be very bad for you." She begins to suspect that he is actually hideous, although he is a good lover. One night she hides a light in the boudoir. She is using her intellect in an attempt to see a god. He comes to her that night, and she quickly takes hold of the light and sees that he really is beautiful.

Amour tells her, "I am sorry you did that, because now I have to leave." He then leaves, but because the princess has seen a god face to face, she becomes a prisoner in the castle. C. S. Lewis writes the adventure of Sister Ugly (as they used to say), who has to leave and try to rescue her beautiful sister, becoming a warrior and leading an army. It's a contemporary retelling of the story within Apuleius' story of *The Golden Ass*. This story within a story is about the problem of love and consciousness; it expands the idea of the clash between intellect and love—the intellect's perception of what love is, how it appears to the intellect, and the shadows cast by the experience of seeing love directly.

This is basically the pivot point of the initiation of Christian Rosenkreutz. A similar theme occurs in the story of Semele and Zeus in the myth sequences of Dionysus. Dionysus' mother Semele gives birth to him, with Zeus as the father. When Hera the goddess wife of Zeus

* *Till We Have Faces: A Myth Retold* (New York: HarperCollins, 1956).

hears about this, she appears as an old woman to Semele and says to her, "You need to question the one who comes to visit you in secret at night. Unless he can show himself to you, he is really unworthy of you. You need to demand that he show himself." One night, Zeus comes to Semele again and says, "I love you," and they make love. Then she says that he should show himself. Zeus first resists but then agrees and reveals himself. Semele, being mortal, is destroyed by the sight of the god , but a great grape vine grows up and protects the fetus. She dies in the revelation of the light of Zeus; however, the fetus is untouched. Zeus takes the fetus and makes an incision in his own thigh in which to incubate, or gestate, Dionysus. Zeus is the Great God, and the story is about the human and the divine, love hidden and love revealed.

This theme describes the delicate task of an initiate. As Rudolf Steiner puts it, true initiation means that the initiate has no opinions. There can be definite thoughts about something, but initiation means to be able to simultaneously think the opposite. This prevents us from getting stuck in an opinion. We can discuss it from one side, but I can also approach it from a different side.

Steiner was criticized during his life for doing just that. In today's political arena this is called waffling or flip-flopping. True political leaders are billed as wafflers when they try to look at both sides of a situation, but we have to bring all sides to the table to truly resolve any issue. Politicians are forced to obsess on a point of view one way or the other, because the public demands leaders who are decisive, make decisions, and stick to them—even when they are dead wrong. I remember Adlai Stevenson, a candidate who opposed Dwight Eisenhower in the presidential elections of 1952 and 1956. Stevenson was a scholar and thinker who had an amazing capacity to consider more than one side of an issue. Eisenhower was the great World War II general. Guess who won.

The initiate is one who, from the popular perspective, seems to "waffle" by being able to think both sides of an issue simultaneously. This capacity is the mark of initiation.

Christian Rosenkreutz is on a ship that is part of a flotilla going to an island where there is a tower that serves as a laboratory for the Great Work. Much of the journey is devoted to numerology and what could be called "cabalistic reasoning." This section is dense and difficult to place in the context of the alchemy that will take place in the Tower. However, the Tower descriptions are marvels of numerology. The various levels in the Tower can be considered symbols of the *chakra* systems in the human body. A chakra is an energy center whose physical center is a gland. The function of glands is similar to that of chakras in traditional esotericism. As a result, the Tower and what takes place there is analogous to the inner journey of an initiate through the levels of organization of the energetic body as they relate to the soul forces of the astral body.

The Tower itself has seven levels. This is the realm of seven, the number of planets that compose the forces of the astral plane. Christian Rosenkreutz and the others are entering the astral body. Within the Tower, only Christian Rosenkreutz can actually see what is really happening owing to the opening of his inner eye in the tomb of Venus. The others participate, but only he can see the spiritual reality behind the physical operations. The Tower can be thought of as the system of our seven chakras.

When they reach the Tower, they enter the lowest chakra and begin the work of distilling and rendering substances. This is the consciousness of the collective, which arises from the digestive organs connected with excretion. After working in the lower chakra, Christian Rosenkreutz goes for a walk outside. Among the planets, he sees that a particular conjunction is taking place. This realization allows him once again to perceive the souls of the beheaded Royals as flames making their way across the sea to enter the Tower. As soon as he sees this, the astral world is disturbed and a wind arises before a storm. He returns to the lower level of the Tower and goes to sleep.

Day Six

Overview

On the sixth day, the ten and the Virgin take a journey to an island, where there is a tower and a tower warden. In the Tower is a laboratory in which alchemy will revive the Royals. Amazing transformations will unfold in the laboratory as the men work through the seven levels of the Tower. Symbolically, the seven levels represent the seven human chakras and the transformation of the different levels of the body and associated soul qualities. Day six offers remarkable alchemical imagery, especially for modern people. It points symbolically at media, belief structures, and the new world order. A principle motif of the laboratory work is the formation of the little homunculus, known alchemically as the *spirit embryo.*

The men go through a complicated process that begins with boiling the dead heads of the Royals to make a liquor. They remove the liquor from the boiling vessel and place it into another vessel where sunshine will digest it in a golden globe. Mirrors around the room reflect the sunlight onto the globe from all directions, and the extract becomes finer and finer as they move up through the Tower.

There is one motif in the Tower that I find particularly useful; it points again to the person of misunderstanding, the activity of grace, and the need for practice—all in a single concept. The motif is the way in which the ten get from one level in the Tower to the next. It's actually rather humourous and even slapstick, but it's instructive concerning the new quality of faith needed for the inner work. In this work, the only one of the ten men who has higher vision is Christian Rosenkreutz; thus, he sees everything from a higher place than the others do. He knows from their comments that they do not see what he sees, but there's nothing he can do about it because, when he tells them what he is seeing, they say, "You don't get it." He's eighty-one years old and considered the slow one. The virgins frequently mock him as a randy old rooster with a lot of intent but very little capacity to deliver. Although Christian Rosenkreutz is the one who can "see," he is perceived as the one who merely tags along while the others do the real work.

Christian Rosenkreutz is kind of stuck here, until the warden comes in and says, "Okay, you did good work on the first level, but now you have to go through the opening in the ceiling to get to the second level. You have three choices. We will have a drawing for the three choices." The warden holds three pieces of paper. Whoever on paper will get wings; another piece of paper means you get a rope; and the other paper will indicate a ladder. Of course, it's the initiate of misunderstanding gets the ladder.

The virgins enter and take those who drew the long straws. They put wings on these men, and the wings miraculously meld to their bodies so they can just fly up to the next level.

Then the men who have ropes toss them up through the hole in the ceiling, and the other men pull them up.

The last one has a big, clunky ladder that he has to drag around, but it doesn't actually reach the ceiling. He has to climb the ladder and then ask the men with wings and ropes, "Can you throw a rope down so I can tie it to the top of my ladder?" This is the picture of the initiate of misunderstanding, representing the activity of grace and the practice of waiting while being spiritually active. He must wait below until everyone else is on the next level. He knows he cannot do anything without them, although he is really the one who is seeing this whole process from a spiritual perspective. His ladder does nothing for him personally, but it is another form of the intellect.

The alchemical tradition is big on the idea of the ladder. We often see a picture of someone climbing a ladder, while an angel at the bottom says, "There's the ladder." A man is going up the ladder, and an angel at the top is saying, "Where are you going to go now?" On the other side of the ladder is a man falling headfirst to the bottom. Then he gets up and has to crawl up the ladder again. This is the way our intellect works.

Because Christian Rosenkreutz is the one with a ladder, he must depend on the others to drop a rope to him, and he has to give up the belief that he is the one who understands. He really doesn't understand, even though he is the one who is able to see the spiritual reality. He must rely the largess of the community to help him through the door to the next level. They pull him up, and together they work on the next level of the alchemical process. This same process is needed again for the next level. Eventually, he reaches the top.

The little homunculus king and queen are born, and the alchemy takes place. Christian Rosenkreutz is the one who makes the transformation possible through his seeing. He is the one who understands how to complete the marriage, even though he's the one with the ladder and cannot do it without their grace. He was actually the one who was able to see what needed to be done. Once he sees it, they can do it, but he understands that this is what needs to be done.

When they finally reach the top and complete the work, pointing to Christian Rosenkreutz the warden says, "Here is the One who made this possible."

The ten men take the little king and queen and put them in a special place on a ship, and then they sail back to the castle.

THE ALCHEMICAL WEDDING, DAY SIX

On the morning of the sixth day, everyone awoke well before sunrise. They sat together in darkness conversing about the strange events of the past few days. Some believed that the beheaded Royals should all be re-enlivened together. Others felt that the purpose was not just to restore life to the ancients, but also to increase the life of the younger ones. Some imagined they had not actually been put to death but that others had been beheaded in their place.

Soon the Tower warden came to them to check on the progress of the medicaments they made the day before. The men had been diligent and careful workers, and he found no fault with their products, so he combined the contents of all of the glasses into one and put it into a case. Then some young persons entered with ropes, ladders, and large wings and laid them in front of the men.

The Tower warden then addressed the group. He told them that they must each carry one of these three things throughout that day. He said that they were free to choose or to cast lots for them. The men replied that they would like to choose. "No," he said, "you should cast lots." The Tower warden produced three pieces of paper and wrote "ladder" on one and "ropes" and "wings" on the other two. These were put into a hat, and whatever each man drew would be his for the day. Those who drew "ropes" thought they had it best, since they could simply coil the rope over their shoulders and be free to move about easily. Those who drew "wings" had them joined to them so easily by the Tower warden that it seemed as if the wings had grown out of them naturally. CR drew the twelve-foot "ladder" to accompany him through the day. It was heavy and cumbersome and taxed his old body frightfully.

After choosing, the Tower warden shut off the fountain. He then left, taking the case with the glass of medicine in it and locking the door behind him. The men imagined they were being imprisoned in the Tower. After fifteen minutes, they saw a round hole appear at the top of the Tower and the face of the Virgin looking down at them. She called to them to come up.

Those with the wings were instantly up and out of the hole. When the first one with a rope finally managed to get to the hole, he was commanded to drop the rope so that CR could tie the ladder to it. Thus, CR and the ladder were pulled up and out of the hole. The remaining men with ropes each had to strain by climbing hand-over-hand up their ropes and out of the hole. This caused many blisters.

After a short while, everyone was out through the hole and once again in the friendly company of the Virgin. The room in which they now found themselves was as wide as the Tower itself. It contained six small anterooms, each raised a few steps above the level of the large room. They were told to enter those rooms and pray for the life of the king and queen.

Once this was done, the Virgin asked for a wondrous object to be brought into the room by twelve musicians. It was large, beautiful, and rather long and oval in shape. The men thought the object was a fountain, but Christian Rosenkreutz could see that it was not, since it was large enough to contain six corpses.

The musicians then picked up their instruments and played delicate music. The Virgin carried a small casket, while the other virgins carried only branches and small lamps. Torches were given to the ten men, who were told to stand in formation around the large, oval object in the following order: The Virgin stood to the south with her attendants spread out from her in a ring around the whole oval. They were carrying lamps and branches. In the west stood Christian Rosenkreutz, with the other men holing torches and standing in a line to the north and south. The musicians stood in the north in a long line running east and west. The rest of the virgins stood in a line in the south, running east and west, their faces covered with delicate white linen.

The Virgin of the ten then opened her casket, which contained a round object wrapped in green taffeta. A series of kettles was suspended above the oval object. The Virgin placed the round object into the uppermost kettle and covered it with a lid full of holes. The lid also had a rim to contain water, into which the Virgin poured some of the water that the men had prepared in the laboratory from the fountain the previous day. As she poured the water, the whole apparatus began to run like a fountain. Four small pipes led from the uppermost kettle to a smaller lower kettle. The virgins placed their lamps on many small spikes under the small kettle, so that together they formed a heat source. The lamps caused the water in the lower kettle to seethe and boil. The boiling water dripped from the lower kettle through numerous little holes near the rim and fell onto the bodies in the large oval object below. The water was so hot that it dissolved them, turning them into a liquor.

Only Christian Rosenkreutz and the Virgin knew that the round object in the uppermost kettle was the head of the dark Axeman of the Royals. It was the influence issuing from the head that caused the water to become very hot and corrosive. In the upper part of the uppermost kettle was a series of holes, through which the virgins placed their laurel branches. Laurel is a very poisonous plant used as a decoction to commit suicide. The water from the upper kettle sprinkled through the branches and assumed a deep-yellow color as it fell into the lower kettle. This process lasted two hours, but the longer it lasted the fainter and weaker the brew became. The Sun had still not risen.

The musicians eventually left, and the men began to inspect the room in which this distillation was taking place. The room was filled with clockworks, organs, springing fountains, and other machines. When the fountain finally ceased circulating, the Virgin commanded that a round globe made of gold be placed under a tap on the side of the large oval. The fluid elixir that came out of the tap and into the golden globe was deep red. The water remaining in the kettles was poured out. The twelve musicians returned and carried away the apparatus, which was substantially lighter than when they brought it in. The amount of water in the golden globe should have been light enough to be carried easily by one man, but it took six men to carry it. With a great struggle, the golden globe was carried outside. The men returned to the distillation chamber and heard footsteps on the roof, which gradually ceased.

Christian Rosenkreutz found the men's various opinions of the strange proceedings very interesting. They all continued to believe that the bodies of the Royals lay in the crypt in the garden back at the castle of the Bridegroom and the Bride. These proceedings remained a complete mystery to them. Christian Rosenkreutz thanked God that he awoke in time to see the inner work of the Virgin in regard to the process of reviving the three royal couples.

After a quarter hour and close to sunrise, the cover above the distillation room was lifted, and the men were commanded to come up. Again, they had to resort to the wings, ropes, and ladders. CR was disturbed by the fact that the Virgin seemed to have an easy way to get to the upper levels, while the men were forced to toil and strain to get out of the lower levels. He supposed that there must be a special reason for this. Eventually, they all got out of the lower room, which closed behind them.

The golden globe was hanging by a strong chain in the middle of the third upper room. Lining the walls of the circular room was a series of large mirrors, each accompanied by a pair of windows, one on either side. Each of these sets consisted of a mirror placed between two windows. The mirrors and windows were cleverly placed so that the mirrors could be rotated by means of hinges to reflect the rays of the rising Sun. The Sun rays were thus reflected in several mirrors facing the window sources. The mirrors then reflected the rays to other mirrors around the circle. Thus, the image of the rising Sun was spread out to each mirror in the room, filling the space of the circular room with the rays of the rising Sun and bathing the golden globe suspended in the center with light.

The golden globe was highly polished and reflected the myriad of Suns to such a degree that the men could no longer look at it, having to look away until the process had heated the globe to the proper degree. The overall effect of the Sun's reflections and the golden brilliance of the globe was that it became more light-filled than the Sun itself and unendurable to the men's eyes. Eventually, the Virgin commanded the mirrors and the windows to be closed, which allowed the globe to cool after a while. This whole process was completed by seven o'clock in the morning.

The men's thoughts now turned to breakfast. Christian Rosenkreutz noticed that no one was overly concerned with either the kitchen or the table; rather, they all seemed to be completely immersed in the work at hand as a contemplation of the Creator's healing forces.

When the simple breakfast was finished, the men returned to work. With great effort, they lifted the cooled globe off the chain and set it on the floor. They were then commanded to split the globe in half, and an argument commenced over the best way to do this. They concluded that a sharp, pointed diamond would be the best tool to split the globe.

Once opened, no redness could be seen. Instead, a snow-white egg appeared. The Virgin cautioned them to be very careful, because the shell might still be too fragile. The men stood around the egg, feeling as jovial and enthusiastic as if they themselves had laid it. The Virgin commanded them to carry it out of the mirror room. After this was done, she had the men reenter the room, and then she locked it and left them alone. The men waited for another fifteen minutes before the roof of mirrored third room opened, and again they had to use their assigned instruments to go to the next floor.

On the fourth floor, the men found a room in which stood a great copper kettle filled with yellow sand being warmed by a gentle fire. The egg was placed into the gentle drying fire, and the sand was raked around it so that the proper heat would mature the egg to perfection. The copper kettle used for this was precisely square, with words written on its sides. On one side was an ancient, indecipherable inscription. On another were the words *sanity, snow,* and *lance*. On a third side was the command "Become!" On the fourth side was this inscription:

With respect to the forces of fire, air, water, and earth
our holy king and queen are now ashes.
They have been taken by force in order to have more
power and influence.
They are now reliable, because they have become a
seed of chaos.
In these funerary urns, they are brought together again.

Now being ready, the egg was removed from the sand. It needed no cracking since the bird within it had already freed himself. He was very jolly, although he appeared bloody and misshapen. The men set him on the warm sand, and the Virgin told them that they should make him fast before giving him anything to eat. This was done, and then he was given food consisting of only the blood of the beheaded Royals. This food caused him to grow so quickly that the men began to fear him. He bit and scratched so strongly that he could easily have killed any of them.

Initially, the bird was completely black, but after he was fed the blood of one of the Royals, he molted all of his black feathers and in their place grew snow-white feathers. With white feathers, he became a little more docile. Nevertheless, the men continued to mistrust him. After the third feeding, his feathers began to show marvelous colors. He was now so exceedingly docile that the Virgin consented to freeing the bird from captivity, saying that the men's diligence had resulted in the perfection of the bird's being, life, and consecration.

The Virgin now commanded that the men be brought dinner and that they should be given time to refresh themselves now that the most difficult part of their labors was over. With this, the men began to rejoice and be merry among themselves. The Virgin was perpetually inquisitive and constantly seeking which of the men she might employ for her upcoming activities. During dinner, her entire conversation centered on the topic of melting, and an alchemist who was conversant in these ideas pleased her with his knowledge of such matters. The dinner lasted three quarters of an hour, during which the men continuously fed the young bird his meal, causing him to grow as rapidly as before.

After dinner, the Virgin quickly departed with the bird. With this, the fifth room was opened to the men, and once again they entered it through a hole in the ceiling.

A bath had been prepared in the fifth room for the bird. It was prepared with a fine, white powder to look like milk. The bath was cool when the bird stepped into it. The bird loved the bath and began to drink it enthusiastically. After the bath began to heat up because of the lamps placed under it, the men found it difficult to keep the bird in the bath, and they had to put a lid on the bath to contain him. There was a hole in the lid, through which the bird pushed his head. Eventually the bird lost his feathers in the bath and became smooth as a newborn babe. The increased heat of the bath did not harm the bird, but his lost feathers tinged the water blue.

The bird then emerged from the bath with a smooth, glittering sheen. Because he was still a little wild, some of the men put a collar on him and led him around the room. The others made the fire even stronger under the bath, and they soon saw a blue stone in the bottom of it. They removed the stone and pounded it into powder to make blue paint, with which they colored the bird. Except for his head, which remained white, the bird was now completely blue.

With their work finished, the bird and the Virgin departed. Now they were allowed to enter the sixth floor of the Tower. There, the men became troubled because a small altar stood in the middle of the room. It was exactly like the altar in the king's castle throne room. The six implements on the altar were also exactly the same, which caused ominous feelings in the men. The seventh implement on the altar, however, was the bird. A little fountain was placed before the bird, and he began to drink from it.

After this, the bird pecked at the white serpent passing in and out of the skull until she bled profusely. The blood of the snake was saved in a golden cup. The men then requested permission to feed the blood to the bird, which he resisted powerfully. Then the men dipped the head of the snake into the fountain water, which revived her completely. She then crawled back into the skull.

In the meantime, the conjunction that Christian Rosenkreutz had been awaiting for two days arrived. The watch struck one. Another conjunction occurred, and the watch struck two. As the watch struck three, the third conjunction occurred, and the poor bird laid down his head and submitted to it being taken off. When this was done, not a drop of blood emerged from the bird. However, when the bird's breast was opened, bright, fresh blood emerged as though it were a fountain of rubies.

The bird's death struck the men's hearts, but what could they do? They removed the small altar and helped the Virgin burn the bird's body, as well as the little tablet hanging near ashes, with a fire kindled by the little taper. They were then asked to purify the ashes three times before placing them in a cypress-wood box.

At this point, the Virgin played a trick on CR and three of the other men. She addressed the group, saying, "There is only one more room to go. For the most part, you have all been good workers." She pointed to CR and three of the men and said, "These four have proved themselves to be lazy and poor workers. I do not want to punish everyone for their poor attitude, so these four will not be allowed to accompany the rest into the seventh and most glorious final room. In this way, the king and queen are less likely to become upset."

CR and the other three were speechless. The Virgin asked one of her attendants to summon the musicians. She asked the musicians to blow their coronets loudly enough to drive the offending men out of the room. The musicians did this with such a vengeance that everyone laughed at the sight. The Virgin was especially scornful and reproached the four men for their weakness, anger, and impatience.

Once the men were out of the room, the musicians told the four to follow them up winding stairs. The stairs led to the seventh room, and under the oddly shaped roof they saw the old Tower warden. He was standing on a small furnace and received the men cordially. He congratulated them that they had been chosen by the Virgin. He laughingly wondered how they could possibly have been so anxious over such good fortune. He said, "This is a lesson to all that we never know how well God intends things for us."

The Virgin returned with her small cedar box containing the bird's ashes. She emptied the ashes into another vessel and announced that she was going to cast a mist over the other artists' eyes, and that we should obey whatever the old Tower warden commands. Then she returned to the sixth room and proceeded to work some magic on the other men.

The four men upstairs were told to moisten the ashes with the water prepared in the laboratory until the ash was the consistency of thin dough. They placed the dough over the fire until it was well heated and then cast the hot dough into two molds and allowed it to cool. As it cooled, the four had time to look through cracks in the floor to observe the others, who were working at a furnace. Each man was vigorously using a blowpipe to make the flame hotter. They were commenting to one another about how fortunate it was that they were so superior to the four whom the Virgin had mocked, because they had to perform the most important task by far. They labored long at this furnace, constantly blowing on the flames and congratulating themselves for their good fortune. Meanwhile, the four men and the old Tower warden rested in the room above while they waiting for the forms to cool.

When the molds were finally opened, two small, transparent manikins were revealed—a female and a male. Each was only four inches long, and their bodies were surprisingly soft and fleshy, as though they were living beings. Nevertheless, for all of their wondrous qualities, they had no life.

The small babes were laid upon soft cushions, and the four men became captivated by the exquisite appearance of the manikins. The old Tower warden warned them not to be taken in so easily by the sight. They were told to instill the blood of the bird, preserved in a golden chalice, into the mouths of the small manikins, drop by drop. This feeding caused them to grow noticeably in size and in the beauty of their proportions. They soon grew so much that the men had to lift them from the cushions and place them onto a table covered with white velvet. The old man ordered that they should be covered up to the breast with fine, white double taffeta.

They finally grew to their natural proportions as if alive, yet they were still not living. The old Tower warden ordered the men's torches to be put in place around the table on which the manikins were sitting, so that the men were unable see the souls of the little manikins enter them. CR, however, could see this, since he had already seen the quality of the Royals' flames twice. Then the old Tower warden told the men to sit on a bench away from the table.

With this, the Virgin returned, accompanied by the musicians. She carried two small, translucent garments that appeared to be made of crystal. She and the old Tower warden began to perform many sleights-of-hand over the table, intending to distract the men's attention away from the table. This was all performed under the roof of the uppermost room. The roof was composed of seven hemispheres, the middle one a little larger than the others. In it was a small hole, shut tight and seen only by Christian Rosenkreutz.

After numerous ceremonies, six virgins stepped into the upper room, each carrying a trumpet covered with a glittering, green foliage-like material that the old man would set on fire during the ceremony. The old man took one trumpet and put it to the lips of one of the little manikins, with the wider end pointed toward the hole in the seventh hemisphere in the roof. He then kindled the green material and the other men watched the manikins. Christian Rosenkreutz, however, looked at the hole in the ceiling and saw that it opened as soon as the material was kindled, and a bright stream of fire shot down through the tube and into the body. Then the hole closed, and the trumpet was removed. The other men were deceived by this device; to them, the fire appeared to arise from lighting the foliage around the trumpet.

As soon as the manikin received the fire of the soul, his eyes twinkled, but still he did not move. The old man repeated the process three times for each manikin, and then all the lights were extinguished and the apparatus put away. The velvet coverings of the table were placed over the manikins, and a small portable bed was brought in, on which they were carried. They were moved and placed side by side on a bed, around which curtains had been drawn so they could sleep in peace.

The Virgin went to see how the other men were doing at the forge below. They were well pleased, since they were to work at forming gold. They thought that this was the highest form of alchemical art, which pleased them, but those upstairs were engaged in making life. The workers in the lower room had also received part of the bird's ashes. In their minds they had received all of the ashes from the bird, as making gold was the highest point of their alchemical art. They thought that the Royals would be brought back to life only through the formation of gold.

As they were thus engaged in the sixth room, the men upstairs in the seventh room waited for the little married couple to awake in the small bed. Cupid appeared in the room and flew behind the curtain of the little bed and began tormenting the married couple until they eventually awakened from their sleep. Once awake, they addressed each other in amazement. They imagined that they had been asleep ever since their beheading. After the renewed their acquaintance with each other, Cupid turned his attention to tormenting the four men. He enlivened the mood by engaging the musicians to play merry tunes.

The Virgin entered, humbly saluted the young king and queen, and brought translucent garments to them, which they put on. In the room were two odd chairs on which they were seated. The four men congratulated them. It was five o'clock in the afternoon by now, and the men brought the necessary furniture and implements to accompany the young king and queen and went with them down the winding stairs, through all of the rooms of the Tower, out across the meadow, and then out to the ship. The ship swiftly left the pier, moved toward a flotilla of stately ships on the horizon, and slipped quickly out of sight.

At five o'clock, the musicians were also brought down to the ships. This activity was accompanied by the old warden's soldiers, who had been garrisoned invisibly along the great wall. Christian Rosenkreutz noticed how well-fortified the Tower really was, whereas it had originally seemed vulnerable to invasion from outside.

After the other ships had been loaded, supper was brought for all of the men. The four were instructed to act in a lamentable fashion so that the others who had labored on the gold in the sixth room would not realize the truth. The gold makers were smiling among one another and nodding their heads toward the four throughout supper, although a few of them were sympathetic toward the four. During supper, the old lord Tower warden mingled among the diners and continuously refuted, corrected, or amended everything that passed from one person to another. Christian Rosenkreutz learned a great deal from the behavior of this man. If each person were to give himself such strict council, much that goes awry and miscarries among human beings would be prevented.

After the late supper, the old Tower warden led the men into his Closet of Rarities, where there were many things that human minds had made in imitation of the most wonderful productions of nature. Exploring this closet took most of the evening, until everyone grew tired. They were lodged in sumptuous rooms within the great wall. The quality of the rooms made the men wonder why they had previously been forced to sleep on the stone laboratory floor instead of in these accommodations.

Christian Rosenkreutz quickly fell asleep and dreamed a continuous dream from eleven o'clock in the evening until eight the next morning.

DAY SIX COMMENTARY

Day six includes a brilliant exposition of a spagyric alchemical process as described in the writings of Paracelsus. If we do a little laboratory alchemy, we could discover a great deal about alchemical transformation just by reading about day six. It is filled with symbols showing how one thing changes into the next. There is an old alchemical saying: *It is easier to make gold than to purify gold*—meaning it's easier to begin a process that eventually achieves synergy than it is to take something that is already in a relatively pure state and try to purify it even more. It is easier to take something in a *prima materia* form (dark and polluted) and get it to move through the necessary steps to become much more evolved than to take something already fairly pure and make it purer still. This is because there is something very powerful in the process of gradually transforming *prima materia.*

In this chapter we gain insight into the alchemy of *spagyrics.* In a spagyric process on plant material, the plant must be taken apart systematically so that it can be reassembled systematically in an "alchemical wedding." There is often an oil or volatile substance in a plant. The oil is embedded in a mineral salt. The most common plant salt is potassium carbonate (K_2CO_3). Salt in a plant regulates how water moves through the sap. Oil and salt are the two polar principles in plant growth. The third principle is some sort of higher volatile substance produced by a ferment, usually an alcohol or acid. Many aromatics in a plant are alcohol–acid derivatives. The initial breakdown of chlorophyll produces *phenol.* In chemistry, the suffix *-ol* refers to some form of alcohol, which is the basis for most secondary metabolites. Secondary metabolites are generally the sources of healing forces in medicinal plants.

However, alcohol permeates a plant in different percentages in different compounds at different stages. Thus, along with oils and salts, alcohol is the third principle of mercury in a plant. *Mercury* is a code word for the universal influence that leads to changes. Alchemically, potassium carbonate in the water-soluble stream is the salt that gives its name to precipitation processes known as *sal*. In plant growth, the end of sequences of alcohol interactions is usually some form of resin or oil. Alchemically, oils are a *sulf*, or sulfur. When fatty acids are metabolized, the result is oil. An oil is a reservoir of energy; alcohols are the means of energy transformation; and salt is the means by which a plant picks up the raw materials to make the energy. These are the forces that create dynamic processes in a plant. In a plant, these three principles—*salt, mercury,* and *sulf*—are embedded and fixed together, and consequently they assume a form in nature whereby they cannot be easily potentized. An alchemist would say, the salt clogs the oil and creates a fixed *prima materia*, or the foundational material nature of the life form.

Using spagyric process as a metaphor for initiation, the *prima materia* can be seen as the condition of a soul that hasn't been worked upon. In this raw state, thinking (salt), feeling (mercury), and willing (*sulf*) are clogged by belief structures and one's temperament. Our thinking, feeling, and willing become fixed together through unconscious habits. When we want to change something in ourself, we are initially unable to do so, because the three soul forces are already formed, or "clogged," so that we are able to live our life and get by without changing inwardly.

However, we reach a point in life when getting by with our old belief structures is no longer sufficient, and we have to separate out the three forces to make a medicine from the thing that's clogging our progress. That clog creates a poison and toxicity, and in poison we find *physic*, or healing. But there is also a lot of pain and suffering. If we can change the pain and suffering into understanding alchemically, we become healers.

In working with plants, we have to take a plant apart spagyrically. Likewise, when working with the soul, we have to take our soul apart spagyrically. We learn to separate the parts of our soul forces, purify each one, and marry them back together in a higher state. This is *The Alchemical Wedding.* What we do in the retort is what we do within ourselves. That is the view of *The Alchemical Wedding.* If we pay attention to what we are doing with the apparatus and focus on our feelings involved in the transformational process, we also find a key to how we can transform our self through what is happening in the physical world. This is called *the Great Work.*

Working with an apparatus is meant to be a mirror that reflects our capacity to separate thinking, feeling, and will to purify them for marriage at a higher level of functioning. In the alchemical wedding, what happens outside (if we work with it in the right way) also happens inside. Working with it in the right way means we have to separate it out and make it more rarefied and purified.

We do this soul work in our sleep. Sleep and dreams become a kind of distillation process for life. We separate out our daily rounds into thinking, feeling, and willing. Then we do an inventory of life and give it to the spirit when we sleep, so that the finer parts can return in a dream. We experience such dreams in our daily waking life; the motif of a dream might come from another person or as we work the apparatus.

My preparation for the content of this volume involved a delicate distillation process with tartar from a grape. I did this for a month and still hadn't determined what this course would be about—that is, until I went through that process. I started to go more and more deeply into the distillation, and the actual day-to-day of this course came to me. I had a little notebook near the still, and there I recorded the next little piece that would take place in the course. What I'm sharing with you is not merely theoretical; it can be a practical guide to living more creatively.

In soul alchemy, the boiling of fixed ideas to separate them is achieved by working with symbolic pictures that arise from the work we do with an apparatus. If we get the symbolic pictures right, our dreams become more productive for us. The pictures we use are what we put into the boiling flask. We "boil" them by forming them in our imagination. To distill and rarify them into their essence, we boil them immediately before going to sleep. This is what Christian Rosenkreutz does throughout *The Alchemical Wedding.* We take the pictures into sleep so they can return in a more rarefied and purified state.

In distillation, the products of rarefaction need to be gathered into a receiver. In our soul, the receiver is the work we do on this side of the sleep–dream threshold, which we feel is related in some way to the images we release in the evening. It doesn't matter what the work on this side involves; the important thing is to do it consciously, with an eye to how it is in some way analogous to the soul process we are working on in the science of initiation by taking things into sleep. Even eviscerating a cow could be called an alchemical process of biodynamics. It could also be a process linked to working with plants—whatever we do. The key is that our work here and the sleep–dream work there are each seen as an analog of the other. The work across the threshold is this distillation process—going into sleep and back through dream to our work in the world.

In *The Alchemical Wedding,* the Great Distillation takes place on the sixth day. It goes through many different levels of the distilling apparatus to make the New Adam. In this particular story, it is actually a pair—a male and a female homunculus, rather than one, as is done in traditional alchemy; it is a hermaphrodite, the Rebis as discussed previously. In this story, the New Adam is both king and queen, but they are the *new* king and queen. They still need *coniunctio* (a term that comes from Carl Jung) when the human feminine principle and the human masculine principle get married and have a child. The human feminine principle connotes the ability to tolerate paradox and say: *Let's keep things open until we understand.* The human masculine principle suggests one's ability to say: *I think this is what this is.* These two approaches to reality have to be balanced.

Carl Jung tells us that we need to get the two parts of us to *coniunctio*—the queenly part, which tolerates knowing we live in a universe that's much bigger than anyone can understand, and the kingly part, which thinks everyone else agrees with what we believe at this moment. Christian Rosenkreutz is the reluctant child of this union when he becomes the guardian of the threshold on day seven.

The king and queen in the soul are linked to a physical division in the heart. In the image opposite, we see a symbolic image of the great retort—sometimes called the human heart. It is an image from the alchemical tradition. A retort is the vessel into which we put something to heat it up and get it to rarify. In human beings, the great retort is the heart.

At the top left of the image of the heart retort, we see a sun with an opening below it into the chamber with a white dove and white key. That is the right atrium of the heart, which receives blood from the liver. The white dove and key indicate that the blood coming in here is from the solar realm of the given. All solar or etheric life processes in the body have put something into that blood. It's all the waste products and the digestive juices. The dead cells, lymph, and the given forces of the natural world enter the right atrium.

Looking at the heart from the front, the image shows the right atrium on the left. The white key is the gift of life from the divine—the given, the ether, the Sun Principle, or etheric. Ether forces enter the right atrium through venous circulation, because now the Holy Spirit holds a key to who we will eventually become when karma is realized. Mostly, however, humans have forgotten who they will be and remember only who they think they are, which is a kind of waste product in the cosmos. Steiner links the venous circulation to the potential future karma, since it is open to the cosmic solar forces of light coming through the skin into the capillaries. Moreover, it is our movements (karma and will in action) that support the venous blood circulation back to the heart. This venous return allows bodily waste products to be recycled, which is a resurrection

Heart retort

of the dead into the living. The transformation to living is constantly carried out in us by the venous blood flowing to the liver (*live er*). Every day that we wake up provides a chance for a new distillate by boiling or recycling the dying part of us. The portal for this is on the right-hand side of the heart. The right atrium receives the venous circulation, the blood and lymph that is spent of life forces. The spent nature of venous circulation allows the blood to be more open to the creation as a given, since it is composed of what has died. Venous blood, especially in the peripheral capillary circulation, is a great vehicle of the divine light brought into the right atrium and down into the right ventricle.

The solar principle of the given enters the right ventricle and becomes a crown. However, consider this old saying: *Heavy is the head that wears the crown.* In esoteric language, our biological inheritance builds in us what is known as the debt to the Creator. We have an existential debt that we know about unconsciously, but it's like knowing you have to pay your credit card while being unable to put anything into the bank. Basically, we are waiting for the angels to show up, because it's January twenty-ninth and if we don't get it there by the thirtieth, we are going to lose credit forces. Human cosmic debt is equally heavy.

The crown is an existential kingly debt, because humans are continuously given the gift of the solar king. It sounds funny to say that being given kingly power is a debt, because today we think of kings as those who exercise power. In the old days, however, the king was the one who assumed the cosmic debt of owing service to the kingdom; people knew they had to take care of the king because he was taking the hits for everyone. It was the king who had to learn to be open to service. Only that sort of consciousness was worthy of being a channel for the divine. Today, however, people don't tend to believe in the divine, so kings are just the boss of everyone. It's a very different worldview.

The crown is heavy because it receives the solar principle from the cosmos, but it is full of karmic baggage. The venous blood has to be lifted and purified to become free of debt. It has to be brought into contact with the world in some way, because it has just been hermetic inside the body. So the blood gets lifted and taken into the lungs, where it meets the outer world.

From the lungs the blood returns purified and ardent to interact with cells owing to the intake of oxygen. In the left atrium (the upper right of the image), oxygenated and purified blood enters the Moon sphere, the realm of the astral body and the seat of desire or craving. Once the blood becomes filled with oxygen and life, it starts to be attacked by the cells and bodily organs that desire the life it now contains. It will be hit on by all that it encounters; it must surrender its life when it's full of oxygen, because everything that has hydrogen and needs oxygen pulls it out of the blood.

As oxygen-rich blood enters the left atrium through the Moon sphere, there's another symbolic key—a black one. We normally think: *Oxygenated blood—yes, it's the source of life.* However, if you were oxygenated blood, you'd see everyone looking for a handout. Every cell you pass would be saying: *Give me your good stuff and take my junk.* For the blood: *It's the end of life as I know it, because I have to give everything out of myself.* That is why the key is black with a black flightless raven on it, indicating a raven that eats battlefield corpses, an old alchemical mantra. Oxygenated blood is the body's sacrificial victim, which goes down into the left ventricle, where there is a skull symbolizing: *Blood, you die, because now you're going out into the body to be totally used up.* This is the great sacrifice. The Golgotha of the "I" is in the left ventricle into the aorta. It is where the "I," the True Self, begins to lose the warmth that is its home.

On the right, venous side of the heart, we see Christ, the great being of the cosmos and representative of divine Word become flesh. On the left side of the heart, we see the devil, representing the grasping physical human body. Bringing these polarities together is the heart's role as the great retort for the conversation between physical substance and soul feelings. Soul feelings need to be purified, because feelings that influence the heart are the source of the healing mercury.

The mercury of rhythmic interplay in the heart is the healer that unites substance and soul. The rhythm arises through a self-adjusting process in which there is collaborative will to get synergy. Alchemists understand that if we want something to change, we need to make it rhythmic in such a way that the rhythms become an analog of how it came into being to begin with. We have to take it apart in the rhythmic sequence of how it came into being. If we find a way to do that, we get synergy when putting it back together; the process self-adjusts harmonically. This is the principle of spagyrics. Rhythm creates the synergy that supports harmonic transformation of substance.

The alchemical work in this is having the imagination of how an entity that needs transformation came to be what it is, so we can imagine how to take it apart without violating its wholeness. In our soul life, we have to discover why a particular emotional pattern arises in a given sensory situation. I do this to separate sensation from reaction. Once separated, we can purify the reaction through biographical referencing of separate soul elements that form the pattern. This alchemy is the basis of therapy and why Carl Jung was so keen on alchemy. He said that alchemists understand the physical process as an analog of the psychic process.

Day six of *The Alchemical Wedding* is a primer for how to take fixed things apart and put them back together. It goes symbolically through every level of an alchemical spagyric process. If we know alchemy, we can say: *That's a salt extraction. That's a fractionating column. That's a digestion distillation. That's a Mary's bath. That's a dry sand bath.* These things that the men use in the Tower are actually alchemical processes. Various cues in the text tell us what is happening alchemically in the sequences of *solve* and *coagula*. The bases of the work in the Tower are the two processes of solve and coagula that must be set into a rhythmic counterpoint, so that the will of how the substance was formed comes to conscious understanding. When this happens the imagination can engage the proper sequence of taking it apart.

When we find the way to take something apart, that's a distillation. We rarefy it rhythmically to begin a self-adjusting process, because the wisdom that formed it—the karmic wisdom that formed the wound—is the healing we can learn to distill out of the wound. The karmic wisdom that caused our suffering is our gift to others when we finally achieve healing. The more we have suffered, the more potential we have for healing others, but first we have to heal ourself. To do this, we have to understand our soul's solve and coagula. We have to understand that rhythm is the key. Without rhythm, we can boil stuff until we are blue in the face, but we won't see many results.

The collaborative will between our higher self and our wound is in an imagination of how the coagula and the solve are connected; they mirror each other. At each step, there's a stuck coagula and a stuck solve element that we have to find. The polarities typically have to do with different levels of warmth. Warm is the feeling that can be expressed in the phrase *"I am That."* Cold is the feeling that is expressed as *"That is not me."* When we have an imagination of how to control these warm–cold rhythms, the processes in which we are engaged become self-adjusting. Once a process becomes self-adjusting, there is synergy, owing to the collaborative will in the polar conditions to move to the opposite pole. The theme here is that it is easier to *make* than to *purify* gold.

The dark will of unconscious impulses in the soul is the womb of the potential true gold of human nature. This is a collaboration between the nature of the will that expects something and the will that expects nothing. The two wills come together in what we can call a *will–imagination.* This will is very dark, meaning that we don't understand what is happening, but we definitely feel connected to what is taking place. As an example, I will share my process in forming the course laid out in this book.

It was two weeks out. I sat at the computer and nothing would happen in my imagination. I couldn't even come up with a handout sheet. I knew the content, but I couldn't bring it into a rhythm suitable for learning. The self-adjusting process told me what to do if I just keep working without knowing the end result. When I told myself that I had to find an answer, my creative process froze. When I finally told myself that I didn't need to find an answer, my mind kicked into my usual method of just doing something to keep flow happening. When flow is happening, the answer shows up. If I don't do anything, I can think about doing something until the cows come home, but I remain stuck.

The self-adjusting process works because the will needs to move. If the process becomes stuck with something and cannot take form, create an inner symbolic image of the variables moving through some sort of morphological transformation; the symbol used is unimportant. Then go and do something—for example, dig in the garden, take a walk, get a crowbar and rip something apart, or pick up a broom. Just *do* something. If a symbolic picture is previously prepared, a moment will come when a feeling of knowing arises. Train yourself in such a way that, when the feeling of knowing arises, stop *doing* and return to *creating*. Knowing will soon fade, so the process is repeated.

Somewhere along the line, the self-adjusting process kicks in, and a whole panorama emerges. It's good to give thanks at that moment and perhaps light some incense. In realty, the solution is already in one's consciousness, but the expectation of a particular solution is in the way. This practice leads to our understanding how rhythm is the essence of taking our soul apart with no expectation that anything is going to happen. Suddenly, we wake in the morning and the self-adjusting process has shifted the problem toward a solution.

This is a little preamble to day six at the Tower. The Tower is where the Great Work takes place. Christian Rosenkreutz went from the castle, through the flotilla, and ended up in the Tower. In the Tower there was a strict warden who represents the Guardian of the Threshold. The Tower is Christian Rosenkreutz's body, his chakras, or subtle body, as he sees them as an initiate. He is going through his own power centers, going up and up. At the bottom they are told, "You have to crush plants with minerals and get the juice out." That is an extraction process of making tinctures. When we make a cup of tea, we are making a tincture. We take pieces of a plant and put it into a solvent; or we take a mineral and boil it in water, and we get something out of it. Taking a bath in Epsom salts is making a tincture. That's the simplest level. If we burn a plant, put it into water, and then remove the water, the water will retain the salt from the ash, and that's the tincture. Such lower-level alchemical activities might include immersing a plant in alcohol, putting a cork in the bottle, and selling the tincture; this is the most basic level of alchemy. This is the traditional way—take an herb, put it in vodka, cork the bottle, and then give it to somebody. That's the bottom level.

In this story, the men engaged in this work make what is called *living water.* They have pulled something from the wholeness of the plant by crushing and using a solvent; they have drawn out a fraction of the plant. They didn't have the whole thing, so that represented the lowest level of alchemy.

The organ that does this kind of extraction in the physical body is the liver. Basically, in the bottom floor of the Tower Christian Rosenkreutz is coming into contact with the liver's function, which is to remove enzymes, catalysts, and so on out of the blood. Thus, when the men do this with the help of the Virgin in the bottom of the Tower, everyone is happy. She praises their work, and then they have a little wine and bread and go to sleep. This is a picture of a *liver rhythm*—eat and sleep.

When they wake up, the Tower warden comes in and tells them they have to go up to the second floor of the Tower and carry out the next process. Getting to the second floor through a small door in the ceiling of the room presents a problem. The warden gives some of them wings and others ropes and ladders, but they had to draw lots to determine who gets what. They thought they would be able to choose for themselves how they wished to go through the door, but they had to draw lots. This is an image of what could be called "menu consciousness," the hallmark of devices. It is the precursor to the iPhone app consciousness. One app will do this, but it won't do that. You choose, but you have to choose from what's offered. If it is not in the menu of options, it doesn't exist for you. In the process of drawing lots, some received wings, some were given ropes, and one got a ladder. Of course, the one who got a ladder is you-know-who. Christian

bird ash / live water level 1 making gold / making life two manikins cosmic fire
snake / bird fountain blood of snake to bird conjunctions beheading of bird / ash
the Mary bath / ripening formation of the stone cosmic thinking reintegration of past
square sand bath lung–coagula dry circulation ash to bird phoenix
heart athanor–solve digestive circulation heart thinking golden globe
kidneys–soxhlet– salt solution fractionation metanoia
liver extracts–tinctures live water

Rosenkreutz, the oldest of the group had to carry the ladder with him, and it wasn't even long enough to reach the door in the ceiling.

The men have to figure out how to get the rope onto the second floor and had to ask those with the wings to fly up through the hole with a rope. Christian Rosenkreutz, with the ladder to nowhere, had to ask those with the ropes to let one down so he could tie it to the ladder and be pulled up. Through this collaboration, all of the men were able to make it up to the second level.

This is a picture of initiation. We cannot do it without involving the goodwill of others. This paradox of being given the power to choose and then having to ask for help is a key motif of this story. The image is similar to the dove–raven scene of choosing a path on the second day. We are free to choose, while at the same time we are bound to our karma and forces of destiny.

The diagram (opposite) describes the seven floors of the Tower. At the bottom is the liver—extracts, tinctures, and making living water. The second floor is the kidneys. Here there is the strange apparatus—a pot with another pot under it. A large, coffin-like object is brought in and placed under the two pots. This is the distilling apparatus. After the men arrive, the Virgin enters and under her arm is a bag in the box. She puts the contents of the bag into the pot on top. Only Christian Rosenkreutz sees this. He can see that it is the head of the coal-black Axeman, who beheaded the Royals. She puts that into the pot and takes some of the tincture they made on the bottom floor and places it into the pot, which now begins to boil.

The lid has little holes in it, and the juice rises and overflows into another pot through small spigots. Then the other virgins enter and place small tapers into holders under the second pot with the spigots, and the warmth from the tapers starts the pot boiling. Overflow from this goes into a big container at the bottom, which is covered. Only Christian Rosenkreutz sees that the bodies of the Royals are in the covered container; it is their coffin. If you know nothing about alchemy, this all seems very strange.

What is being described here are two different alchemical apparatuses. One is called a *soxhlet* extractor (see image on the next page), which is designed to extract essential liquor from a salt through a recirculation process. In the bottom of the body-tube of the soxhlet is a vent. The middle tube chamber is sealed and contains a paper sleeve for holding solid salt-containing material. A flask with the solution is then heated, and steam flows over the salt and is repeatedly recirculated to gradually extract the more resistant contents of the salt.

The condenser, the second device (at the top of the soxhlet), condenses the vapors. A boiling flask filled with water is placed over the heat and the steam travels through a vent into a slender steam tube. The steam tube is encased in a larger tube (the water jacket), in which cold water is circulating. The cold water condenses the steam traveling through the steam tube into a fluid. Frequently, a condenser is mounted over a soxhlet like this to condense the water that falls through the soxhlet into a boiling flask.

This laboratory device clearly represents the work in the second room of the Tower—extracting the head of the Axeman into the living water. They extract a solute from the head of the Axeman. The

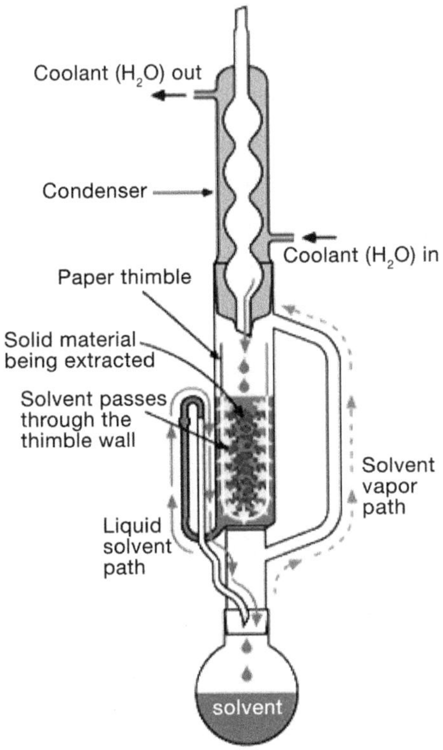

particular apparatus in the story is ingenious. The text describes a tube that comes from the bottom of the solution chamber, which will eventually fill with fluid and rise until it reaches the top, which connects to another tube that carries the solution down to return into the boiling flask. As it falls through a siphoning action, it draws all the water out of the solution chamber and returns it to the boiling flask. Then it starts again and empties. This is a self-adjusting extraction of salts. As the salt becomes stronger in the solution and is boiled and purified, the solution becomes permeated with salt. The Soxhlet extractor is a brilliant device and a clear picture of the work on the second level of the Tower on the island.

In the story, the Virgin extracts the salt of the Axeman's head. In alchemical language, the head is the alchemical salt. It is the salt of the Axeman, the one who says, "Cut off your head if you want to come in here." In other words, clean up the salt of your thinking. Then the Axeman's head is cut off and made into a salt solution. The solution then drops down into the second little column, a fractionating device.

This image show a typical fractionator. A boiling flask is placed under it and connected at the bottom so that the steam rises through the tube. Inside the tube, little glass fingers disturb the steam column as it rises. These cause a local drop in temperature at those sites. As the steam rises past each next set of glass fingers it cools further. When it finally emerges from the top of the fractionator, the temperature of the steam is much lower than when it entered.

Thus, water is continuously shed in the fractionation process. With less water in the mix at the top, volatile substances such as oils will be richer in the steam This happens as the cooling process at each station sheds water and concentrates the volatile substances. The fractionator is an image of the Virgin's second little boiler. Thus, we have a salt extraction and now an oil or volatile extraction through fractionation. The juice that emerges from this process dissolves the bodies of the Royals, making a liquor that they gather and put into a golden globe. The process with these apparatuses in the second stage is to prepare a miraculous liquor; it combines the Axeman's head (thinking–salt) with the bodies of the Royals (willing–sulfur) to make them into an essence.

The men then go up through the roof again into the third level, where they find another alchemical device—an *athanor* (right). It is used by alchemists to create a "digestive" circulation. An athanor is also known as an alchemist's furnace. Its purpose is to digest what has been fractionated. The athanor is an analogous image of the heart, the true digestive organ for sensory experience. Things have been taken apart in the fractionating process, but then, in spagyric processes, they are put back together. By putting them back together, there is a rhythm of solve and coagula that happens for a specific time in what is known as a digestion. The whole question for a medicinal essence is this: Can the body accept it at a high level? If the medicine is at a low level, such as in a tincture or tea, the body has to break it down to assimilate it. A spagyric process does this before the remedy is taken. The

men in the third level are trying to make a material that is digested in a rhythmic way. The athanor uses gentle heat in a closed vessel, whereby the fractionated essence is warmed and circulated within the vessel. They have the golden globe hanging in the center of a room, and sunlight (the Sun is on the horizon) enters and strikes the twelve mirrors arranged so that sunlight reflects onto the golden globe and heats it. After an hour or two, the Sun passes, and that is the end of the digestive process.

They then take the golden globe and go up to the fourth level where the golden globe is put in a sand bath. In the square sand bath at the next level, they coagulate what they have now digested. So they put it in what is known as dry or coagulating heat using sand. The picture of the rhythm of going up through the body is the alternation in physiology of processes of solve and coagula. In the sand bath it is a drying circulation. What happens is that in the drying heat, there is an egg formed that has a bird and a stone in it. Here we get the famous alchemical stone. The egg with the bird (a bird always represents thinking in symbolic lore) symbolizes new, living thinking. The coagulated essence gives life to a bird. They begin to feed the bird with some of the juice that came from the dissolved bodies of the Royals. This gives a new will to the bird of the new thinking.

In the fifth level we reach the Mary bath (*bain Marie*), which provides wet heat and is digestive. Dry heat, by contrast, coagulates. Wet heat in the Mary bath represents assimilation or nutrition. The process here opens and coagulates, opens and coagulates. This is done at increasingly refined degrees until a new, creative being forms in thinking—the bird. Now they have to feed the bird of new thinking with the best parts of the past to form a foundation for creative thought. This is very elevated alchemy. At the end of the work, the bird and the Virgin depart.

At the sixth level is the small altar that was present at the beheading of the Royals, with the white snake passing in an out of the skull. The bird sees the snake and immediately attacks it until it bleeds. They had to force-feed the snake's blood to the bird, which resists taking it. Creative thinking resists the given qualities of the sensory world. The bird pecks the snake, which dies but is revivified by dipping the snake's head into the water of the fountain. However, the snake immediately creeps back into the skull. Birds arose from reptiles, so this image is a complex metaphor for the transformation of instincts based on sensory impressions into the capacity to think creatively and free of sense memories.

The Virgin then asks the men to decapitate the bird, save its blood in a golden chalice, and burn it's body to ashes. They are then told to purify the ashes three times and to place them in a cypress-wood box. When this is done, those who wish to make gold are separated from those who actually want to perform the alchemical marriage. This is the great challenge of initiation science. One's feeling that gained insights are the result of personal achievement is a fatal flaw in alchemy. It is the fatal inflation of the worker's egoism that ignores support from the spiritual world.

The Virgin's way of dealing with this is pure psychology. She tells Christian Rosenkreutz and three other men that they have been lazy and impatient and that their anger has been disruptive to the process. She sends them out of the room, causing the six other men to laugh and mock them. The four who have been pushed out encounter a little stairway, which allows them to ascend to the seventh room, where they meet the warden of the Tower, who represents the Guardian of the Threshold.

The Virgin then brings in the little cedar box with the ashes of the bird. All of these four men except Christian Rosenkreutz have had a mist cast over their eyes. The four men in the seventh room are told to take the ashes of the bird and mix them with the water that they made on the bottom floor to make a kind of dough, which they put into a small mold.

Then the Virgin goes down to the sixth room and tells the six men there that they were chosen to make gold. There is a little furnace in the room, and the six are told that they need to blow on the flames in the furnace to increase the heat, which will eventually make gold. Thus, the six men in the sixth room are blowing on the furnace to make gold while the four above are peering down at them through cracks in the floor of the seventh room. This a trap that alchemists have fallen into for centuries.

When the molds cool, Christian Rosenkreutz and the other three remove a tiny king and queen—little manikins that are transparent. They are placed on little velvet pillows and, with the help of the warden, fed the bird's blood that was saved in the golden chalice. This causes the little king and queen to grow in beauty and proportion, though they are not yet alive. Then the warden returns and begins the process of breathing life into them. The essence of this is that all of these processes go through alternating solve and coagula; this is the key. It is the rhythm of the flow that eventually instigates a self-regulating process that carries through to the end. The men cannot actually do it, but they can allow it to happen. In the alchemical wedding, humans can't do it on their own but need to collaborate with the spiritual beings who can.

The Tower is us; we are the Tower. The different levels represent the organ systems or the chakras, but however you want to read it as a symbol, *the Tower is us*. Going through the different rooms of the Tower alchemically with the various operations is also analogous to the esoteric school. We have to separate our instincts and drives; we have to take apart our desires. We take apart the soul's features piece by piece and purify each part separately.

We do this by turning one soul force that has been separated from the others back into the others after it has been purified. We separate thinking from automatic will by consciously willing thinking. When thinking is willed, it is no longer automatic; will and thinking separate. When thoughts happen automatically, will and thinking are mixed together and create problems. We need to do a spagyric process of solve and coagula on these two soul forces so they are lifted to a higher order.

This is the idea. It is everywhere in Rudolf Steiner's works, but here it is in symbolic language. Each step in the Tower involves the solve and coagula of a soul force. Some are a little more primal (the liver and kidneys), and others are closer to cognition (the heart and lungs). In the ancient world, the heart was the organ that made decisions, not the brain. The brain was simply a mirror, or monitor, for what the heart went through. Esoteric work is employed to make the heart recover its capacity to think.

In this image of "The Tower" from the tarot, men are bailing out of a tower, which is being struck by a lightning bolt from the Sun. It blows the crown off the Tower, and little pieces of the Tower are actually small pieces of gold. The image shows that the work of self-transformation attracts lightning from the cosmos to our Tower, or body. It blows the lid off, and we have to bail out, but gold starts pouring out with the shock of being struck by cosmic insight. This is the metaphor, and it's a sticky thing. As we begin to do this work, we realize that the work we are doing draws the ultimate thing to us that we do not wish to happen. We begin to have spiritual potential, which makes us into a lightning rod for the adjustment processes needed by the progressive forces in the cosmos. When the bolt of spiritual insight comes down, it blows the lid off along with thoughts of being the king and crown of it all. However, the bolt of spiritual insight also creates a shower of gold given by the cosmos.

On day six, Christian Rosenkreutz made it to the top of the Tower, and he could see the other men on the lower level intent on making gold, which exemplifies the great alchemical trap of believing that the highest goal is to make gold from lead. In alchemical language, there used to be what were called "puffers" and "blowers." They spent their time at the bellows, cooking up things to make gold, but the gold that really needs to be formed is in the soul.

True alchemists understand that the operations done outwardly in lab devices affect who they are in their souls. Through spiritual insight, they also understand that such transformations become subtler with each level, until at a certain point a synergy happens, and something inevitably takes place that will blow the lid off the Tower. When this happens, it's a little like *The Sorcerer's Apprentice*. They are able to begin operations, but then the operations self-adjust to higher levels of power. What you begin to see in the spirit attracts the attention of a being from the other side.

This is the reading and simultaneous writing in the astral light that Rudolf Steiner speaks of. What you begin to see attracts a being who sees you. Steiner expresses this in the most potent mantra for esotericists: *Christ is seeing us*. All alchemists know that, if you really want to understand a mantra, you need to work it in reverse. If we work that potent mantra backward, we have this: *Us seeing is Christ*. This is a great mystery.

In our transformed sensory activity we manifest the Christ principle in the sensory world. Steiner calls this process *the human phantom*. The phantom needs to be understood by esotericists when they get to the higher rooms of the Tower. In the lower rooms, one is just doing and wishing and hoping, but in the higher rooms of the Tower it's not about wishing but about willing. We have to make sure that what we will is what needs to be willed by the needs of the spiritual world, because when our will starts to become more powerful, things happen, and then we surely need to be in contact with what is happening. This is pictured in the Tower attracting cosmic lightning. The old woodworkers' phrase "measure twice, cut once" means spending more time planning what you want to do when the will moves. Rudolf

Steiner discusses this in his book *How to Know Higher World.* He calls it "building a hut"—making a spiritual home by transforming one's dream life for a continuity of consciousness.*

These are the three steps in the higher realm of the Tower. Building a hut, transforming one's dream life (everything in a dream is a symbol of our feelings); and continuity of consciousness. Continuity of consciousness is the intent behind doing something. The irony is that the intent has to be open. If it is focused on an outcome, it will not bring spiritual insight, because it leaves no opening for the spirit. This aspect of esoteric work is difficult to explain. In our culture today, we think that *intent* implies the end result; we expect things to happen because we are doing something. This is *earthly intent.* Spiritual intent is this: *I am offering my will to be so engaged in my love of the process that the outcome loses importance.* I'm okay when lightning hits the Tower. I pay attention to the gold rather than to the fact that I had to bail out of the Tower, losing my crown.

Bailing out of the Tower is just a given—it's called meditation. We have to leave our body. When we leave the body, we experience death. If we are anxious about death, we are looking at the lightning bolt, not the gold. The gold means we pay attention to the integrity of what we're doing rather than where it's going to get us. This will is the will that needs to be separated by the thinking so that it can be purified spagyrically. When this happens, what we do here without expectation of reward goes out to the periphery and creates waves of interaction with people I don't even know. They magically resonate with the intent I have by clearing myself of expectations.

Rudolf Steiner calls this "motive." It is the force of will in the "I"-being, the True Self. It is the perception of why I do something. If I grasp why I'm doing something, it's like it says in the *Tao Te Ching:* "Do nothing; leave nothing undone" (verse 37). This is Zen. All traditions speak of this state.

---

* Chapter 7, especially pages 157–158.

In teaching, the rule is this: Prepare 150 percent, deliver seventy percent, and the things you get wrong are the things your students are trying to share with you. So, prepare 150 percent, deliver seventy percent, because you're not going to deliver 150 percent. You won't even deliver a hundred percent, because you're dealing with people. They let you know what they don't understand, and that becomes a seed for your research. After a while, you have a huge reservoir that you think is undeliverable until you have to go to the next level in the Tower. Then, what was undeliverable in room four is the key to room five.

Preparation is where the will lives; so, when the lightning bolt hits the Tower and blows the crown off, you are okay if you have prepared. When what you think needs to happen doesn't, you are still okay. The more capacity we have, the scarier it gets, because after a while we can't blame anyone else for anything that happens in our life. According to Rudolf Steiner, Christian Rosenkreutz is the most highly initiated Western person. He is the one needed to complete the work in the seventh room of the Tower. Even the other three men in the seventh room are not where he is, because Christian Rosenkreutz is able to see the spiritual reality behind phenomena.

The warden has a little trumpet, and he puts the trumpet to the lips of one of the little manikins, and then he has some greenery and lights it on fire near the trumpet. All the other men look at the burning greenery, but Christian Rosenkreutz looks at the opposite space and sees a hole in the roof that opens up when the greenery is lit and a bolt of light comes through the roof, down through the trumpet and into the little manikin. He is the only one who sees it. This is St. Paul's letter: "If I speak in the tongues of mortals and of angels but do not have love, I am a noisy gong or a clanging cymbal" (1 Cor. 13). Like Paul, Christian Rosenkreutz is being initiated in light and love, because he has seen love directly. The other men are being initiated in the alchemical technique, and he is being initiated to evolve his soul, although they are all doing the same thing. In alchemy it all depends on where you are observing. That's the work. In the middle of the flow, can you remember what your intent is?

So the men make the manikins, the Tower warden causes them to come to life, and the group in the upper room complete the wedding. They take the two manikins, a male and a female as the new king and queen, and bring them on the boats back to the castle of the ancient king and his queen. By the time they return to the castle, the young king is now fully grown and talks with Christian Rosenkreutz. He and the others are given medals. On one side of the medal are the words: "Art is the priest of nature." On the other side is: "Time is the daughter of nature."

Time is a code word for life body, the time body, the daughter of nature. Behind nature is the entity we call time. The being time is an etheric goddess, so to speak. The men learn that time, a being, is a result of nature manifesting; nature's corpse is not real nature. It is old nature, but the daughter of nature is *the becoming*. Time, the becoming, the ether body, flow, evolution. And that's one side of the coin.

The other side of the coin is this: *Art is the priest of nature*. Alchemists have always been called artists. The royal art is alchemy. Essentially, this art means I have to learn how the daughter works. What is the function of time in nature? What is the function of the life body in nature? How can I understand time? How can I enter time? How can I study time? How can I perceive time so I can work it instead of being a slave to it? The highest alchemy is about time. It's about when to do something. This is then planetary motion—putting things we say in time and retrieving them in time, so that we get a synergy from the time body. That's the art.

By getting synergy from the time body, one becomes a priest. This is biodynamics. It's the other side of the coin. The great secret and significance of alchemy is that it's not only about what we do, but also about when we do it. There are times when we can do things, and there are certain times when we cannot do that same thing.

Science has yet to learn this. It was once common knowledge but had to be forgotten it when became merely superstition, fear, and sorcery. Now we have to return to and revivify knowledge of time and rhythms. This understanding has to come back by working with rhythms that guide nature's changes, because we are reaching the limits of nature to endure.

Time is the daughter of nature, and art is the priest of nature. When we wish to turn our soul, we have to understand where it gets stuck in the timing of things. This is usually because we have an expectation that is inconsistent with the way the cosmic pattern of our life needs to unfold. The cosmic pattern of our life will continue to offer things that help us understand that any impulse we think is coming toward us is actually coming from a part of ourself that knows where we will be twenty years from now. This is a great key to turning the soul.

Day Seven

Overview

The ten men return triumphantly. All the king's ships are out in the harbor. Here they come—they have done the great work! The highest initiated person in the whole world, Christian Rosenkreutz, comes back and enters the castle, where the king and queen, the Bride and the Bridegroom, praise him. The king says to him, "You are my father."

Everyone is full of joy and having a great time. On day two, the king had been told by the original Guardian of the Threshold that someone had seen Venus naked. Now that Christian Rosenkreutz has gone through the whole process, the Guardian comes and tells the king that it is Christian Rosenkreutz who has transgressed. The king was about to give Christian Rosenkreutz the Great Book of the Order, in which the members of the order write an admonition for posterity. Because Christian Rosenkreutz is of the highest order, he is expected to write his epitaph for all of humanity. He will record his admonition to them concerning the path through *The Alchemical Wedding*. What he writes will become the principle of initiation for the ages.

Prior to this, the king had received the message of the transgression, though without anyone named. The king was smiling, but now, he suddenly appears solemn. Christian Rosenkreutz stands there with the Book, and everything is silent. The king comes down to Christian Rosenkreutz and says, "We have a problem. There is a difficulty, because something has happened. We will finish your ritual here in a moment, but we have to attend to this first."

Christian Rosenkreutz asks the king about what has happened, and the king replies, "Someone has seen Venus naked, but don't worry. We will surely discover who it was, and when we do we will deal with him." Christian Rosenkreutz asks the king what the penalty will be for the transgressor, and the king explains that the penalty is that the perpetrator must free the Guardian from his burden as Gatekeeper by taking his place. This goes to Christian Rosenkreutz's heart.

Leaving Christian Rosenkreutz with the Book, the king goes to meet with his astronomer about the issue. Rosenkreutz is a good man and a bad man at the same time. He's the success and the failure. He's the savior of the mysteries and a betrayer of the mysteries. He is the true person of misunderstanding. In this condition, Christian Rosenkreutz writes his epitaph for posterity: "The highest knowledge knows nothing."

The king's astrologer has asked for a meeting with the king, and when they meet Christian Rosenkreutz confesses his guilt. Thus, according to the great law, he must now serve as the Guardian.

Christian Rosenkreutz just wants to go home after all of this. The others are looking at him and shaking their heads, lamenting over how terrible this is. He then goes to sleep in a small room, with the warden of the Tower on one side and the astrologer of the king on the other.

And right there—mid-sentence—the book ends. The kind of feeling you have at such an ending is... *What?* There is a short disclaimer at the end, saying that the last few pages of the manuscript are missing but that Christian Rosenkreutz went to sleep in the castle and awoke the next morning at home.

This is a remarkable alchemical story of, we could say, the modern initiation practice of *understanding that one doesn't understand.* That is Rosicrucian alchemy whereby the world and my "I"-being have to be married, because when I separate my "I"-being from the world, "the whole creation groans and suffers." The marriage requires my humility. This is the key to Christian Rosenkreutz's deliverance. Even though he knows he doesn't understand, it brings into his soul the kind of humility to say, "I am in God; in me is God." That meditation, given by Rudolf Steiner to people who work with therapeutic modalities, is a deep meditation on the humility of modern initiates, whose success sometimes does not allow the people around them to cooperate fully; their success does not allow their buildings to withstand jealousy and arson and ill will–this is the role of the new initiate of misunderstanding.

The healing in this book is about the experience that, if we can get in touch with the cosmic I Am—the I Am shining into our "I"-being, our "I"—then I can heal the polarity between uncertainty, which leads to depression, and hubris, which leads to inflation. Healing these polarities is, to me, the real work that Rudolf Steiner brought to us, especially through the thirty-six Rosicrucian aspects of anthroposophic practice. Bringing the marriage of the spirit and the soul together so that my True Self—our "I"—and the world can connect through imaginations such as those needed for biodynamic work, working with children, and in the arts requires the participation of my "I" in the world and the world's participation in my "I."

This, then, is the perfect picture of *The Alchemical Wedding*. What I understand from this book is the motif of *understanding that I don't understand*—I don't want to cultivate or promote misunderstanding. I need to understand, in my humility, that what I consider absolutely certain has another aspect to it, as well as another aspect to that, and so on. My task is to include as many aspects as possible—meaning that whatever I think I understand from one perspective is actually a deep misunderstanding, because it causes me to form a premature judgment. I am too small to judge—especially too small to judge another person. If I want to judge something about my own life, that's fine. If I must judge something about a medicine or the like, okay. But judging another person's soul is no good. The line between judging an action and judging a person is very fine, and it's exactly the line being blurred today in politics and many other aspects of social discourse where image is far more important than substance.

If we do not develop an organ that's sensitive to how humility works in relation to misunderstanding, we tend to polarize human interaction. In today's world, if I form a judgment and keep repeating it over and over, I expect my judgment to rule. This is a kind of psychic poison. It becomes poison for the soul because it lacks humility. The greatest struggle for people today is to be humble in their misunderstanding and uncertainty. This doesn't mean that I'm a stupid or bad person. There will always be more to a situation than what I think I know. Goethe said that all of my knowing can be only half-knowing; my half-knowing prevents me from fully knowing. What I think I know for certain prevents me from learning things I don't know. The struggle for people today is to move past what we think we know.

Rudolf Steiner's spoke of being ten-percent open-minded, which resolves this problem. Even if you are a hundred-percent certain that the steeple of a church cannot stick out from the side of the church at ninety degrees, and someone tells you that the steeple is sticking out ninety degrees, Steiner suggests we practice holding ten percent of our consciousness in abeyance, because that is our deliverance.

Our terrible certainty is our prison. It inflates us. In psychology, *inflation* refers to a kind of tunnel vision in life. We see only what we see, and we believe this is what everyone else is seeing. This is one side. The other is depression. We can be crushed like bugs by our inability to be grateful if we awake to the impeccable organization of natural world and realize how we have disregarded it in daily life or have taken it for granted. We would become depressed, because we would see our complete lack of gratitude. If all we can see is our own concerns, we are "inflated." By contrast, St. Augustine said, "I am a worm." The world is so great, and God is so great in the world that we are merely worms, or less than worms. Between *inflation*—seeing only the radiance of our own concerns—and *depression*—seeing only that the world is much greater than we are—we can have the experience that our "I"-being lives in both conditions at once.

When we experience being in both places at the same time, we awake to what Rudolf Steiner calls the process of forming a mental image. We wake to the fact that our soul constitution is made up mostly of pictures that are continuously active in us and have their own pattern; they have their own life, independent of our own will. Waking to this, we begin to train our consciousness, which begins as we pass our thirty-third year.

Rudolf Steiner has said a kind of recapitulation of the Crucifixion takes place in our thirty-third year of life. Naïve dreams and the idealism of youth are crucified in the thirty-third year. We awake to the fact that we have mortgages and commitments and so on. We are probably not going to become millionaires or the most beautiful people or whatever we consider ideal. We will simply grow older. During our thirty-third year, we put on glasses and begin to see that we have reached a turning point. At this turning point, our "I"-being begins to see its origin in the great I AM, the being of Christ. We realize that we all have this experience, which is both worrisome and liberating. Some people observe this only momentarily and remain inflated and concerned only with worldly matters. Others see this and think: *That's interesting.* They begin to study and meet others who are also occupied in this way. They begin to think: *There is something beyond me that is real and has something to do with me, and I with it. If I can get in line with that, the split between the world and my "I" comes together a little better.* The rule is this: *If I do this myself and bring things together a little, this is the alchemical marriage.*

Jungians call this condition *individuation.* By integrating the world with our self, we also make it possible for others to do this. Steiner might call this the "mystery school," whereby we learn how we have separated the world from our true self by holding opinions and judgments about others and what they should do to confirm our own points of view. When we realize that we don't understand everything, we begin to be more malleable and allow both sides of the world to speak within us as images. Such images often take the form of fairytales, myths, and legends, as well as the pictures Rudolf Steiner provides for biodynamic agriculture and education, speaks of in his lectures on the Gospels, and so on. These are all images and nutrition for the soul that continue after our life on Earth.

When we finally decide to "take up our bed and walk," we are beginning to get a feeling for our I Am and having the tools needed to do the work. Then we are "anthroposophists." To me this is the message of Christian Rosenkreutz in *The Alchemical Wedding.*

The Alchemical Wedding, Day Seven

Christian Rosenkreutz awoke early in the morning and, wishing to set off for the Tower, made his way through a labyrinth of passages in the great wall. This took him a long time, and it was much later that he finally made it out of the wall and entered the lowest chamber of the Tower. There he met the others, who also had a difficult time getting out of the great wall. They were all given yellow habits to wear and their golden fleeces. The Virgin told them that now they would be known as knights of the Golden Stone. After that they all went to breakfast, where the old warden of the Tower gave each of them a gold medal. On one side were these words: "Art is the Priestess of Nature," while the other side had the words: "Time is the Daughter of Nature." The old man cautioned them never to do anything against these admonitions.

After breakfast they went to the ships and set sail. The ships were twelve in number. Six were theirs, and six were the ships of the warden of the Tower, in which were many soldiers of the warden. The musicians were placed in the first ship to play music for the voyage. The twelve ships flew flags representing the twelve signs of the zodiac. The ship of Christian Rosenkreutz flew the flag of Libra, and aboard it was a wondrous clock. The journey began in a pleasurable way on a calm sea, with the old warden giving discourses on the history of things. Christian Rosenkreutz felt as if he could sail with the old man for his whole life. After sailing for a while, a sailor called out that he could see the lake of the castle, and that it was filled with numerous ships that had come to meet them.

As soon as they sailed from the sea into the fjord, they were surrounded by five hundred vessels, one of which sparkled with gold and precious stones. On that ship were the king and the queen, along with lords of high birth and the most exalted Virgins. At the approach of the flotilla of the warden, the other ships discharged cannons and sounded trumpets and kettle drums in a stirring salute. As the flotilla approached the Royal ship, they came together, and the Royal astronomer Atlas delivered a handsome oration of welcome. He asked if the rest of the Royal presents were available. This question caused a stir among the six men who had worked on the gold, for they had no idea what was meant. They still believed that they had to go to the castle garden to wake the Royals. The four who had delivered the Royal couple in the seventh room acted as if they had no idea what was meant by this request.

After the oration by Atlas, the old warden of the Tower stepped up and, with great flourish, wished the king and queen all happiness and increase in their lives. With this, he brought forth a small casket and gave it to Cupid, who'd been fluttering between the Royal couple for safekeeping. The cannons on all the ships set off a volley to celebrate this event, and the ships all sailed to land at another shore. The area of the landing place was very close to the first gate that Christian Rosenkreutz had encountered when he first approached the castle. Many members of the Royal Couple's family had gathered there with a large herd of horses. As the men debarked from the ships, the king and queen shook their hands, and they were mounted on horses. The men were given places to ride with the other lords and relatives of the Royals. But Christian Rosenkreutz, who felt least worthy, and the warden of the Tower were given a place to ride beside the king himself. They each bore a snow-white flag with a red cross.

Christian Rosenkreutz had fastened his medal onto his hat. The young king noticed this and asked him, "Are you *he* who redeemed his tokens at this gate?" Bashfully, Christian Rosenkreutz answered in the affirmative.

The young king replied, "If this is the case, there needs to be no further ceremony between us, since you are my father." Then the young king laughed and asked him, "How did you manage to redeem the tokens to get through the gates?"

Christian Rosenkreutz answered, "They were redeemed with salt and water." The young king marveled at how Christian Rosenkreutz could possibly be so wise.

Now they arrived at the first gate, where the Gatekeeper in the sky-blue uniform had met CR. The Gatekeeper was still there, holding a request in his hand. As soon as he saw Christian Rosenkreutz, he approached him and passed the request to him. The Gatekeeper wanted Christian Rosenkreutz to tell the young king how well he had treated CR when he passed through the first gate. He asked the young king to tell him about the situation of the Gatekeeper.

The young king replied, "He was once a famous and rare astrologer always held in high regard by the old king. But he committed a fault against Venus by seeing her naked in her bed. His punishment for this impetuous act was having to serve as Gatekeeper at the first gate until someone comes along and relieves him of this debt to Venus." The young king continued, "If anyone can be found who has committed such a great transgression, he must stand in his stead and this Gatekeeper will be free."

These words bit deeply into the heart of CR. His conscience revealed that he was the offender, and yet he remained calm and delivered supplication to the young king. As soon as the young king read it, he was shaken.

At that moment, the young queen approached, accompanied by the virgins and the unnamed queen of the hanging of the weights. The young queen asked the young king, "What is in the letter?"

The young king acted as if nothing was amiss. He put the paper in his coat and began to talk about other things, and then he turned to return to the castle. After about three hours they arrived, and CR accompanied the young king into the great Hall. The young king immediately called for Atlas, and they both entered a private chamber, where the young king showed him the paper. Atlas immediately rode out to interview the Gatekeeper.

The young king and his queen sat with Lords and Ladies of the court and the virgins. The Virgin of the ten began to commend the diligence the men had demonstrated on the Island of the Tower. She asked that they be royally rewarded. She also asked that she be allowed to honor her commission and finish her duties to the old king. The warden of the Tower also spoke on their behalf, suggesting that the men be allowed to stand and each make a request. He said, "Those such as these, with such great understanding, would ask for only what is the best for all."

During these speeches, the young king and queen started to engage each other playfully in a game resembling chess, but instead of black and white armies it involved vices and virtues as opponents. The game was skillfully organized, so that the laws of engagement revolved around moral instead of military values.

During the game, Atlas entered the court and made his report to the king in private. CR felt himself blushing all over; his conscience would not give him rest. The king returned and gave the porter's written request to CR to read. It began with the Gatekeeper wishing the king prosperity and increase, so that his seed might be spread far and wide. He then asserted that the time of his service as the Gatekeeper was now coming to an end, and that he should be released from his punishment. He went on to say that Venus had been uncovered by one of the king's guests. He knew this, because his observations did not lie to him. But if he was in error, he would remain at his post at the gate. He asked to be able to attend the gala supper that night so he could point out the offender to the king.

CR felt these words cutting into his soul like a dagger. He asked the king, "Is there another way that the Gatekeeper can be relieved of his punishment?"

The king replied, "There is no other way, because there is a special consideration in this affair." The king then sent word to the Gatekeeper that he would be permitted to attend the supper that evening.

A spacious, well-appointed room was chosen as the place for supper that evening. Christian Rosenkreutz and the other men entered the hall with much pomp. He noticed that Cupid was not in attendance. He had heard that Cupid was so angry about the transgression toward his mother that he chose to be elsewhere. CR's offence and the Gatekeeper's request had cast a distinct air of sadness upon the festivities. The young king was perplexed as to how to allow the inquisition of his guests on the night of a banquet in their honor. This was especially so because none of them knew that trouble was brewing. The young king asked the Gatekeeper to be quick about his survey of the guests. The banquet was held and the young king did his best to act merry.

After the banquet was over, the tables were quickly taken away and a circle of chairs for the curious was arranged in the hall. The young king and queen, Atlas, and the warden, as well as all of the virgins sat within the circle. Atlas began to speak of the unusual circumstances. He said that the young king had not forgotten the service that the men had done for him and his queen. For this he had elected them all to be Knights of the Golden Stone, and as such they were supposed to swear to the following articles.

1. You knights will at no time ascribe fealty to any Devil or Spirit, but only to God your creator and his handmaid, Nature.
2. You will abominate all whoredom, incontinency, and uncleanliness and not defile your order with such vices.
3 You will apply your talents to any and all who are worthy and have need of them.
4 You will not desire to employ this honor toward worldly pride or positions of power.
5 You shall not be willing to live longer than God will have you.

The assembly all had a good laugh at this last article, as it seemed to be added as a conceit. The men were installed as knights by the king's scepter and given power to deal with ignorance, poverty, and sickness. These events were ratified in the young king's private chapel. They were each to hang their golden fleece there with their hats in an eternal memorial.

The men were now asked to write their names in the great book. Christian Rosenkreutz wrote:

THE HIGHEST KNOWLEDGE UNDERSTANDS NOTHING
BROTHER CHRISTIAN ROSENKREUTZ
KNIGHT OF THE GOLDEN STONE
THE YEAR 1459

All of the men wrote what they deemed would offer the greatest good. After writing, they were all brought into the hall, where they were instructed to think about what they would wish for. The young king and his party retired to a small chamber to hear individual requests. Christian Rosenkreutz thought he would like to be able to demonstrate great gratitude as the thing that he wished most to have. With this thought, he resolved to free the Gatekeeper, whom he now considered to be his Benefactor.

When it was his turn to have audience with the king, Christian Rosenkreutz was asked first if he had any observations or suspicions about who the guilty party might be. At this, Christian Rosenkreutz began to explain how the whole business in the chamber of Venus had developed. He admitted that he had fallen into that mistake because of his ignorance, and that he was ready to submit himself to the punishment that must arise from this offence.

The young king and all assembled were taken by surprise at this admission of guilt from Christian Rosenkreutz. They asked him to step away so they could confer. When he was called into the circle again, Atlas told him that it was particularly painful that he had fallen into disgrace because he was most beloved of the young king. Since the laws governing this were ancient and came from God, the young king was forced to free the Gatekeeper and pronounce sentence upon CR. The young king told him that he wished someone else would soon be apprehended so that CR could soon go home. However, he knew that no release could be hoped for until the marriage feast of his future son.

The sentence weighed heavy on CR and, at first, he hated himself and his loose tongue and his inability to hold his peace. But after a while, he took courage and, since there was absolutely no chance for a reprieve, he reflected on how the Gatekeeper had given him a token and sent a letter commending him to the second Gatekeeper. In this way, the Gatekeeper had opened the door to him for a tremendous experience and great understanding and entry to a high place. Thus, Christian Rosenkreutz worked his soul into appreciation and gratitude for what had happened.

Christian Rosenkreutz told the young king, "If I were to wish for anything, it would be to return home once again." The young king answered that he had no power to do that.

The Gatekeeper was freed, and Christian Rosenkreutz was obliged to step aside as he left. The rest of the men were called out, and they laughed and were joyful at the prospect of returning home. This caused CR to burn all the more in anguish. He imagined that he would end his life standing under the gate. He then thought about the fact that he was old and did not have many more years left, and that a melancholy life might be quickly ended by his old age. He hoped that by a most happy sleep he would go to his grave and put his doorkeeping days at an end. It occasionally bothered CR that he had seen such wondrous things but was robbed of them by this terrible fate. He sometimes felt that the worst part was that he had been so close to great joy in his old age, and that his life would now end in shame. His thoughts continued along these paths for a long time.

At the end of the evening, all of the others were led to accommodations except Christian Rosenkreutz. However, the young king told him, "Because you are now a knight, you should bear your trials bravely." The young king then kissed Christian Rosenkreutz and took him in his arms. He was escorted to a glorious lodging...

The remainder of this manuscript is missing, except for the ending in which Christian Rosenkreutz, imagining that in the morning he must be the Gatekeeper, was returned home.

DAY SEVEN COMMENTARY

Christian Rosenkreutz is now back with the new king and new queen, who were the manikins but have now grown up. There is a scene in which the young king is riding with Christian Rosenkreutz and asks him if he was the one who redeemed his tokens with the Gatekeeper. Christian Rosenkreutz responds that he was, at which the young king exclaims, "Oh, you are my father!" Christian Rosenkreutz is the father, because he was the midwife for the king's delivery. He is the one who made it possible for the young king to be born.

The young king then asks, "How did you redeem the tokens to get through the gates?" Christian Rosenkreutz replies that they were redeemed with salt and water. The king marvels at how Christian Rosenkreutz could be so wise. *Salt* and *water*—code words for the "I"-organization, which monitors how the life body (*water*) is influenced by the formation of thoughts (*salt*).

Now, Christian Rosenkreutz understands that his thoughts have a relationship to his life forces. His salt has a relationship to his water. The things he thinks about affect his given life forces, transforming them into the *not-given*. This kills life in the thought process. Thinking can be freedom or slavery. If our intent is correct, it is freedom; if we are not in contact with our intent, it is slavery—confusion and repetition of old patterns.

However, Christian Rosenkreutz gave salt and water to the Gatekeeper for the tokens needed to pass through the gates. Having the tokens was necessary for him to be able to perform the transformation in the Tower, and be was able to understand how his salt and his water were related. The Gatekeepers recognized that he was the One who had to do the work. This is the ability to recognize one's intent, or motives of one's will's impulses. This is the secret to turning the soul.

Here, the king mentions it, and Christian Rosenkreutz answers it. All of this is connected with the Gatekeeper, because he is the key to this story.

Near the end of the story, the Virgin asks the young king and queen for permission to honor her commission and to finish her duties to the king. This is Sophia meeting the Holy Spirit and rejoicing that human beings have done it—we am free. When humans perform the alchemical wedding, Sophia is freed from the human illusion that nature is composed only of corpses. Humans do this by seeing nature's activity as the activities of spiritual beings—not through visions, but as inner cognition. This is the key: If we want to see nature as visions, there are many ways to do that; if we want to have it as cognition, we have to remove the scales from our eyes. We must experience a Damascus event.

The young king and queen are playing a chess game when the court astronomer Atlas enters and reports to the king in private that the Gatekeeper had given Christian Rosenkreutz a letter when he arrived at the castle. The original Gatekeeper (day two) goes right up to Christian Rosenkreutz and gives him a letter that says, "Please tell the king that I was very good to you."

When Christian Rosenkreutz sees this, he begins to have pangs of conscience. He asks the young king what the issue is with the Gatekeeper. The young king tells him that Atlas was a well-respected astronomer at one time, but then he committed the error of seeing Venus naked. For that indiscretion, he must serve as the Gatekeeper. Anyone who commits such a grave transgression must assume the position of Gatekeeper. This deeply shocks Christian Rosenkreutz, but he gives the letter to the king anyway. Now, his conscience will give him no rest.

Here we get to the real issue—having done the Great Work allows Christian Rosenkreutz the capacity to see, and now that he sees at that level, he is also responsible for what he sees. When he first began to see, he hadn't yet reached the level he was at when he did the work in the Tower. His eyes were opened when he saw Venus. After that, he could see that the Royals were not really dead—that they were still alive but in a different state of consciousness. By seeing Venus, however, he jumped from *imagination* to *intuition* without having developed a consciousness strong enough to protect himself. When he saw Love directly, we could say that it accelerated his spiritual development. However, it was also inflation, because he thought that his understanding was a gift from a spiritual being. According to Rudolf Steiner, all of our thoughts are really the will of other beings.

When Christian Rosenkreutz went down to the tomb and saw Venus naked, he was not yet at the level of being able to cognize what was really happening. His curiosity, inflamed by the page, led him to an expectation that caused his undoing. "Curiosity" means that he had *an expectation*. The odd thing here is this: How can we use our curiosity to become *incurious?* How can we do spiritual research without expecting that what we learn is the truth? The next day, we might awake and realize that what we saw is not at all what we thought it was. The safeguard against misunderstanding is to *continuously rethink what we think*, because what we think is true only for our present level of understanding.

So there it is; Christian Rosenkreutz has accomplished the Great Work, but he has also made the huge mistake. Paradoxically, these two situations can be the same thing. When he gave the letter from the Gatekeeper to the king, Christian Rosenkreutz was about to be honored by the king and was asked to write a thought for posterity in the Great Book.

We have no record of what the other men wrote, but we have a record of what Christian Rosenkreutz wrote, because he was the most highly initiated person. This is significant. What he wrote was this: "*The highest knowledge understands nothing.*" Like everything in alchemy, this has two sides. We could say that the highest knowledge understands nothing at all. Similarly, I can say that *the highest knowledge understands the significance of nothing*. This could mean that no matter how much knowledge we have, we still do not really understand higher truths. That's one way. We could also say that *the highest knowledge understands the implications of the concept of nothing*. Thus, the highest knowledge *understands* what nothing is. Each way uses the same words but has a different intent.

This is the book, and I choose to read it this way: The highest knowledge *understands* the great importance of nothing. This *nothing* is the great spiritual dimension of the invisible—understanding the great nothing (*void/pleroma/entelechy/devachan*) that allows us to turn our soul. It is the understanding that everything comes down to a null point that eventually allows a person to have gratitude for life's trials. This is the epitaph of Christian Rosenkreutz.

Then the young king and queen grant each man a request. Christian Rosenkreutz asks to be able to demonstrate great gratitude. This is subtle. He hops to request from the new king and queen (his new thinking and his new soul) the gift of being grateful.

The astronomer returns at this point to speak with the king. The king tells Christian Rosenkreutz that the Gatekeeper was aware that one of the men had seen Venus naked, and he would come to the dinner that evening and reveal the perpetrator. After he writes, *the highest knowledge understands nothing*, Christian Rosenkreutz asks the king for the ability to experience great gratitude. He requests this because he knows that great gratitude that will allow him to free the Gatekeeper by considering him to be his benefactor.

During an audience with the king, Christian Rosenkreutz begins to explain how the whole business developed in Venus' chamber. He admits that, owing to his ignorance, he fell into that error and that he is ready to submit himself to the punishment that must arise from his offense.

The king and everyone assembled are surprised by Christian Rosenkreutz's admission of guilt. They ask him to step away so they can confer. Then the king says, "You know, you are my father; I love you, and you did the Great Work, so it is painful for me that you have fallen into disgrace." However, since the laws of governing were ancient and came from God, the young king was forced to free the Gatekeeper and pronounce sentence upon Christian Rosenkreutz, his benefactor. This is like a great tragedy—everyone is dying; everyone is in pain.

This sentence weighs so heavily upon Christian Rosenkreutz that, at first, he hates himself and his loose tongue, wishing that he had kept his peace.

Because now there was absolutely no chance for reprieve, he reflected on how the Gatekeeper gave him a token and sent a letter commending him to the second Gatekeeper. He had opened the door for Christian Rosenkreutz to a tremendous experience and great understanding, as well as entry to a high place.

Here is a key sentence for the whole book: "In this way, Christian Rosenkreutz worked his soul into appreciation and gratitude for what had happened." I understand this sentence as an encapsulation of the whole book. It represents the new initiation: Working the soul into appreciation for the fact that all of this had to come to pass. This attitude purifies the will. The great formula from Rudolf Steiner is this: *When I will my thinking, it leads to freedom.* When we take our thinking in hand and actually will ourselves to think a certain sequence of things, we lead ourselves to freedom. It means that, if we find ourselves in error, we can actually think of what that error has taught us. This is *turning the soul.* But we have to *will* our thinking to do this.

As an initiate, Christian Rosenkreutz is the teacher of the proper attitude after having a failed initiation. His initiation is a failure in this story. Nevertheless, he was able to work his soul into appreciation and gratitude.

Christian Rosenkreutz tells the king that if he were to wish for anything it would be to return home, and the king says, "I really can't do that, because this directive comes from lofty spiritual realms. God made these rules, and I am just a king. I love you, but I really can't make that happen for you. You have to do it yourself."

Then the Gatekeeper is set free, and Christian Rosenkreutz is obliged to step aside as he leaves. The other men are called out, and they laugh with joy at the prospect of returning home. Christian Rosenkreutz—at eighty-one years of age—did the deed, and now everyone will recognize him for not doing the deed, even though he did.

Then the manuscript says, "At the end of the evening all the others were led to their accommodations, but not Christian Rosenkreutz. The king kissed him and took him in his arms, and Christian Rosenkreutz was escorted to a glorious lodging.

The rest of this manuscript is missing, except for the very end. Christian Rosenkreutz, imagining that he must become the Gatekeeper, is returned home the next morning.

Coda

The abrupt end of this work is a bit of a disappointment on the first read; it seemed a bit contrived to me. However, I have gone over this work many times since then, and the ending now seems totally in keeping with the idea of misunderstanding as an initiation process.

The past year, 2020, has introduced a worldwide wave of uncertainty regarding health, the economy, social issues, politics, and the future. Truth has become toxically relative and partisan. From the perspective of Rudolf Steiner's work, this is a symptom of a necessary human watershed development that he called *consciousness soul*—that is, the soul condition in which each human individual unilaterally asserts and expects a high degree of social autonomy. Numerous symptoms point to this, such as social media platforms on which hyper-individualized points of view are broadcast to legions of followers, giving rise to tribal allegiances to individually targeted fanatical worldviews pushing fantasies as a basis for social dialogue. Such hyper-individualism manifests even in disease patterns, composed of particular individualized combinations of comorbid symptoms.

These pathologies are seen as spectrums of interrelated symptoms, with the result that each point on the disease spectrum must be treated as an individual pathology. Ironically, individualized adaptive strategies are now rising among the pathogens themselves, which are in turn targeted by unique individualized remedies that might or might not alleviate the symptoms. To make a full circle, the effectiveness of such remedies depends on unique, individualized prior comorbid conditions that depend on tribal beliefs. These hyper individualized patterns and others point to the action of consciousness-soul conditions. Steiner has stated that consciousness soul is deeply antisocial.

What are we to do?

The overriding posture of Christian Rosencreutz in the face of ridicule, exclusion, uncertainty, and ultimately unredeemable error is to become authentically humble. It is his humility that shines out through his trials. His true human humility draws spiritual beings to him. They see him as the one who has the potential to affect such a complete transformation of self that he himself becomes the spiritual Guardian of the Threshold between worlds. They continually test him to help him become stronger. His humility is based on his knowledge that he doesn't understand; *he knows that he doesn't know.* This is his path through the forest of darkened minds. Thus, he points the way toward the future human. The irony is that he is already walking that path when the fatal verdict of his failure is passed to him on the seventh day by his Son, the young King. His spiritual power to turn his soul during that time of dire uncertainty is the hidden gift developed through the challenges he received from higher beings. Through steadfastness in knowing that he doesn't know, he overcomes uncertainty. It is a practice of *radical unknowing.*

As I understand it, this is his gift to all humans for their future development. The humility of knowing that one does not know is a saving grace against the violence of the economic war of each against all and all against each. This conflict arises from the storms of misunderstanding that, by destiny, accompany the worldwide hyper-individualism of human souls in the age of the consciousness soul.

In his small mind, CR went to bed shamed as a failure. At the same time, Christian Rosenkreutz advanced to being the Guardian of the Threshold, even while he was at home in bed.

OTHER BOOKS BY DENNIS KLOCEK

Colors of the Soul

Physiological and Spiritual Qualities of Light and Dark

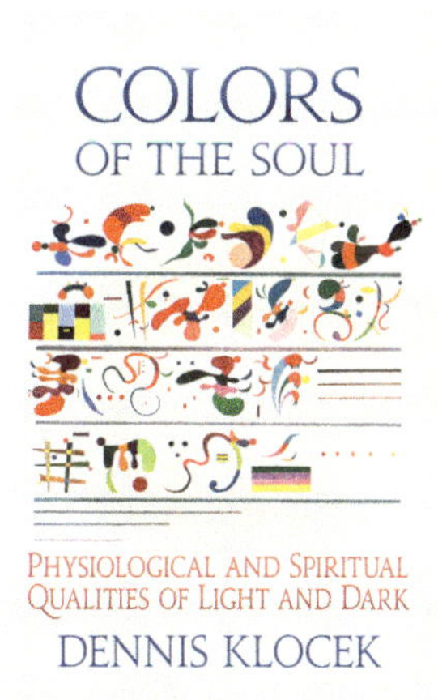

Colors of the Soul is illustrated in full color, featuring numerous helpful diagrams and examples of art from the Middle Ages to the twentieth century. Like the author's books on physiology, climate, and agriculture, this book brings knowledge and surprising insights to the nature of color, a topic that is integral to our everyday life and development.

ISBN 9781584209607 • PAPERBACK • $35.00

Esoteric Physiology

Consciousness and Disease

"In healing processes or in the general growth of the body, the formation of bone or the formation of a tissue from a fluid is a sclerotic process. We can call it the formation of tissue from fluid growth, but technically it is sclerotic. Sclerosis, which is considered to be a disease process, is therefore a natural process in the body. Inflammation and infection that can kill you and sclerosis are both the body's natural healing processes. Steiner mentions this and asks, So, where does the illness come in?... The answer he gives is this: Illness is not in the body and its life forces. Illness is in the thoughts we bring to the body and the life forces. Illness is in the soul." — Dennis Klocek

ISBN 9781584201922 • PAPERBACK • $25.00